The Dean's Demise

The Dean's Demise

Sexual Harassment in a Divinity School

A Novel

Richard Fletcher

RESOURCE *Publications* · Eugene, Oregon

THE DEAN'S DEMISE
Sexual Harassment in a Divinity School

Resource Publications
An Imprint of Wipf and Stock Publishers
199 W. 8th Ave., Suite 3
Eugene, OR 97401

www.wipfandstock.com

PAPERBACK ISBN: 978-1-4982-9901-5
HARDCOVER ISBN: 978-1-4982-9903-9
EBOOK ISBN: 978-1-4982-9902-2

Manufactured in the U.S.A.   10/06/16

This is a work of fiction. The persons, places, processes, and events described in this novel are entirely products of my imagination. They do not describe any actual person, place, process, or event.

Characters in *The Dean's Demise*:

Karl Wolfe, dean and husband of Emily

Emily Wolfe, librarian and wife of Karl

Madison Byrne, mentor of Karl Wolfe

Adrian Tanaka, university president

Thomas Metcalf, divinity school senior faculty member

Megan Metcalf, psychologist, Thomas' wife

Martin Evans, interim divinity school dean

Norah Evans, nurse, Martin's wife

Edwin Diaz, Kevin Walker, Sharon Henderson, and Rebecca Swingle—
divinity school faculty

Kylie Raven, Tyler Jamison, and Jennifer Logan—
divinity school students

Clayton Heron, retired seminary president

David Karns, current seminary president

Molly and Max Hoffman, seminary faculty

Jack Curtis, local church pastor

Annie Nicholson, confirmation class member

Melvin Jackson, denominational official

Prologue: 1979

"There is no trap so deadly as the trap you set for yourself."
RAYMOND CHANDLER, *THE LONG GOODBYE*

WHEN KARL WOLFE GAVE a speech, he was always sensitive to the audience's response. No matter how provocative his words, he sought the audience's approval, and when they reacted positively, he fed on that response. Riding an emotional high, he would embrace them even as he soared above them. Tonight he was not certain about his audience. He had never failed before, yet tonight on this big stage he realized that anxiety was overtaking him. Nearing the conclusion of his talk he paused, then caught his breath and hopefully moved into his concluding remarks.

Emily had said it was a dangerous, even a radical speech, but he had paid no attention to her words. Perhaps he should have listened to her. No matter; he had not listened, and now the end was near—perhaps in more ways than he realized. He wondered what the several hundred academics who had come for the conference's opening keynote address were thinking. He knew his words had surprised them. Radical suggestions about the origins of the Bible, and how seminaries and university divinity schools had deep-seated differences regarding such things, were probably more than just a little distasteful to this crowd. Some things needed to stay hidden. He knew his words stepped over this line—personally, theologically, and politically.

Was their silence born of intense interest or a dismissal of his words? He found their quiet presence unsettling; had he misjudged them? With only a few words left to say, he slammed both hands hard upon the speaker's wooden podium and stepped back. Shaking off his doubts, he rose onto the tips of his toes to his full height while working a verbal cadence that slowly built, ending with a double-edged question: "If this be true, what comes next; and, what should we do?"

Finished, Wolfe half-stepped away from the podium and stood, head bowed before the crowded ballroom. His challenge hung in the air. There was a moment of silence, then sudden, unexpected, enthusiastic applause. Raising his head in disbelief, Wolfe realized he had dreamed of such a day happening and of standing inside such a moment, but now that it had arrived, it had caught him unaware. As the applause continued, the man in the gray suit and charcoal tie quickly stepped to the stage. Turning toward the audience, he asked for quiet and: "A few questions for Dean Wolfe?" Several hands popped up, and the intense level of what were powerful exchanges led to more affirming applause. Again he asked for silence, requesting: "one more question." Following this last exchange, he addressed the crowd: "An excellent, provocative keynote address." He continued: "You have challenged us, Dean Wolfe." More applause. He leaned toward the audience: "We look forward to the rest of our time together and, in particular, we look forward to our keynote speaker's presence on our afternoon concluding panel, but for tonight"—turning first to Wolfe and then back to the audience—"let us again demonstrate our thanks to Dean Wolfe." More applause followed Wolfe as he made his way off the speaker's stage through the crowded room toward the vestibule outside. He was aware of several pats on the back, the shaking of numerous hands, and the occasional comment: "Great speech."

The hotel lobby was an oasis of calm, but Wolfe did not pause, instead hurrying through the revolving exit door into the wetness of a coastal city's dark night. The mist he stepped into penetrated his light suit, a suit purposely chosen for his speech and the heat generated by the inevitable spotlights, but not for protection against the cold dampness of the weather. Still caught in a euphoric high, Wolfe nevertheless physically embraced the coldness and the nighttime mist. Taking a deep breath, he exclaimed: "It went well." He said these words out loud, as if he were alone and not standing in front of a startled doorman. And then he shouted: "It went very, very well!"

Fronted by a river channel linking the port to the ocean, the hotel's sidewalk ended in a ribbon of greenery near the base of steps leading up an embankment holding the channel in place. He took these steps two at a time, quickly reaching and grasping the top rail of an iron fence overlooking the hurrying waters. Breathing deeply, Wolfe wrapped both hands around the wet railing and leaned back, stretching the accumulated evening kinks from his body. Intermittent black clouds and a continuous gray mist shrouded the lights of a few ships, still visible against the outline of the city. Earlier that same day, he had stood at this exact spot and watched a single dolphin making its way downriver toward the sea. There had been a deliberateness to that solitary dolphin's forward movement Wolfe had applauded, even as he now considered his own journey.

He was forty-two. Still young, or at least he still felt young. A kid out of a hardscrabble small town existence. Maybe a hundred and sixty-five pounds, soaking wet. He'd stayed in reasonable shape. Not handsome, but he'd been called "good-looking," and that—coupled with raw intelligence— had given him enough of an advantage to escape the circumstances he'd been born into. Early on he'd tried to protect his ma from the sullen rages that often accompanied his pa's drinking. Pa had died in a bar fight when Wolfe was twelve, and his ma from pneumonia that had caught her during a cold, unrelenting winter. But what he remembered most about early childhood was his pa beating him with a belt while repeating again and again: "You ain't nuthin', boy. You ain't nuthin'."

School provided safety from the beatings he received at home, and he quickly became a student of behavior, comparing what happened at home with the expectations and practices of his teachers. He soon recognized there were signs and ways by which he could read the onset of pa's drunken moods, as well as responses he might choose to either push pa into a violent rage or periods of calmness. By fourth grade he realized that his nodding at the right time and only occasionally commenting on academic subjects made him look smart. Moving into junior high he found he could easily manipulate adults and peers by consciously adapting his conversational tone and content to fit their expectations. Always polite, he worked at positioning himself in conversations to meet his desired outcomes. Molding exterior behavior to other's expectations earned him the reputation of a smart loner, someone who didn't quite fit, but who, nevertheless, was competent and who probably would go far. Adults he met as a child or a youth called him "precocious." In high school he'd been voted "most likely to succeed" out of forty-two classmates, and he'd puzzled over that description. Wolfe laughed. He'd come a long way. The speech he'd given this evening was the kind of thing that would carry him further.

Pulling himself away from the river, Wolfe descended the steps and moved down the tourist-filled street. He was hungry, but food could wait. When he was a kid, food had been scarce, so much so, that without realizing it, as an adult he'd frequently skip meals. "Like tonight," he thought.

He had not eaten before his speech. He'd been too anxious. And when he'd finally stepped into the banquet hall, he'd been stunned at how his body responded to the elaborate dinner. Everything he'd never had, but all before him now. He'd caught himself—food would wait; he was there to give a speech, a speech that just might determine his future. He remembered the dolphin, and with deliberation he'd eased his way through the tables in the packed room, making his way toward the front and a table positioned close to the speaker's stage and podium.

Three men sat at the table, two wearing blue blazers and gray slacks; the third was dressed in a solid gray suit, completed with a charcoal tie. Graysuit stood, locking eyes with Wolfe; he asked: "Are you Karl Wolfe?"

"I am."

"Thank God," one blue blazer said, "We've been worried."

"You've missed the meal," said the other blazer. "But look, desserts just arriving, and we're pretty much on schedule. So no harm done."

"I'm sorry; I was a bit nervous, and lost track of the hour."

"No matter," said Graysuit, picking up a paper from the table. "But you ought to read this." Handing Wolfe a half sheet of cream-colored parchment, he said: "Hope you like it. We've decided to up our game a bit." The top of the paper carried an embossed conference logo. It caught and held Wolfe's eyes. He said: "Impressive." The three men made no response, but continued to observe Wolfe. Wolfe looked down, saw his name in heavy, black type followed by the title of his keynote speech. Still further down he read the titles of his book and three current articles.

Wolfe wondered at all this. His resume seemed slight. Vision blurred, he skipped to the last line ". . . currently Dr. Wolfe serves as the academic dean of. . ." He read it again: "currently," it said. He'd read it correctly. It was as if someone was suggesting that even though he served (now) as the academic dean of a small, somewhat back-water seminary, his future was open, and after all was said and done, a question could be posed: "what might the future hold for this impressive, young scholar?"

Stunned, Wolfe remembered sitting down. No one spoke. Then Graysuit asked: "Want to eat Crème Brule before you speak?" "No," Wolfe responded, "I'm set to go," and both he and Graysuit rose from their chairs. At the time it had seemed a long walk to the stage and the centered speaker's podium, but he had made it without tripping or dropping his speech. And his speech was not just ok, but a rousing success. Wolfe shook his shoulders. He danced down the street, shadow-boxing some imaginary opponent. Anxiety gone, he felt as if the world was his. Hurrying along the street outside the hotel, he spoke out loud—"Maybe I 'weren't nuthin'" to you, Pa, but by God, I am somebody now."

*

Earlier that same day, he had taken time to walk around the hotel. He'd been able to locate a café with an indoor phone, and now he pushed open the café's door and stepped into the phone booth. He dropped in the correct change and made the call. She answered on the third ring. "Emily," he fairly shouted, "It went perfectly."

"I knew you'd do well, Karl. Were you nervous?"

"Absolutely. The room was packed, and there were a lot of follow up questions. Lots of folk from my old graduate school days. It was hard to pull away, people seemed to want to grab onto my hand or arm. I've never had that kind of response. I'm still wound up, but I wanted to call."

"That's wonderful, Karl. Things here are fine. I miss you."

"And I you. But I need to cut this short. I'm expected to attend the annual get together of those of us who got our doctorates at my home university, and then to bed. I am exhausted."

"Enjoy yourself, Karl. And I love you."

"And I love you, Emily. Good night." Wolfe walked back to his hotel. His suit was damp, but not yet soaked. He decided it would be ok to wear it to the third floor university open house. As he entered, several people turned to him and began to applaud. "No. . . please," he entreated, waving them silent, but they persisted. He tried to be amiable, but soon tired of the press of bodies who seemed bent on keeping close contact with him. He had only wanted to put in a brief appearance and then ease his way to his room, but near the rear of the darkly-lit room sat his old mentor, Madison Byrne. In non-verbal tribute, Byrne lifted his wine glass to Wolfe. Wolfe could not leave without at least one or two words with this man.

Byrne had retired two years earlier. He'd been the senior professor at the university when Wolfe had studied for his doctorate, as well as his thesis advisor and the chair of Wolfe's doctoral committee. Retirement had not been kind to Madison Byrne. Here he was, returning to an event where he had once been honored, but now, as Wolfe observed, his mentor appeared disheveled and more than slightly inebriated. Wolfe cautiously approached the table. Byrne sipped a drink, his eyes never leaving Wolfe. "How did I do," Wolfe asked. Byrne responded: "You were flashy, charismatic— as always— and technically well put—as always—but flashy, ruthless, and cold."

"I take it you did not like my speech?" There was no response. Wolfe grimaced, but continued: "You said 'flashy' twice. 'Flashy' seems showy. Perhaps you're suggesting I was also arrogant? I concede—all that may be true. But what about the argument?"

"The argument. Ahh, yes. The argument. A good talk can give both you and your audience an erotic high. Certainly this is what occurred tonight. Yes, it did. I see you raising your eyebrows. I am not drunk, well, at least not so much that I could not see this and understand how such applause could occur. And it did occur. Let me say that a good, honest, heart-to-heart talk is like a speaker's making love with the audience. Not *to*, but *with*. I mean that. If you speak from the heart, the soul, and what is said is true, then a connection occurs—is bodily made—with those who see and hear and want to touch, to embrace, to be near you. Love is at the very core of a good talk. But you, Karl, you have always found it hard to love. For you it is as if a good talk is a battle, a place of winning and losing, a performance. For you a talk is a mere fuck, one more encounter on your ladder of success. And you performed well, more's the pity." Addressing Wolf, Byrne's voice grew louder, face flushed. His hand swept the small tabletop, knocking a glass of wine onto the floor.

"You judge me."

"You asked, and I responded. In all honesty, you were technically merely correct. But you know that. What was missing? Humanly, you were arrogant. You mentioned this. I agree. You were cold. That's either a sad miscalculation for a speech like this or, if not recognized, a huge weakness. I mean, if one were to dig deeper, what would be found? Maybe a better question: Do you, after all is said and done, do you believe in God?"

Wolfe angrily turned toward the door. A half step from the table, he heard Byrne quietly say, "I will pray for you."

A marvel of polished mirrors and plated glass, the hotel's elevator lifted Wolfe away from new admirers and Byrne's (slightly sloshed) judgment. As the elevator rose, the outside lights of the city and the river traffic became clearer, as if the mist and incipient rain had never occurred. Stepping off the elevator, Wolfe had to remind himself to turn left. Some six rooms down the hallway, he found himself standing outside his room. He had no key, having requested only one when he had registered that day, but his knock merited a quiet response: "coming," and the door opened. "So," Molly said, "the conquering hero arrives. Your talk was wonderful, Karl. Now come to bed with me."

*

Wolfe was an early morning person. Emily might stay up all night, reading a book from the library, but Karl was always up and about. He embraced such early moments. It was as if the bright newness of the day was made for him (and only him). The infrequent walkers Wolfe might meet on his early morning walks were, for the most part, ignored, but Wolfe would always try to make eye contact with young, well-dressed, attractive women. He knew "attractive" meant different things to different people, but for him it meant a certain carriage coupled with a graceful walk and a young, well-maintained body. When such a woman made eye contact of a certain sort with Wolfe it was if the stars had aligned and she willingly was engaged in the fantasy world buried somewhere deeply within his mind. Yet this morning was different. Molly, a supple, attractive (and wayward) young professor, who with her husband Max, also a professor, was on the faculty of the small seminary where Wolfe was dean, remained sleekly curled under the down comforter in the king-sized bed they had made their home after several hours of conversation and sex. On the pretext of a denominational dean's meeting piggybacked onto the conference, Wolfe had informed Emily and his office that he would stay over and return a day later instead of coming directly home following the conference.

Sensing Wolfe's readiness for his morning walk, Molly pushed herself into an upright sitting posture, leaning, one breast exposed, against the bed's headboard. "You coming back?" She asked. "Absolutely," Wolfe responded, noting how her long, blonde hair managed to cover the second breast. "I'm going for a walk by the river. Back here by eight thirty. When's your plane?"

"At one. So I'll stay here. I'll put 'do not disturb' on the handle, but I'll leave after you get back." This was said with a smile, as if she was confirming something they had long ago agreed to do. "Of course," said Wolfe. "I'll miss you." Taking the key, he stepped back outside and made his way outside.

Molly and Wolfe had a set routine born of two years of conference connections such as this one. Molly would be the first to leave. She would check out of her own room, a room she used during each day, leaving the bedcovers in a disheveled state and using the shower in "her" bathroom. Some cursory shopping, a quick taxi ride to the airport and she would be on her plane about the time Karl was checking out of "his" room at the hotel. This was an agreeable arrangement for both of them. And there was no retribution. Molly's husband was ineffectual. He had ridden on Molly's coattails into a temporary appointment at her school. She was the star. A bit precocious and often unpredictable, Molly was not in any way like Karl's wife, the predictable and homebound Emily.

Wolfe dozed on the plane, still picturing himself in bed with Molly. He was four years her senior, and he knew she wanted both couples to divorce that she and Karl might marry, but this was not going to occur, not if the luncheon Karl had just experienced with a seminary search committee panned out. Once again he considered the twists and turns of that conversation. He had few doubts about what had been inferred. He was on their "short list," and if things went well —every school first had to perform "due diligence"—he might be asked to serve as this (much bigger and more important) seminary's academic dean.

Some weeks passed, but no call came. Apparently, Wolfe mused, the search committee had located someone else for the bigger seminary's deanship. Subdued, he settled into the routine of his own seminary and his role as academic dean. Not that he didn't find himself thinking about what might still happen. In those daydreams Wolfe turned his back on all seminaries, instead imagining a call from a much bigger university divinity school asking him to serve as their dean. At a university a dean was more like the president of a seminary, one dean among the several schools making up the full university.

Occasionally Wolfe would turn away from his desk and project the room he sat in, and all the books that surrounded him, into a plush university divinity school setting. He would be a star. But the reality was that no one called. Maybe he'd been too young when he gave that keynote speech. Maybe someone was just waiting for him to age a few years. But he was bored. He was moody, on edge. Emily had remarked on his moodiness and apparent disconnection from the church. He'd sleep in on Sundays, and did not seem interested in the comments Emily brought home from her work or from the church they used to attend together. Maybe it had to do with failed expectations. He wasn't happy.

One Monday morning he'd stopped at a store to purchase some boxer shorts. When he'd picked out a package of four shorts, he made certain he wound up in a particular cashier's check-out line. An infrequent shopper, he'd some weeks back noticed this cashier's slim, shapely frame, and often found himself stopping for a minor purchase like gum or soap and the invented opportunity to casually flirt with her. Today when it was his turn at her register, he'd said something he thought was witty, and then found himself muttering: "would you be willing to perhaps, maybe, I mean sometime—get a cup of coffee or go to dinner some evening with me?" Even now he remembered how he had trembled at his embarrassment, his wimpy question, a fumbling teenager's query laced with "perhaps" and "sometime." She had looked at him and calmly dismissed him: "I'm pregnant. And didn't you forget—you're wearing a ring."

Stepping back from his purchase, Wolfe ducked his head downward from her accusing eyes. He saw the slight bump at her waist and, for the first time noticed that she also had a ring on her finger. His face flushed; he did not like playing the fool. Laughing at his obvious discomfort, she turned away from him while completing his transaction. Head bowed, he stepped away while quickly retreating, leaving the boxers in her hand. Slamming the car door, he wrestled the car out of the parking lot and away from her and his pitiful overture. As he merged in traffic, he crossed off that particular store. He would not go there again.

Ahead was the seminary and the daily trudge up the thirty-eight steps into his fourth floor office. There he would greet his secretary and the sheath of pink slips regarding persons who were calling for recommendations, disciplinary concerns, or the endless issues a dean dealt with concerning students, faculty, and an academic unit's financial sheet. Linda, his secretary, stuck her head into his office. "Oh, Dean Wolfe, Professor Munson is on his way up to see you."

"Why?" asked Wolfe. As always, Linda had the answer: "He knows Howard is retiring, and he wants Howard's office. He will plead seniority." Wolfe thought: "This is my job. No one here considers me their close friend. I'm dean not because of the faculty's great love, but because no one else on the faculty really wants the post. Further, the faculty fears the governing board's long reach. They think appointing an outsider as dean might break up their cozy arrangements. And it is true— an outsider's loyalty would lie more with the board than with the faculty. On the other hand, even though I am an 'insider,' I have not played favorites or backed any particular faculty group. And that favors me—I'm the devil that the faculty knows. So they will keep re-electing me as their dean, and my day is filled with the weighty issues of who gets what office or parking space and who doesn't want to teach evening courses."

At home, he and Emily occasionally talked about their failure to conceive children. This was usually brought up by Emily, who kept suggesting adoption as a possibility, but Karl was not interested. He continued to sit silently in his study, and whatever comments she could elicit were short ones. Emily thought he was depressed. "Not clinically depressed," she told a friend, "but definitely in a kind of melancholy state."

Things changed, however, when Karl was asked and accepted a mentoring position with the young confirmands of the church he and Emily attended. "I actually suggested this to Pastor Jack," Emily confided to a friend. "And it seems to be working." Emily continued: "Since Karl's involvement with the youth of the church, he seems rejuvenated." Karl himself confessed to Emily—"I like helping them with their questions about the Bible and what it might mean for them to be 'Christian' today."

*

Pastor Jack Curtis was dying, and he knew it. He'd already used up three of the nine months his doctors said he had left, and now he was settling accounts, writing last letters and working on the worship order for his funeral service. He'd also made arrangements with a hospice program: "I know the people there, and they will help me die at home." He'd no more than two appointments left with his lawyer for the updating of his will, then he'd be ready to check out. Jack knew his brother was a bit troubled by the way he was going about preparing to die, but he'd been close to dying before, and given the steadily increasing pain, felt he would welcome death. He did not fear it. He welcomed the idea of a rest from what had always been a busy life. As for the pain, his doctors regularly upped his medication. His doctor had told him: "You'll not have enough time left to worry about addiction."

So he hadn't worried; instead he'd spent the time left him by wrapping up some concerns and carefully easing out of a number of responsibilities. He'd cut way back on a lot of things he'd been doing, like keeping track of some sick people and several classes he'd agreed to teach. Not that many folk knew he was dying. He didn't want the sometimes pitying conversations that often dogged those who were dying. He remembered being a kid in a freshman class where a weepy conversation had centered on a beloved professor who was known to be dying from prostate cancer. Jack happened to be at a lunch table when the talked about professor sat down at the table next to him. He'd found himself overhearing a conversation in which the professor complained to a friend about the "intrusive concern" that came because he "had mentioned his cancer" at a staff meeting. "Before I knew it," he said, "my prostate was being prayed for in the Sunday church service," and "after that I was besieged with phone calls."

As a college student Jack had tended to keep personal concerns tucked deep inside. That disposition had not always helped him in his relationship with his wife, and once he'd figured out how relational love involved being more open, he'd peeled away some of his camouflage. But that was when he was with her. In most public situations Jack Curtis was protective of his innermost feelings. Now his wife was dead, and as a general rule he felt that at least some of his integrity had to do with not unduly undressing his private concerns in front of others, no matter how badly they wanted that to happen. So only a very few folk knew that he was dying, and he intended to keep it that way, at least for now.

When he'd retired, he'd had people come looking for him with job offerings designed to fill their needs. Some of the offerings involved a lot of money, but instead he'd become a dollar-a-year part time associate minister for a friend's small town parish. There were reasons for this move, but he wasn't going to post them on his door. He expected to resign his position after Easter, a celebration that was only three weeks away. As that date got closer, he'd been writing a letter. He'd worked at what he needed to say. It would go to the members of the parish and his friends.

But today he sat in his office, a good-sized room filled with books and enough chairs for the after school confirmation group. This was the one thing he had held onto, perhaps because their youthful exuberance took him back to his initial work as a youth minister, some sixty odd years ago. "I was never that young," he murmured out loud, as one of his favorites named Annie entered the office. An attractive child, bold and physically mature beyond her years, at fifteen Annie Nicholson usually carried herself in a confident fashion that often made her look more like an adult than a peer. But not tonight. Tonight she looked like a troubled teen-ager. He could see Annie was not sleeping well. There were dark circles under both eyes.

At times Jack knew that Annie looked to him for fatherly support. She and her dad had issues. Annie and her mother were sometimes alone, and often struggled to make ends meet. The father had left, come back, left again. Might as well say that Annie and her mom were really on their own.

The father provided little or no help. That wasn't so unusual with this group. Five of the nine youth came from single-parent households.

Throwing her backpack under her usual couch, Annie peeled away a jacket and dropped into the chair beside Curtis's desk. A frown marred what usually was a happy face. "Why can't you trust anyone, Rev. Jack?" she asked. "Annie." Curtis greeted her. "You're telling me you can't trust anyone?"

"Yeah. Maybe; I mean why are boys—and men, I guess—why are they so untrustworthy?"

"Can you say more?"

"Well, I don't know. I mean I'm not a child anymore, but the way most boys act toward me is scary. And then there are the older guys, and some really old guys. They look at me like. . ."

"Like they want to take you somewhere and have sex with you."

"Well yeah! And my mom says that I have to watch out. She is always telling me about my aunt who didn't watch out and how she 'made her bed and had to lie in it' and that kind of stuff. . ."

"Annie, it sounds like you are being pressured to. . ."

Just then, Shawn entered the room. Shawn bounced across the carpet and kissed Annie on the head. As Shawn and Annie continued greeting each other, Curtis interjected. "Annie," he said: "We need to talk later, ok?" To which Annie nodded, and then turned back toward Shawn and the other teen-agers entering the room. Curtis mentally filed Annie into his appointment book for a telephone call and a talk sometime later that week.

The confirmation class ended well. Each week Annie was usually among the first to leave, but tonight she hung back, seemingly intent on being the last one out the door. He had noticed that she had seemed more vulnerable in the way she phrased some of her comments. Given her usual up-beat enthusiasm, Jack wondered if something more serious than dating peers was on her mind. As she left the room —and it seemed to Curtis that her leaving was done in a hidden way that was not really as covert as she might have intended— she paused by the door and dropped a double-folded, small square of paper into the wastebasket. "She wants me to read that," thought Curtis.

After receiving final goodbyes, Curtis stepped back into the room and bending down, retrieved the folded sheet. Opening it, he first saw lavender ink, easily identifying Annie's girlish hand in what was just one written word. That word had been placed dead center in Annie's twice-folded sheet of paper—and that word was "Why?"

Five days later Annie's mother called; Annie was dead. As best they could determine, somehow Annie had swallowed a lot of drugs. When contacted by the police, a pharmacist said that the kind and quantity of drugs she had taken were easily capable of killing her. Her mother had located the father, and he was coming home. She alerted Jack as to the father's anger. "He hardly ever was here, but—you know—she was his little girl." Her voice breaking, Mrs. Nicholsen told Jack that Annie had left a note asking Reverend Curtis to "do" her funeral. "Annie said you were kind and that you'd understand." "Neither of these things is true," he thought. "And suicide for this girl makes no sense, no sense at all."

*

Ten Years Later, 1989

Fall Academic Quarter

One

CLAYTON HERON WAS AN angry man. He'd picked up the coffeepot and the handle had broken, almost burning him and spilling at a minimum two cups of coffee onto the kitchen floor. "Darned modern junk," he exclaimed, "now I've got to get me a new one." He'd risen early. He'd thought the day might be orderly, but now the coffee spill unsettled him. Once the floor was cleaned, he moved toward the door, calling his dog, Sassy, a Springer Spaniel of high energy. "Maybe a walk will help," he told himself.

Tall, his white hair unruly, in gait Clayton Heron matched his name. A retired academic and ordained minister, walking for Heron involved an uneven positioning of both legs, accompanied by a tugging arm motion. Under a beat-up baseball cap, bright blue eyes peered out of a strongly lined face. On occasion he'd been mistaken for a retired schoolteacher, farmer, and automotive mechanic, but rarely as the president of a theological seminary.

Wearing well-washed khakis, worn dock-siders, and carrying in his jacket pocket his great-grandfather's pocket watch, Clayton watched as his dog ran unleashed through a neighbor's field. After Sassy flushed a small rabbit, Clayton affectionately whistled her back to his leash and their continued walk through the awakening neighborhood. Turning into a side street, they collected a newspaper at the corner store, and he now sat alone at the kitchen table he and Kate purchased forty years earlier. This was the home in which they had raised two children, a boy and a girl, and where he would remain until God called him home. "And that soon enough," he spoke out loud.

He was in his late sixties. Kate had passed ten years earlier, but he had soldiered on, not yet ready for full retirement, whatever that was. He knew even his close friends would never understand his love for his church, but he remained entwined with his denomination and its ministry, its churches, and its seminary.

Seminary presidents were an odd lot, but on the whole the little country seminary located in the town of about six thousand residents had been blessed with administrators and faculty members who cared more for the good health of the school and their students than for the prideful enlarge-ment of their own egos. He'd been president for twenty-eight years, and now the man who followed him into the presidency, David Karns, contin-ued to see in him a rich oral repository of the values and the principles that had, over the years, shaped the school into what it was today. He'd often call Clayton and ask him for his opinion.

And in his retirement, Clayton had been careful. When David asked, he'd sit and talk with him, but he didn't butt in. He knew, without apology, that he'd been gifted with some smarts and some social graces and the good sense to use them in helpful ways, so he and the new president got along just fine, thank you.

Which, with Kate dead, still left a lot of time, and he occupied a good bit of those hours as the part-time "calling" pastor at the church where he helped the pastor. On Tuesdays and Thursdays he'd normally swing by the hospitals, and then on Fridays he'd stop by the denominational office and spend about an hour with Melvin Jackson, the district pastor, a man who found that troubled congregations often meant dealing with ministers who got themselves and their churches tied into knots. Clayton often wondered why some folks seemed to have no common sense at all. Some people he knew called a lot of what went on "sin;" Clayton simply called it "dumb."

But yesterday, a Monday, when most pastors (and even seminary presidents) took time off for rest following busy weekends, he'd gotten a call from seminary president Karns, who'd said, "Clayton; got a bad one. Can you spare some time, maybe walk down here today?" He'd said "Yes; how about nine?" And with that said, he'd fed the dog, finished his coffee, brushed his teeth, and headed away from home, moving his creaky body toward town and the seminary, about a mile from his house.

As he walked, Clayton caught the first hint of winter in the blustery, chill wind. The northern hardwood leaves were coming down. Some of the oaks, seemingly unable to let go of brown, dead-looking leaves, cast dreary shadows as occasional rays of the sun broke through an overcast day. He shrugged deeper into his jacket. "Bout time to get the winter gear out," he said to himself, even as the momentary sunshine warmed his brow. Touch-ing his forehead, Clayton noticed that his hairline, much like his father's, was receding at a rapid rate. "I'll soon be bald," he noted.

November could be a dreary, cold month, and Clayton catalogued some of the simple things he would miss this winter— simple things like sidewalks clear of snow and a light jacket warm enough for an early morning walk. He'd also miss Kate, and the fact that she knew how to make the best coffee. "And not break the damned coffee pot," he grumbled. By now he could see the seminary, and it always soothed him, raised his spirit, helping him to quit feeling sorry for himself.

Back in the day the seminary had acquired the high ground across the river. It had been a smart move. No question that the seminary was a noticeable part of this essentially rural, small town community. Everyone could see it up there, a kind of earthly vision of God's presence. It was on top of a high ridge, and Clayton took his time crossing the bridge and climbing that last uphill quarter mile. Walking through the seminary gate, he glanced at his watch, noting with some pride that he could still do this hike in just about forty minutes, "not bad," he muttered, "for an old geezer".

The administration building was of sandstone, put together in an 1850's kind of quasi-Victorian style, with green stained copper flashing, red tiled roofing, and an occasional gargoyle downspout. Taking the entryway steps quickly, he could see David Karns pacing outside his office, and Clayton could see that the president was deeply bothered. "Coffee, Clayton?" David asked. He grasped Clayton's right hand and embraced him in a warm hug. "Nope; had some earlier," Clayton smiled.

"Come on in then; let's sit."

"No calls," President Karns instructed his executive secretary, and the door to his office was pulled shut. Clayton said, "So now the news."

The president said: "Clayton, our former academic dean, Karl Wolfe, has several nasty rumors about him publically circulating." He continued: "Maybe these rumors are the stuff of daily gossip in the church, but I had not heard them, perhaps because they are not complimentary of either you or me." Karl Wolfe had been academic dean under Clayton; "He did a good job," said Clayton. "He sometimes needed me to rein him in; he could be too authoritarian, but I'm not aware of his mistreating faculty or not doing the job asked of him. I guess I'd have to say that I'm not aware of any involvement in bad behavior that occurred on his part while I was president."

"All true," said the president. "I inherited him from you, and I've trusted him with significant work, and he did that work competently. But," said the president, "Wolfe got that offer, as you know, from the big city university divinity school, and he jumped at it. In fact it was a good offer and he took it and became their chief administrative officer. You and I can understand that—the university job was a plum. Here we're a small, confessional school primarily educating pastors for our denomination. There, well, Wolfe could hob-knob with Nobel prize winners and be the head of a well-known divinity school that has students in a PhD program and ministerial degrees, as well." Clayton knew something bad was coming because this president rarely used a last name when speaking about someone. Usually it would be "Karl," and certainly never "Wolfe." Today it was just "Wolfe." Clayton heard the anger under the surface of the president's comments. So he just listened.

The president clenched his teeth and continued: "The rumor that I heard yesterday from a trustworthy source is that Wolfe can't keep his hands off several of the university div school's female students and at least one faculty member." He continued: "I don't know how much of this is true, but I do know that our professor Molly Hoffman, wife of professor Max Hoffman, came to me last week with not only accusations of Wolfe's having an affair with her while he was dean here, but with a pile of letters that seem to prove it. Some of those letters were written on our seminary stationery. Others were written on divinity school stationery. On both sets the 'office of the dean' is part of the header and Wolfe's name is prominently displayed. Almost as if the fool thought he was invisible and untouchable."

"I'm stunned," said Clayton.

"Indeed." President Karns paused, took a sip of what, by this time, had to be cold coffee, and continued: "It seems that the two of them, or at least Molly, had a fantasy going with him about getting a big city div school position and then divorcing his wife, Emily. Once that happened, Molly would divorce Max, and then she and Wolfe would marry each other and live happily ever after." President Karns paused; then he continued: "This started on your watch. It became a full-blown affair under my watch. At least if we can believe Molly." He wiped his brow, "Sounds crazy, doesn't it?"

"It does; it does indeed," said Clayton. "I'd have put most of it down to Molly. She is a bit of a strange one at times, but that stack of correspondence from Wolfe sounds like he shared—or at least led her to believe he shared—that they were soul-mates and that this idea could become reality. Damn fools." Then he asked: "But why has she come forward now?"

"She came forward because some of the university divinity school faculty—I don't know which ones yet, but I'm sure I will, soon enough—some people at the div school have been checking up on Dean Wolfe. They found out that he has been dipping his cock into several of their female students; and, in addition, they heard that Wolfe and Molly Hoffman (from our little seminary) were in some kind of long-term sexual relationship. So out of the goodness of their hearts they decided to call Molly Hoffman at her home to find out if she knew that Wolfe was messing round over in the big city with students from their school. And the short answer is no, Molly did not know that the good dean had moved on to younger pickings." Clayton had risen to get a fresh cup of coffee; he was pacing back and forth. "Not good; not good at all."

"And Molly went ballistic. I mean I think she's called just about everybody she could think of who might be able to clip Karl a good one. In a way I can't blame her, but hanging all his and her dirty laundry out for everyone to see it?" Karns sat down. Shoulders hunched, he raised his head and plaintively said: "Clayton, I just don't get it."

"Makes you wonder, doesn't it," said Clayton, "something about a woman scorned? Tawdry stuff. Wolfe must have thought (must still think) that no one ever talks with anyone else. Maybe he thinks he's invisible. Not for long though; that div school bunch have proved to be pretty good researchers, after all, and if they follow Wolfe's scent, he won't get far. But why would he do this kind of thing?" There was a pause in the conversation; nodding at Clayton's summary, President Karns said: "I can't really answer that, Clayton. All I know right now, not to be blunt, is that when it comes to women and sex, it seems Karl has no shame. We teach our ministerial students that they are to love the people in their churches, but Karl seems to have taken that literally. And he thought he could get away with it." Clayton responded: "And when Molly heard that Karl was chasing div school women students. . ."

"She lost it; I think she called Emily Wolfe and after talking with her got in contact with some members of the div school faculty. When she saw me she alternated between tears and rage. I'll say one thing: she will not be silent about this. It's a mess."

Clayton had resumed sitting with both elbows planted on his knees. Now he looked up at the president. "David, we should be expecting a call from the div school. They will want to know what you know, what I knew, and if we knew any of this before Wolfe left here. They will want to know if we sent them damaged goods. And even if he is messing with div school students now, we need to find out about our own. Sally Hoffman is an adult, that's one thing, but if he messed or is still messing with our students we're liable, and I mean we're theologically, spiritually, and ethically liable in addition to legally liable."

"I think I should call our lawyer."

"I agree; but I want to emphasize that this is more than a legal matter; before we agree to do what a lawyer wants, we've got to talk this through and come to an understanding as to the moral issues it may present for us." After several phone calls and a series of difficult conversations well after business hours, both men finally left the office.

Muttering "Damn fools," Clayton walked slowly down the hill toward his home.

*

Holding onto the cuffs of his long-sleeved shirt, Tyler Jamison inserted both arms into his blue sweater, tugging it over his head and then pulling it down to his waist. Stepping outside his room, he double-locked the door and bounded down two flights of stairs. The old apartment building's tattered green wallpaper and brown staircase weren't much, but it had become home. It was a crisp fall morning, most of the leaves on his tree-lined street were down. Winter could not be far off.

Tyler had come to love this part of the city, the university part. On his right, he could just make out two short blocks of older apartment buildings like the one he lived in, while on the left was the low outline of the university lab school, and beyond them the taller, gray buildings of the university itself. Ahead lay the tennis courts, the quadrangle, and tucked in one corner, the university divinity school.

Having reached the quad, Tyler joined the constant flow of students and professors hurrying toward morning classes. Reminding himself that his mid-point review would occur next week, he once again asked himself what the future might hold. If he was successful in passing this review, he would no longer be understood to be a student; instead, he would be declared a candidate for the degree. But how would he use the degree? Where was Tyler Jamison headed?

The problem was his own indecision; would he declare for ministry, or would he aim for the doctorate? Not that he was over confident; his professors had been clear that they saw no reason for him to fear the mid-point review, and further, they had tried to tell him that he could successfully go either way. Both paths held certain stipulations he would need to meet, and he was not certain what he should do.

Early on he'd had his share of hard choices. He'd been nine when his dad died in his sleep with lungs filled with water with the disease from his time in the coal mine. Trying to help, Tyler had been strong enough to dig at the exposed seam behind their house, scrabbling chips of hard coal with a mattock and pick-axe before winter set in that year. And he'd figured out his dad's axe, cutting downed trees and sawing them into two foot lengths that fit into their ancient furnace. By spring the family was a regular for the Salvation Army's box stuffed with government canned pork, cheese, beans, and margarine, a white lard-like substance made yellow by breaking and kneading into the margarine a small yellow tube of coloring. He remembered the canned pork. His mom made gravy with the pork, serving it over biscuits. Thinking about it made him remember that he'd skipped breakfast.

He considered how far he'd come, from a tiny, crossroad town in north central Pennsylvania through a community college and then a state school where he'd met a conservative campus chaplain, gotten involved, and now found himself in the div school. An intramural basketball player had started it all by inviting Tyler to a party at the home of the campus chaplain. Tyler had been surprised that something as frivolous as a party was somehow connected to the church and religion. As he'd grown up, neither he nor his parents had contact with formalized religion, but he'd been in the mood for a party, even one sponsored by the church. He had been surprised. He'd behaved somewhat cautiously, but had enjoyed the evening. The chaplain did not fit Tyler's image of what a minister "ought to look like." He was skinny, wore blue jeans, Frye boots, and had more hair on his head than some of the girls at the party. He was also low key and, more to Tyler's liking, he was a very interesting conversationalist.

As Tyler was leaving the party that night, the chaplain caught his arm and said: "Tyler, we've a discussion group every Wednesday night at six. There's good food and better conversation. Come join us. I think you'd like it." "I'll see you then," Tyler said. Later, in seminary, he'd found that the Presbyterians had a word for it—predestination. As Tyler heard it being explained—God apparently not only knew who Tyler was and where he would wind up, but knew it well before Tyler did. On one level, Tyler liked this idea; he especially liked it when he considered how far he had come without having any great plan in mind. Somehow he had wound up here, and who could really say how that had happened. But maybe he was just lazy when it came to not looking ahead. His theology professor noted that, historically, people who were doing well liked the idea of predestination and were somewhat arrogant in their belief that God was being favorable to them (and against others who were not faring as well). That professor,

Dr. Thomas Metcalf, was at pains to always point out the pros and cons of theological convictions like predestination, and that was one of the reasons Tyler was taking most of Metcalf's elective courses.

Tyler had given himself and the div school a year, one year to convince himself that he could find his way in the world as a teacher, minister, or maybe something he'd never thought about. That first year had been good, no questions there. But he was still in seminary, and this was his second year. "Damn it," he exclaimed out loud; he still could not decide. The questions remained. Maybe he should simply commit; do this thing he feared, and dive into ministry. That would mean looking for a position, most likely in a church, and he'd need to start that process next year; on the other hand, the pursuit of a doctoral degree could keep him here four or more years. "A penny for your thoughts." Tyler jumped. He'd been daydreaming. A young woman named Kylie was walking beside him, a smile on her face. "You're a million miles away."

Kylie. Tyler's brain suddenly engaged. Kylie had been a surprise. He wasn't certain what the people who attended divinity schools were supposed to look like, but never in his wildest imaginings would he have imagined Kylie. On that first day at the seminary he had stepped into a room where a man was holding forth—this was their mandatory "orientation"—and there was this dark-haired, lovely, almond-eyed girl, sitting across the room looking at him. He had tried to play it cool by acting surprised at seeing the empty seat next to her. He had negotiated a path through the twenty or more student-filled chairs, interrupting the speaker, finally managing to fall into the empty seat and whisper: "Hi, name's Tyler. You are?" "Kylie Raven," she responded. "Who's he?" Tyler asked, nodding at the speaker. "Dr. Karl Wolfe," Kylie whispered, "He's the University Divinity School Dean."

*

Two

THERE HAD BEEN DREAMS. No, they were hallucinations. Maybe they were real. He was not certain where reality began and what he was experiencing ended. Awake, Wolfe asked for water. Sipping from a bent straw, Wolfe marveled at how much work was involved in the simple act of drinking. Exhausted, he fell back onto the pillow and into a drug-addled moment when he and an old hag were riding a train. Try as he might, he could not see her face. She said nothing to him, but instead took his arm, pulling him close to her body in a wild kind of dance. Collapsing onto the gray, metallic floor of the train-car, they kissed, but he still did not see her face. She suddenly stood, pulled him upright, and chortling together, in high spirits both danced as they rode the train round and round until it finally shuddered to a stop.

Exiting the train, Wolfe discovered blood running down his face. He turned toward the woman, but she did not get off, and as the train doors closed he saw her face looking back at him. Her ugliness dissolved into the angry face of a divinity school student at the university, a beautiful almond-eyed girl he wanted to touch, to hold, to ask if she would ride with him, but as he reached for her, she became an old hag who pushed him away, a hard enough shove so that he fell backward off the elevated platform, into the path of a second train. A searing white light woke him from his dream. "Let me increase your dose," the nurse said.

Doctors had ended one of Wolfe's meds after lions, tigers, and multicolored snakes had come out of the hospital's walls trying to rip him apart. But he was still confused, not sure who (or what) was visiting him, and prone to long, disturbing periods of sleep. Always there were women in his dreams, but none came to calm him or to love him. Some were beautiful. One in a black caftan came calling more than once. She offered curses, and knew of things he had done.

Wolfe's dreams were closed loops always involving women. The loops played over and over, exhausting him. In one that he tried to unpack while awake, he remembered dreaming about being in *The Thoughtful Bean,* a coffee-shop frequented by professors and students. He had been observing the back of a young woman whose jeans were tight and whose laughter occasionally floated back to where he was sitting, sipping a cup of coffee and reading that morning's newspaper.

He could not see the young woman's face, but the fullness of her body was visible over the shoulder of his wife, Emily, who never realized how far away he was from her and everything else. Emily moved her chair, bumping the young woman, who turned and, so he thought, caught his eyes on her. She was Pamela Wilson, a thirteen year-old whose breasts he had cradled in his hands as the two of them stood in neck high water in a rural swimming hole on the river near their homes.

This was impossible, his mind kept trying to alert him, because Pamela had died at age thirty-two from breast cancer and, in any case, all that had occurred nearly forty years ago, and how could the woman in the coffee-shop, now in her thirties, be Pamela Wilson? No matter. . . the girl in his drug-addled dream had the same dark eyes into which he, a thirteen-year-old in love, had gazed, knowing only that he held a mystery in his hands even as the hag whispered: "I know what you did." But what had he done? Morphine eased his pain, but did not provide an answer.

When he was young he'd been clumsy and inept with girls. While dry humping a blonde cheerleader on her parent's basement sofa, his adolescent body had ejaculated a burst of semen. At home he shamefully hid his soiled underpants until he could take the burnable trash to their outdoor fifty gallon drum and set fire to them with the rest of the rubbish. He flirted with girls, but never fucked one until his first year in college when a senior sorority girl had invited him, a lowly frosh, into her sorority suite to "look through some of the pictures of sorority activities." They had been at a mixer dance, and he had been bold enough to ask her to dance with him. He'd actually kept up with this woman for what she called "a fast dance," and when the music ended she had said: "whew; I'm glad I wore my knickers." Puzzled, he'd said "What?" She had raised her pleated shirt with both hands, showing him soft-green, longish boxer panties. Later, alone with her in the sorority suite, he said "you surprised me." She raised her eyebrows. He continued "I don't think I've ever seen anything like those. They look so soft. "Here," she said, "touch them here." And he did.

*

He was surprised he was still alive. Rarely sick, all his life he'd been good enough to be mediocre at sports. He could still beat younger colleagues at racquetball. But when he had grabbed for and missed his desk and slid onto the office floor, face down, hard, he had no doubt that he'd seen the last of his fifties and that he was to die, and die that very day, that very minute. "Heart attack," a man said as the room slowly faded away. And in that minute, face pushed into the brown carpet, he'd thought about Emily.

Emily had caught him unawares. Karl had met her on a campus retreat. He was lonely. Life had not gone well, but he had—nevertheless—thrown himself into his study, graduated well, and had been hired. In that job he had met Emily, and though she was prim and proper, she had struck up a conversation with him that had led to evening conversations on her folk's back porch. Her dad was the president of the college that had hired Wolfe, and there was a porch swing they could sit on, talking while gently swinging back and forth. She was attractive, willing, and they were both young and lonely. Marriage followed. There had been no children, yet those early years were still full. But something happened— he'd grown apart from Emily even as his eyes increasingly fell on younger women. It was unplanned, yet this nexus, this troubling location that Wolfe sensed had to do with something incomplete inside his soul, had to do with an empty hole in him that he tried to complete, to fill, to control, to be at peace with.

Now he was in his fifties, often unable to have an erection. He wasn't certain if it was a physical or mental issue born of frustration and stress, but yesterday doctors had split open his chest and cut out his heart, placing it in a stainless steel pan. Even as they were stripping replacement tubing from legs and arms, four rotten vessels were thrown into a garbage can and, once things were stitched together, a battery shocked him back to life. He felt different. For some time, even before all the cutting, his sexual drive was weaker. Only hours after this process, he had awakened with the certain knowledge that he would soon die. In one of his dreams he felt the dirt coming down onto his casket and him screaming inside.

He'd not yet met God, and if there was one he'd share a laugh with him when he was dead. Dead. His life would leave no mark except perhaps a footnote in some obscure text. There it was. He'd worked hard, pushed himself to the limit, and he was at his (almost) final moment. And no God to save him, even in death. The heart attack was a step into that final blackness. How ironic that he had worked all his life in texts that proclaimed a living God, yet he had never met the God he so easily proclaimed. A final indignity, a wire that ended just above his belly button was attached to his heart. If his heart got erratic or, God forbid, were to stop, a battery could be put in play again, shocking his heart once more into action.

He remembered a recurring dream in which he was handcuffed to the safety bar across the seat of a Ferris wheel. No one else was in the seat. He was alone. The wheel had stalled at the peak of its trajectory. Around him a late night fireworks show erupted into colored blossoms, targeting circles filled with vivid colors. Looking down he saw a clutch of people gathered into another tight circle. The eyes of colleagues and women stared upward, searching for his face. He felt he was being accused, but why—what had he done? There was a gun in his hand. In his dream Wolfe flinched with each pulling of the revolver's trigger, but what were his targets—the firework patterns? Or the eyes of those who stood beneath him near the base of the Ferris wheel? But there was no answer. He heard screams as the colored blossoms centered by watchful eyes disappeared. "Damn," said Wolfe. "It was just a dream."

Wolfe had watched old men sleep. Perhaps that was to be his fate. Maybe, like them, he'd dream the last few years away. Dreams, after all, were his secret world. He knew Emily would not miss him, not really. The spark once there between them no longer existed, and he and Emily remained together not by choice but for convenience; no other option was really there for her now. Once she had options, but no longer. Not now. And there was no one other than Emily who might miss him. Nevertheless—Emily stayed. And what had once been love of some sort now to Wolfe seemed filled with contempt, if not on her part, at least on his. Why would anyone stay with him in his miserable state?

Perhaps that was too harsh a judgment; perhaps she did not feel his contempt. Her staying with him was after all, her choice. A choice of sorts, but a lot of what went into her being with him was connected to her pride at being the wife of a minister, a respected man, Karl Wolfe, the dean of a university divinity school, one known throughout the world. Emily Wolfe prized continuity, the sameness of each day, a litany of months rolling into years. She had been there when he had labored in the hinterlands, crawling through the mean times, but now the two of them were past all that, and whatever accusations there had been in those years, now she had her role as "the Dean's wife," and her garden. Nothing seemed better for Emily than a good book, a pot of tea, and a bouquet of fresh-cut garden flowers on the table. She had stood by his side for thirty-two years. He had always been there for her, but he did not cherish her. Perhaps he cherished no one.

He realized that today was a Sunday, and he could see Emily getting ready for church. He closed his eyes. Bible class always started at 10 AM, and Emily Wolfe tended to be an "early bird." In his mind he saw her making certain the coffee pot was on, that napkins were in place, and that the chairs were arranged in a comfortable circle.

*

On Sunday Emily wore what she called her "blue outfit." Today a dark blue skirt, a floral patterned blouse, and a warm, light blue cardigan sweater felt just right. From her garden she'd picked some of the last mums to bloom before the inevitable late fall frost. As she placed them in vases onto two tables strategically located at either "end" of the circle, she heard a noise, and turning saw Jill Adamson enter the room. "Jill," Emily said, and turning back to her flowers said, "a little color to brighten this old room." "Oh Emily," Jill responded; "I'm surprised that you're here, what with Karl in the hospital. Is he ok? I heard the news from Sylvia Masterson, and I couldn't help but think that I'd miss Karl's leading our Bible study next week. Such terrible news."

"It's ok, Jill. Karl's heart attack was not a major one. God was with us. They discovered that he needed bypass surgery on four diseased blood vessels leading to the heart. They did that surgery the day he went in for the heart attack. After his surgery he was full of strange stories about riding a train and an encounter with a mugger and a knife, but I think that was the drugs. He never has done well when the doctors give him drugs." She paused, adjusted a wayward flower, then spoke: "He'll probably be home Monday or Tuesday, and I'll be going in to see him after church today, so I'll carry your concerns and prayers to him today. Never fear."

"Well, it's a shame. When everyone is here, we'll offer prayer for his safe return home."

"He'd like that."

Finished with the floral arrangements, Emily claimed a seat as the rest of the class settled in anticipation of remarks to be made by Dr. Kevin Walker, a new professor at the divinity school. He'd come to the church because Karl had suggested to the group that as a good speaker and a new professor, Walker needed to get acquainted with some of the churches that over the years had been supportive of the divinity school.

"Sin most easily is understood as broken relationships," Walker said. A youngish man of perhaps forty, Kevin Walker was good-looking and an instant hit with the Bible study group. Gretchen Anderson was first to ask a question. "Doctor," she said, "If God created a good world, why are we so broken up by this thing called 'sin'?" The class had a lively discussion, concluding that creation was good, but that humans "messed it up," as one member so inelegantly stated it. The class agreed that "the church spent too much time protesting the sins of individuals while not willing to confront systems that needed confronting." Emily wanted to talk this over with Karl. Theology was perhaps the one place that she and Karl still actually had conversations. She quickly made her good-byes, found their car in the church parking lot, and drove to the hospital.

But her enthusiasm was dampened when she saw Karl. He seemed stressed. He also still seemed somewhat befuddled by his drugs. Nevertheless, she pressed on, telling Karl: "You missed a good one." After hearing Emily's recounting of the morning class, Karl obviously had a different agenda. He didn't want to discuss sin or what the church "ought" to protest. Instead, he was anxious that Emily hear, once again, how he had been mugged on the way home after one of his downtown meetings. "I dreamed about it again, Emily. I was scared," said Karl. "I understand how you feel. I don't feel safe when you're out of town, Karl," said Emily. He backpedaled: "We're safe at home, Emily. The crime reports suggest we're living in one of the safest neighborhoods in the city."

But Emily was hearing none of it. "I hear the sirens every night, Karl. Don't tell me there's no crime here. It's visible outside our bedroom window every day. I see it near the train stop. You weren't here when two men got into it right outside our window. One man shot the other man. The police were all over the street, but he got away. I know there's violence here. I've seen it, Karl, and I don't want it inside our home." "We'll get a home security system", said Karl. Emily shook her head. "No, Karl. Today in our Bible study several people talked about how brutal this city has become, and I agree. I've seen too many movies where those home security things can be disconnected. I'd feel safer if we kept dad's old pistol in the drawer beside our bed."

Karl didn't like guns, but he knew that Emily's family still delighted in recalling the story about Emily's mother and her pistol. Living alone in the country after her husband had died frightened Emily's mother, so she had taken to sleeping with the family pistol tucked under her pillow. If Karl had heard this story once, he'd heard it a dozen times. Usually Emily's brother would chuckle, and as her mother would run into the kitchen he'd whisper: "You won't catch me knocking on the door of this house late at night. She'd probably shoot me. No way I'd risk that!" And he was right, thought Karl, but his concern really wasn't the pistol. "If keeping a pistol in the drawer beside the bed makes you feel better, then no problem, we'll do that. In fact, you can do that before I come home." Emily looked relieved. After a pause, Wolfe remembered that Emily earlier wanted to discuss theology. "And you were saying, Emily, Walker gave a good class today. About sin, right? And prophetic action? Sorry to distract you. Would you like to talk about it?"

*

The next morning; 4:30 in the morning. Wolfe rolled over; no longer in a deep sleep. A slight shudder, a twitch ran across both shoulders and down his spine. He had been dreaming. Again. He'd been back in the hospital. There was a hospital bed, a plastic-covered, metal contrivance that was one of many situated on both sides of a long rectangle of a room, dimly lit and with no windows. Aside from that one twitch, he'd had no awareness of his body. Wires led to eye-high monitors, slowly becoming less visible.

It was strange to have no immediate work ahead of him other than "getting better," as the doctors termed it. He looked at the clock. 4:35 AM. Nights were hard. Days were harder. He rolled back, under the covers. He had almost died. He remembered. He had surfaced slowly, floating upward as if pieces of one of his bad dreams held him down. One eye caught movement beside his bed, and a man's voice—a male nurse— had asked if he was ok with his pain, and he felt his twitching arm.

He remembered. He had finished his class, closed a window, and while collecting his papers began to feel out of sorts, as if he had an upset stomach and had just carried a full suitcase up several flights of stairs. Outside his classroom he'd stopped at a men's room, but despite his best effort, he could neither void his bowels nor throw up. He had found himself grasping his office desk when someone asked: "Are you all right?" And he'd slid face down into the brown carpet.

That had been what had happened, but the day after his surgery he knew that something still seemed wrong with his arm. It had twitched. And his body had seemed out of sorts, not really connected, kind of floating. He told himself that what he was experiencing wasn't a dream. He could not tell what was real and what had been imagined. Wolfe had been given a sip of water. Was the water real? Wrapped in warm blankets, in his mind he saw medical students and doctors gathered at the foot of his bed. As they talked about him, he became aware of a loosening of his spirit, a letting go of the energy that held him together, a shaking that started as a shiver in his spine and built into a trembling, and his words were: "something is wrong; I'm not ok, I'm losing it." He was shaking and the bed was bouncing and he was dying. This was reality. His body was wrong; wrong—something wasn't working. "Help me," he whimpered. A doctor pointed at the two drip bags on the steel pole and asked: "What's in that?" A nurse said something; pointing, the doctor said: "disconnect that one." The nurse did something, squeezed a plastic clip. The shaking stopped. Exhausted, he closed his eyes.

Later he was hot, too hot. Wolfe threw off the bed covers, sat straight up, and made his pronouncement to an orderly: "Living and dying are connected by a very fragile thread; break or badly fray the thread, and everything collapses." The orderly called for a nurse. Another needle entered Wolfe's arm. He was not well. He had almost died twice, that much was clear to him. Again he was hot; it was as if his insides were burning. He pressed his emergency call button. A new nurse arrived. "Your vitals aren't right," she announced. But he did not hear her. He had fainted, and he did not know that he had been a code blue, and that he was back in surgery.

The night nurse was back, and once again he was in a large darkened room. "Sleep," said his nurse, but he did not want to sleep. It was dark; he could not see the nurse. He wondered why God had abandoned him and why his nights were filled with nightmares. The old hag regularly visited him: "I know what you did." He wondered what she knew and why she never leveled with him. "Tell me," he screamed, "tell me."

In his mind he got up out of the bed and moved to his desk chair where he sat with his head in his hands. Pamela Wilson. Her again. He was dreaming, but he no longer was afraid. Perhaps he needed to confront the dream. Perhaps he could dig deeper. The recurrence of the dream could not be a coincidence. It had played after the three times he almost died. Maybe it all started there, with her.

But he'd been just a kid. He remembered: there was a turn in the river just before the spillway. The water backed up, forming an eddy. On either side of the river were high banks, shielding the eddy and providing plenty of safe parking up top. On hot summer days, "Highbanks" had everything that might be of interest to young men, including liquor, cars, and girls. He might have been just a kid, but everyone at school had let it be known via the town's efficient grapevine that the place to be that Saturday was Highbanks.

He'd hitched a ride with Frank, played softball, ate a hotdog—but all that paled before his encounter in the water with a girl, Pamela Wilson by name. Close-cropped hair, brown eyes, a tanned body inside a white, two-piece swim suit—Pamela effortlessly cut him out of a pack of boys playing chicken in the neck-high water. In his mind he again watched as she splashed him, caught his eye, silently inviting him, and then turned away, as if to say: "Want me? Come get me." He had followed.

Facing her, both their heads above the brown river water, his hands encircling her waist, her hands encircling his. Slowly his hands moved up her perfect waist until, heart pounding, he held both breasts. As they stood, close together, his penis became erect. An electric realization hit him—this was what life was all about. Watching his face, she slipped both hands under his swimsuit and, clasping his erection for a long moment, smiled. Just before swimming away, she looked in his eyes and said: "I'm not that kind of girl."

He did not follow; he could hear Frank yelling at him, and he was afraid to chase her. If he caught her, what would he do? "Time to go," Frank yelled again, and he found himself moving with deliberate slowness away from Pam, leaden legs carrying him away from whatever catching her might mean, away from all those realizations that might carry him beyond the set boundaries of his adolescent life. He hoped his erection would subside before he reached the edge of the water. He was grateful when Robert Kelly bumped his shoulder. The two of them wrestled in the waist deep water, allowing him to emerge unembarrassed.

In that moment he realized that women had a kind of power in life that he'd never fully understand. And now, looking back at that moment, Wolfe felt sympathy for that young man, not sure of who he was or what he should do, even as he saw the boy crawling up the riverbank and disappearing from Pamela Wilson's life forever. He thought: "I could have, I should have taken the chance, gone with her and ignored my ride home." But he'd been like that in those days. Less assertive, he'd been raised to not expect much, to look down when talked to, to fail in school and in all the important things of life. He was "nuthin," as his pa had told him. After

Highbanks he'd gone home, and twenty years later Pamela Wilson had died from cancer, just like he'd no doubt die from having diseased arteries. And here he was, three days after they had cut him open, still trying to understand what made a life worth living and searching for some signs that he was alive, kicking, and still able to do it (whatever "it" was). In his mind he stood up, exited his room and wandered the hospital's hallways, adding and subtracting the choices leading to this moment. He would not die today, but he knew his death was not some far off, unrealized event, but instead was something daily occurring over a set of consequential small steps that were finally coming together into an unavoidable terminal moment. He named them. . . impotence, diseased arteries, age. . .where had it all gone? What had he done? He'd lived his life, and today doubted the worth of that living. He went to the bed and crawled back under the covers, but he could not fall back asleep.

*

Three

Tyler's mind re-played his luck (or laughing, maybe his "predestination") of meeting Kylie that orientation day. While much of the first part of the year was a blur, Kylie was never far from his awareness, and now here she was, one more time, this time a golden fall day. He knew that he was more than a little in love with her. "Kylie. Hey. It's good to see you on such a beautiful fall day." Leaning toward Tyler, Kylie touched him lightly on the arm. "It's good to see you, Tyler; I'm glad you're here." He responded: "It's good to be seen, Kylie, especially by you. What's up?"

"I thought I'd try to catch you before class. Last night Karen called me late. Have you heard? Dean Wolfe had a heart attack. Nearly died. He'd just ended a class, went into his office, collapsed onto the floor, and then everyone started running around, calling the university police, getting blankets and generally going crazy." Open-mouthed, Tyler stopped walking and faced Kylie, almost as if he needed to see if this was a joke, but no, Kylie was dead serious, no smile, a painful aspect infusing her usually cheerful face. She looked as if she was expecting someone might come into class today and suddenly notify everyone that the dean had died. "Were you there?" Tyler asked. "No," Kylie responded, "but I was coming into the div school when an ambulance pulled up, lights flashing, siren wailing, and then university police were running and I was really, really frightened." Kylie continued: "They did the whole thing. . . EMTs, stretcher, oxygen. . . then off I guess to university hospital. Before I left, I was told by one of the professors that he'd be ok, that he had talked with him, and that while he was in a lot of pain, he seemed to be getting some color back."

"Wolfe has always struck me as tough. He'll make it."

Kylie didn't look so sure; a small frown creased her face, and Tyler said, "What? You don't want him to make it?" Kylie made eye contact: "Maybe you don't know. He has a kinda bad rep among the women in the div school; he hits on students." Tyler stopped, pulled Kylie to the edge of the sidewalk, away from the flow of those students heading toward the school. Tyler blurted: "He's married." "Silly boy," she responded, "That doesn't always mean what you think it should mean."

Tyler didn't consider himself naïve. He'd grown up in a small semi-rural setting where people knew everybody's business. There was the occasional scandal, but for the most part folk led what he believed were straightforward lives. Hell, he thought, most of the people he knew worked so hard they didn't have time to cat around. But maybe he was naïve. . . because now he was here, and in some deeper way he did not understand, this news about someone he admired depressed him, sullied this day, and a glance at Kylie and her discomfort brought words unbidden to the surface: "Kylie". . .(slowly now; very deliberately). . . "you said he hit on some of the students. You?"

Kylie, head down, took several steps and then sat on a campus bench. She was distraught, no longer composed. There was a long pause; "Maybe I shouldn't ask, Kylie, but I mean if that happened to you, I'd expect you to be spitting mad."

*

Professor Tom Metcalf stood at the window of his office in the University Divinity School. He wondered how the faculty were dealing with the idea of Karl Wolfe in the hospital with a heart attack. Since the academic year had just started, he'd bet that the administration would be going crazy. Probably they would appoint someone from faculty as the interim dean. If asked, he'd say "no." Not that he hadn't on occasion admired the dean's office. His own office view included a fraternity house where aluminum beer kegs, buried under successive winter snows, in each spring took on the appearance of odd-shaped Easter eggs, forgotten but slowly emerging with the early thaw. His office was small. One wall held a single chair, often filled by a student. It stood next to a well stocked floor-to-ceiling bookcase. Opposite the bookcase was Tom's desk, piled high with papers. His radio on that desk was tuned to a local jazz station, and a picture frame on that same desk displayed wife and children. Still— it was student papers that threatened to overflow the desk. "But that's my job," he mused, "and I like it." A Korean watercolor and his doctoral diploma hung at eye level. Other than the one window and the door leading to the hallway, there wasn't much more to the office.

He often wondered at his good luck at being where he was. A treasured job, a strong marriage, and happy children. . . he felt blessed. Looking back he knew he'd been lucky to have his parents. They had loved and raised him with positive expectations. For all that, he'd still remembered that his had been a solitary, reflective kind of childhood. His aunt called him an "old soul," someone who seemed to know more about the world and his place in it than others his age. Not that Metcalf was socially backward. He got along with peers, even being considered by many to be a leader. But suggesting this to him would have brought a puzzled look to his face. He did not consider himself a leader, and he was comfortable in rebuffing overtures made to him on behalf of the administration. No, he did not want to serve as the school's ombudsman; no, he did not want to become an assistant university dean. He was happy where he was, thank you.

But today his happiness seemed fragile, and he knew why. He'd had another argument with Megan. These seemed more frequent than usual. Mid-morning found him in his office, sitting at his desk and feeling sorry for himself. Not that there weren't reasons—the argument with Megan and his mother's health high on the list. But the increasing number of arguments were a real kick in the gut. And he knew why. Six months earlier he'd been asked if he would join an accreditation committee that would make a visit to a west coast school. He'd accepted. The trouble was that the visit brought up memories for Megan of a similar visit he'd made to an east coast school some years earlier. The accreditation agency sent a professional staffer and the committee was composed of peers from member schools. In advance of the visit, each committee member had received the school's "self-study," a paper that would provide the visiting committee with an intensive snapshot of the school. He was surprised to discover Karl Wolfe, then the academic dean of a nearby seminary, serving as the chair of the visiting committee.

He'd flown into the airport located near the school, been picked up by a student, and had arrived at the committee's hotel an hour before they were expected to have an initial meeting. He'd registered and was walking toward the bank of elevators when things had fallen apart. Alex Clark had surprised him. They had slept together.

When he'd returned home, he'd had to sit down and tell Megan that he'd spent the night with one of his earlier students. That had not gone down well, and today Megan had dropped the hammer on him—"not another 'accrediting' trip, Tom?" He remembered. He remembered Alex Clark standing in the doorway to his office, smiling at him. He thought that hers was a smile that could light most rooms, especially rooms where there were men present. She stepped toward him, shoulders squared, a half-smile on her face, leaning—ever so slightly—toward him. He thought that there would be no stopping her once she set her mind to do whatever was in front of her. He'd said: "Hi, Alex. Can I help you?"

"Tom. I hope so." She had been comfortable calling him by his first name. "And why not," he thought. She might be several years younger than him and a student, but being addressed in a more familiar way by a beautiful woman was appreciated. She wanted help with the topic for her final paper. He helped her. She appreciated his help. She was all business, straightforward, to the point. But he could not help but think that there was more going on here than met the eye. No flirting, nothing obvious, but there was a kind of electricity that smoked whenever he looked into her eyes. "Watch yourself, Tom," he'd warned himself.

He had watched her instead. Another day he'd had to move a coffeepot and an assortment of food and papers into a newly assigned meeting space for a committee, and he'd recruited several students, including Alex, who were helping. He found himself trailing the group, and he could not help but notice Alex as she walked in front of him down the long hallway. It was her walk that tripped him up.

She'd glanced back, saw his face, and laughingly said: "I know what you're looking at." He knew his sheepish smile confirmed what she was thinking.

Alex had been in her last year of study in the div school. He told himself: "Hold on, Tom. She'll be graduated and gone. . . soon." That would be a good thing. Not that he minded the frisson her smile produced in him whenever their eyes met. Not that he minded the occasional image of the two of them in bed that sometimes entered his consciousness just before he fell asleep or sometimes as he was awakening. But he'd been chaste. He'd told himself that it was the act and not the fantasy that counted. There had been no affair. And when graduation arrived, he'd shaken hands and gotten hugs and thanks from many of the graduating class. He'd bumped into Alex. They were hurrying and had turned at the same moment and there she was, right in front of him. She tightly hugged him and whispered: "You and I have unfinished business."

He remembered her voice calling his name before he got to the bank of elevators and his first accrediting committee meeting. Surprised, he'd said: "What are you doing here?" And she'd said: "I heard on the grapevine that you were going to be in town, so I decided to look you up. We've some unfinished business."

"Here? He stumbled. You're here? In this hotel?"

"Yes. Nice coincidence, isn't it. I'd love to talk." Without thinking, Tom replied: "I'd like that. I'm in a meeting that will go through dinner. I'd be free after. Say around nine. How could we meet?"

"Ring me. I'm in room 509." Nodding, Tom left her and pushed the elevator button. Karl Wolfe was standing there. He'd apparently overheard some of their conversation. "Good-looking woman, Tom. Old friend?"

"An alumnae, Karl. Didn't know she worked in town here."

"But she knew you were here, Tom. Sounds like you've some catching up to do." He was with Alex until four am, then he went to his own room, showered and made ready for the work of the new day. There had been a blinking light on the bedside phone. There was a message from Wolfe: "If you can tear yourself away from the lissome blonde, we'll meet downstairs at 7:15 for breakfast."

He'd been as honest as he could be with Megan. She had been angry, but had forgiven him.

He'd often wondered what Wolfe might do with his suppositions.

*

Four

PROFESSOR MARTIN EVANS ROLLED over in bed, bumping up against the back of Norah, his wife. "You awake?" he whispered. "Yes" she responded. Martin said: "I know what's going to happen. Lying on his back, he pushed himself up against the headboard onto a folded pillow. As he sat up, he said, "The senior divinity school faculty is going to meet tomorrow morning for breakfast at *Nikos,* the Greek restaurant, and they will authorize Tom Metcalf, our senior faculty member, to carry a simple message to President Tanaka." Wriggling onto her back, Norah sat upright and joined Martin on the folded pillow. "What is that message going to be?" she asked.

"Given Wolfe's heart attack, they will have looked each other in the eye and said 'not me' and quickly decided that Martin Evans would do just fine as an interim administrator; in other words, I'll be asked to become the interim divinity school dean. Funny, but a university dean, even an interim dean, immediately becomes an administrator, joining that side that sits between the faculty's concerns and the university's priorities. The negative would be that my day would be filled with meetings and budget issues. I'll have no time to do research, and unless over time I could see this as my vocation, my calling, I'll fall well behind my peers. That's the bad news."

"Martin, that doesn't sound good. No research. How do you feel about that?" Looking Norah in the eye, he said: "Don't know if it's good or bad news, but I'm betting that President Tanaka will be either calling me or will drop by my office by 10 AM. Between now and then I've got to think this through. Truth be told, I think I'd like to do it."

"He'll call."

"Yeah; you're right. He'll call, and I'll be asked to come to his office. Depends on how he sees this as to whether or not he gets out from behind his desk or stays there, but our talking will take place inside his office, and his door will be closed."

"I need to translate what you just said. You think that if everything is just as it seems. . . that Wolfe's heart attack is the only issue that needs to be addressed. . . then President Tanaka will sit across from you at the little conversation nook by the big bay window in his office, and the two of you will talk like the friends that you are. But. . . and it's a big but, I'm guessing, if there is more to it than the heart attack, he'll get formal and 'be presidential' and sit behind the desk, the loci of his authority, and he'll keep things business-like."

"You are not only good looking but good at reading me. Yeah; I'm not so certain how the President feels about his dean. In public he and Wolfe play their roles, but this may have more of an edge to it, and I'm really not certain as to how Tanaka sees this—is it simply a pragmatic issue; or, is it an opportunity?"

"You're thinking there may be more to it than the heart attack?"

"Wolfe has been here more than three years. He's not really liked by the faculty. He's. . . well, frankly, a bit odd. Wolfe seems to start conversations somewhere in the middle of an argument that's only going on in his head and that only he knows, and then the person being talked to, and I mean *to*, has to figure out what's going on. I mean figure it out as if they were there, at the beginning of the mental conversation that only he's been having inside his head. I think it has to do with control. It's like he always works at controling the conversational boundaries and we have to figure out the context so that we can join him there. It's not easy. There's that."

"Ouch."

"And there's something else, something that drives the women faculty crazy. I think it has to do with the way he talks with women. Actually, maybe it's more than that. Sometimes I can be far off observing him in conversation with a woman, and for the life of me, what I see looks like an intimate, almost sexual conversation. But nothing explicit has surfaced on that account, and I don't put much faith in rumors. Don't want to encourage them."

"You have a good antennae, Martin."

"I usually think so. But—and you can hear it in my voice—I have some doubts. I can see him flirting, but he's married and he's not the most handsome guy in the world. So. . . I think I'm wondering if he uses his office to hit on women."

"Sexual harassment; here?"

"I don't know. I do know that he has a wandering eye. Whenever I'm with him I can tell he enjoys watching attractive young women. Nothing wrong with that, but when I get into conversation with women from his old seminary, that small denominational school where he was on the faculty and then, by most accounts was drafted to be the school's academic dean,

I get a sort of undertone of dissatisfaction along those lines. I am good at catching the nuances, but no hard facts. No real narrative that tells much. Just a faint buzz. More like: 'I'm glad he's in your shop and no longer with us.'"

Norah's face had what Martin called "the look." Taking her by both shoulders, he said, "Something's bothering you; tell me." They were still in bed. Norah turned to him and said, "That buzz you heard doesn't surprise me. I never told you, because two years ago we were new here, and President Tanaka and Miriam had the div school faculty Christmas party at their house, and everyone was there, and I wasn't sure, and I didn't want to accuse him of something that was more my imagination than reality."

"What happened?"

"You remember that it was a lovely evening, and toward the end of dinner, President Tanaka rose and introduced the new dean, Karl Wolfe. Tanaka indicated that there had been some maneuvering done in order to acquire Karl. Part of the lure had been the promise of a position in the library for Wolfe's wife, Emily. Another part was the promise of a new institute dedicated to on-going projects in biblical archaeology, not an inexpensive idea, but backed by at least one significant donor plus the university's promise of serious work from its development office. Tanaka suggested that, I think he said: 'the scientific approach to the Bible that Dean Wolfe embodies will attract people to the university, and the divinity school and the department of religion will work together in this new endeavor.' Then, to applause, Wolfe stood, and seemingly unsure, fumbled a couple of lines and said that he was glad to be at the university and hoped that 'we' —the div school and the university department of religion—would 'work well' together. There was polite applause; he sat down, and dessert was served.

"At the time his hesitancy seemed, well, peculiar. Almost as if he felt he'd been hired by the wrong department. I understand, Martin, that the div school educates ministers and professors within the Abrahamic traditions while the department of religion offers a much broader range—everything from Buddhism to shamanistic pre-modern practices. But Wolfe came in part because of his modern ideas about the Bible. I know that his approach does not sit well with some of the div school's faculty—I got that there might be some tension for Wolfe at that dinner 'introduction,' and I sensed that he was unsure as to his reception. Like he might have realized that there could be some issues focused on his presence. But when people milled about following the meal, some at the piano singing carols, others in the atrium having drinks, and still others helping students carry table dishes into the kitchen, he was less unsure."

"Say more."

"At one point the two of us were alone in the kitchen. I had placed some dishes into the kitchen sink, and when I turned to leave, Wolfe was standing directly in front of me. He took my hands. I was surprised. He said: 'Norah, we have not really met, but I have to tell you that you are such a beautiful lady and I hope we will have occasion to talk—at some length— one day soon.' I said nothing, but I was shocked. He was very close. He had intentionally invaded my space. Had I smiled, he might have kissed me. As it was, he let go of my hand and touched me on my shoulder. I brushed past him, leaving him standing at the sink."

"My turn to translate," said Martin. "He propositioned you."

"He was so polite about it, I had to wonder if I was imagining it, but when I happen to see him now, I feel like he is seeing me lying beside him in bed, so I avoid him like the plague." With a sideways glance: "You men are all alike."

"Hey, not true. I have known some women who hit on me, so it goes both ways." Norah quietly said—"You're remembering Lisa Banks. She did come after you, Martin. I'll give you that. I think Ms. Banks felt that by getting close to the minister, she was getting closer to God."

"Maybe so. I only know that at some social event at the first church that I served, this very sexy young woman came up to me, put her hand on my arm, looked me in the eye and said: 'Hi. I'm Lisa. You must be Martin Evans, our new minister.'"

"Not much of a come on."

"You had to be there."

"And you were there."

"I was there, and I found myself instantly aware of her. The bells went off."

"And you needed to be on guard."

"Right. And I don't know why I'm telling you this."

"But I'm glad," Norah said, nestling against his chest. "And you need to know that if you ever act on those urges, I'll rip out your eyes." This was said quietly, followed by a gentle punch on Martin's shoulder.

"Ouch. Look. . . I'm trying to say, badly, I know, that I've always ad- mired your competence, beauty, and bravery and I hope you always know that I love you."

"Even when the grass looks greener. . . ?" Long pause.

"Can we go back to bed now?" from him, plaintively.

"I could be persuaded."

Much later. . . "Martin, do you want to be the interim dean?"

"Yes. But I'd be silly not to consider the rumors, what we've been calling 'buzz.' I think educational institutions can be sexual pressure cookers. If the kind of sexual escapades we've been talking about are happening to our faculty, they won't remain hidden forever. And if, or when they pop, watch out."

"I know that; be careful. You know. . . I can believe some men make mistakes. They—for a peculiar moment—jump out of character. Then they feel guilty. They know shame. They recognize what they did was a mistake, and they honestly seek forgiveness."

"Got it. But that isn't Karl Wolfe. He's not that romantic about himself or, for that matter, about the world. Even though what you just said lies at the heart of religious tradition—confession and forgiveness—it doesn't fit his worldview."

"Agreed. Wolfe is more cynical, more pessimistic. But there is, I think, a second category. This is the hopeful opportunist; that is, someone who, given the opportunity, will take the opportunity every time. In another era, this guy would be called a 'rake,' someone who openly and enthusiastically celebrates multiple 'conquests' of the fairer sex. A sensualist."

"You have a dim view of men."

"Not all men. But let's consider—Wolfe may use opportunities, but he doesn't count on them. He likes to perform in secret, away from prying, judgmental eyes. He's no flamboyant rake, either. If I had to label him, I'd say he's a predator. That's my third category. He likes to hunt. And he uses age, position, and the weight of his influence—all those power imbalances—in his hunting. The congregant sees the pastor as being next to God. In business we can define some as worker bees, and then there is the CEO. Guess who comes out on top. The executive officer wins every time. The same with schools. Students rarely win in power tussles with professors, deans, or presidents."

"You're saying be careful of Wolfe?"

"He's a dangerous man, Martin, I don't like him. If I was a psychologist, I'd say he pretty much fits what I understand describes a sociopath."

"And I don't like him coming on to you."

"Believe me, I'll never put myself in a closed room with him again."

"But Norah, why would he do such a seemingly blatant thing?"

"I think he was fishing. I could have blushed and gone all giggly, even flirted with him. I think he'd have liked that, and I'd be willing to bet that if I had done any of those things, in a few weeks he would have called me to ask if I'd like to have a cup of coffee with him."

"But that's so dangerous for him. I don't get it."

"Oh, he's done this before, and he's gotten away with it. He'd assume that I wouldn't talk with you about it. And he'd take it just as far as I'd let him take it. No. I don't like your dean. Even with a heart attack (how appropriate), I think he's a dangerous man. Be careful, Martin. If President Tanaka does ask you to be the interim dean, be careful. Wolf tried me, and it did not work. He will not forget. And I am connected. . . closely, I might add. . . to the new interim dean, so he will be suspicious. I think he could be very dangerous, not only to me, but to you."

*

Five

At 10 am Martin's office phone rang. It was the office of the University President, Dr. Tanaka. His secretary quietly but firmly suggested: "The president would appreciate it if Professor Evans would come to his office ASAP."

A trim man of no more than five foot four inches in height, Adrian Tanaka always wore dark clothing and leather, European shoes. In his late fifties, during his lengthy presidency he'd been recognized as a competent administrator and was respected by both faculty and the university Board of Trustees. Martin had met Tanaka before he knew Norah, at a time when he was working on his doctorate and a part-timer teaching religion classes at a small mid-western college. At a luncheon during a conference on liturgy and ritual process, he'd found himself seated with Tanaka. They engaged in a conversation that was at once wide-ranging and at the same focused on what Martin was working on for his degree. By the end of the meal, Tanaka had invited Martin to come visit the university so that they might pursue their common interests. Martin left the luncheon aware that he had just had a very positive interview with the president of a university that housed both a department of religion and a well-known divinity school. "Of course I'll visit," he heard himself saying to President Tanaka, pinching himself at his good luck.

That had been a long time ago, and he'd been surprised to get a phone call one fall day from Tanaka, alerting him to a search for a scholar at the divinity school where he was president. During that conversation, Tanaka said: "This position is tenure-track and sounds very much like what you were working on for your doctorate." One thing led to another, he got the position and he and Norah arrived at the university filled with anticipation and somewhat giddy at their good luck. In addition, Norah, a nurse with solid recommendations, quickly found herself awash in job offers, most coming with signing bonuses.

Martin picked up his coffee cup, turned off the office light, closed his door and, after partially re-filling his cup, walked to the third floor elevator. At the ground level he exited the elevator and the divinity school. Turning left, he crossed two quadrangles and entered the university administration building.

Five minutes after leaving his office he was sitting in front of the president's desk. Tanaka pushed back his chair, placed both hands behind his head, and slowly stretched. It was a practiced gesture, almost as if he was saying he was now done with desk work and was ready to deal with those human issues that he often found filled his office chairs. Shaking hands with Martin, he placed his hand on Martin's shoulder and quickly jumped into his business mode. "Martin. I'm sorry we're getting together just because of this emergency. I assume you know that Karl Wolfe is in the hospital? Quadruple bypass surgery. They call it the 'cabbage.' Not a nice term. But he will survive. The doctors informed Emily that he would be home this week."

"That's good," said Martin. "I was at the div school when he had the attack. They got him into the ambulance and out of there awfully fast. Since then, Tom Metcalf has kept us up to speed. He told us yesterday that Dean Wolfe was to be released very soon."

"Looks that way, but what with rehab, exercise, a new diet, and less stress, don't you know, we really won't see him until the next academic year, I'm afraid, so that's why you are here. I'll be candid: we are deep into the fall term, and winter is coming quickly. The various schools of the university are well in hand, but we need someone to head the div school. The university, as you know, has eight separate colleges, each one headed by a dean, all under our academic provost. You know as well as I that things are running smoothly, but we can't afford to have someone or something take one of the wheels off. Not to blame Wolfe, but we need a functioning dean in charge of each school. That means we need a steady hand taking responsibility as the interim dean until he can return."

President Tanaka stood, went to the coffee caddy sitting on a sideboard, and poured a cup. "Want a cup?" He asked. Martin gave a negative shake of the head, and Tanaka returned to his chair. After a brief pause, he continued: "I can tell you that the senior divinity school faculty members are of a common mind: they think you're the man to serve as interim dean. I agree. I want you to do this. If you say 'yes,' there would be a nice bump up in salary and you'd need to know that in all likelihood you'd be dean beginning now through the remainder of this academic year till the end of next summer. Beyond that is anyone's guess, but if Wolfe does come back, you'd at least have had a taste of administrative work, and that experience might help you sometime in the future."

After one or two beats, he continued: "If you agree, and I hope you do, I've got to poll the trustees, of course, but the confidence of the senior faculty will go a long way with them. They trust you. The students know you. We'd like no surprises. And I know I'm pushing you on this, but will you do it?"

Martin understood that this moment was the best time to ask for Tanaka's response to several issues that might arise were he to accept the Interim Dean's position. He said: "I'd be willing to do it, but I'd like to know what you think about our working together. I know you're the president, but I also count you as a friend. My becoming interim dean would be a new relationship, and the wheels you're worried about can come off at times rather quickly, so I'd like to know what might happen if something happens on my watch. Is your door open to me? That's important. I might disagree with what you're considering in a specific situation, but I think you need to know I won't disagree with you in public, and if major issues come up, I'd want to be heard by you. I know that's a bold thing to say, but I need to say it before we get onto the playing field."

"Martin, I've always been pleased that you accepted a faculty position here. That's first. And in that process you've become a good friend. That's second. If things go topsy-turvy, I know we could work together. That's third. Beyond those three points, I think I understand how to do the work of a university president. That's fourth, and that's perhaps the most important answer to your concerns. I've been here ten years. We've survived faculty wars, almost going bankrupt, and, at least as I saw it, made it through one governance failure. Most of your colleagues will testify to my trustworthiness. I like to believe that I seek advice and that I don't act hastily. I'm not known to behave like a dictator, and I can honestly say that I'd want your candor in whatever comes to us. My door is always open to you, and from what I know about you, well, let me say that I think we'll do fine together."

Both Martin and Tanaka stood and Martin leaned across the president's desk. They shook hands. Martin said: "OK; let's say I'm on board; what next?" Tanaka said: "I'll get the trustees on board, too. By Friday the school and all our friends will get a letter regarding the health and prognosis of Dean Wolfe, his medical leave, and your new position as interim dean. You'll get a formal letter detailing your responsibilities, new salary, all that detail. You'll get two copies, both signed by me. Keep one. Sign and return one. And my cabinet, of which you are effectively a new member, meets Friday at 9 AM; be there. We'll be looking at several initiatives, the background papers which you'll receive by this Wednesday. I'll count on your response as to how these moves might impact the div school. That's probably enough now. But by next week you'll be knee deep in administrative work."

Martin turned to leave, but Tanaka stopped him; "Oh, one more thing. If you and Norah are free Friday evening, we are having several of the university deans coming to our home for dinner around seven. Check with her and if you can make it, please contact my executive secretary." With that, Martin exited. Back in his office he called Norah: "We were right. He asked me to become the new interim dean. There was nothing mentioned about Wolfe concerning the things we discussed. Maybe the wolf has changed, become the lamb." "I doubt that," said Norah. "I think Wolfe's behavior will become an issue, but that should not stop you. Go for it."

Martin sighed, perhaps for the first time becoming aware of what saying "yes" might entail. Then he exhaled, and said to Norah: "And by the way, if I sign the papers that appoint me to this position, you and I are invited to dinner Friday at President Tanaka and Miriam's home. I think it would often be like that—you know, my being the face of the school at meetings here in the university and out there with other schools and agencies. I'll be busy. If I sign the paperwork, do you think we can cope with an even busier year? And don't mind me if I sound excited, because I am excited."

"Congratulations Martin," Norah exclaimed, "Of course you're excited. Sign the papers. You'll make a wonderful dean. And of course we'll go to the President's dinner Friday night. And don't worry—we'll be able to work things out. Just know I love you."

That evening Martin called his parents. Both sets were still alive, and he and Norah tried to keep them "in the loop." He knew that all four were proud of the two of them, and as he'd grown up he'd come to appreciate them more and also need and use their advice. That hadn't always been the case. As a seventh grade rural kid in a city school he'd of necessity become something of a scrapper, but running with the wrong group didn't last long. He'd always played catch with his dad, and as he came into his height and weight his role on both the basketball and baseball teams grew. At one hundred eighty pounds and six feet two in height, Martin's athletic frame was topped with a shock of unruly black hair. While not handsome, his gray-blue eyes, strong features, and a calm steadiness suggested both competence and dependability. Sports left little time for rowdiness, and he gradually came to understand that life might offer him more if he went to college. So he went. College had been less than he hoped. He'd found the state school drew a crowd of seemingly aimless youth who seemed satisfied with drinking themselves senseless every weekend. After six weeks his roommate went home, and for the rest of that first semester he had a room to himself, which suited him just fine.

One of his four classes that initial year had been taught by a middle-aged history professor who challenged most of what he'd learned about history in high school, and who was the first to open the door and show him how the world worked for some and hindered others. Once that door had been opened, he'd walked through it. That first Christmas home from school he'd sat for a long time with his parents, trying to let them in on what he was excited about. Most of what he said was said with the zeal of youth, but knowing his parents always were in his corner, he also knew that even if they did not really understand what he was trying to say, they would always love him and would always be proud of him. He told them that his goal was graduate school and his becoming a professor.

Martin had met Norah while he was in graduate school. One night he'd dropped a glass on the kitchen floor in his bachelor apartment. By this time he'd taken a half-time job with a struggling suburban church. It was summer, and the stress of studies and ministry was getting to him. He had scheduled a day off, a day he now found himself using to repair a leaky faucet in the apartment. It had been unbearably hot, and he was wearing a pair of worn shorts and no shoes. He'd swept up the glass, but apparently missed some of the tiniest shards, one which nailed his instep. "Damn," he said. "Tiny things like this can become a big problem." He went to the hospital.

The emergency room nurse was a slender, intelligent woman named Norah. Later he would wonder if it was her intelligence or her beauty that attracted him, but in that moment he only knew that he was in pain. She was all business. He remembered having his foot propped up on a pillow and the nurse named Norah probing for the glass slivers: "Does this hurt?" She asked. Two years later Norah and Martin were married.

So much had happened since then, but in the things that mattered, both Norah and his parents were always there. He was thinking of all this as he talked on the phone with his mother. "But what does the dean of a divinity school do?" was her question. "I'm not really sure yet, mom" he replied, "but ask me at Christmas and I'll have a better answer." He wasn't dodging the question; he really didn't know very much about this new position.

President Tanaka had been clear as to the various layers of authority. "You'll need to primarily work with and for the faculty," he'd said. "And you'll need to temper that working by understanding what the Board of Trustees wants to do with the university." Martin knew he stood under the Board, the president, and the provost, a man responsible for the educational "product" of the university. That was a job Martin would not want—the provost had to ride herd on eight deans.

Martin had heard Tanaka, a veteran, emphatically talk about "chain of command." "In the military the chain of command is clear and unambiguous; here it's always muddled," said Tanaka. "I don't understand," replied Martin. "Well," said Tanaka, "here that chain isn't always understood or followed. One way to look at it is to recognize the difference between 'I' and 'we,'" said Tanaka. "Now you've lost me," said Martin.

"Sometimes a person's personal desires or ambitions lead to an overstepping of the role that person might play within a big organization," said Tanaka. "That's the stuff that ends in either tragedy or comedy, and usually it winds up being a mess for the person who was guilty of overreach." Martin said: "The Greeks called it 'hubris;' theologians call it 'sin.'" "Whatever," said Tanaka, "There's a fine line here. On the one hand, I encourage people to want to do better, and that means—sometimes—that they step over the line. But when that occurs, there comes a judgment, and at the same time an opportunity, if you will, an opportunity to assess how that person's line-stepping has impacted the institution, positively or negatively. And if it can be seen to be negative for the institution's mission. . ."

"And only profitable for the person who has stepped over the line," said Martin. "Then the institution will come down hard on that person."

"Exactly," said Tanaka. "That might be cynical, but I would look at something like that as a breach in the chain of command."

That evening Martin was reflective. His first day as interim dean under his belt, Martin was trying to unpack where he was in the chain of command. He'd decided that he was somewhere in the middle. Already faculty members were lining up to have him carry their concerns "up" the chain. At the same time the provost had him carrying the board's concerns "down" the chain to the faculty. He had tried to say all this to his parents. His dad was on the second phone line, and he weighed in: "I'd bet you'd be like a foreman in the mill; you'd have to work with the folk that are there, and if things don't go right, you get the blame and when they work well, then if you're lucky you'll get a little bit of the praise."

"That sounds about right, dad" Martin said. "Sounds like you've been there. I think that being Interim Dean will certainly have some big surprises in store for me, and I just hope I'm capable and wise enough to deal with whatever happens."

Their conversation went back and forth about friends and relatives until Martin said good-bye. After he'd hung up the phone, he realized that he felt nourished. Norah wanted to know how his folks were doing, and he answered positively, feeling not for the first time that when they were no longer alive he would deeply miss them.

*

Six

At home, Clayton sat in his favorite chair thinking about his mother. She had been a city girl, but when his parents had discovered a small frame house they could afford, she had willingly moved into the country. Clayton's dad labored in the mill while she tended the animals, canned vegetables, and worked at raising two rambunctious boys.

Theirs had not been an easy life. Clayton had several black and white photographs of the small, wooden-framed, one story house. It sat on a mud flat; there were no other visible houses. But while the picture looked desolate, the photographer obviously was pleased. "This is ours," the picture shouted, "It might not be much, but it is ours." A wilderness lay beyond that back yard, and as the two boys grew, the exploration of its ravines, streams, and wildlife drew both boys. At lunchtime one day the dog would not stop barking and Clayton's mom almost stepped on the coiled rattlesnake that was drawn up near the back steps. While she made short work of the snake with the sharp end of a shovel, that night she and his father had given both boys a short lesson on how to safely walk in the woods. "And," she finished her comments, "under no circumstance are you allowed to go past the fallen tree." This was in regard to a huge pine tree roughly one mile into the woods that had fallen during that summer's biggest lightning storm.

Clayton loved those woods. He knew where the ruffed grouse hid, came to expect the sudden intrusion of a pileated woodpecker's drumbeat, and treasured his occasional glimpse of a small red fox's litter, birthed in a tiny cavity under a rocky pile left behind by the depression years' Civilian Conservation Corps. The woods gave him solace, a time and place away from the older boys in school making fun of his name and his ungainly approach to all things athletic. While tall, he had no aptitude for basketball, nor could he throw a baseball with accuracy. But as soon as he got off the bus and was home from school, he'd greet his mother and was immediately released out the door, down the steps, and off on yet another adventure in the space he knew so well. As a young adult that love of the woods took him into the Boundary Waters between Canada and Minnesota with five summers spent guiding groups within that wilderness. Through that work he'd learned a lot about human nature. But now he found himself on uncertain ground. It was as if he had climbed over a fallen log and stepped onto a poisonous snake. How had he missed Karl Wolfe? Maybe he'd figured that someone capable of doing this kind of stuff would have to look more evil than Wolfe.

If asked yesterday, he would have described Karl Wolfe as a reasonably put-together man who got along well with his colleagues and who was admired for his scholarship and administrative talent. If asked today, he'd have to add a large "but" to his earlier statement. "*But* the man is sexually active with the wife of a colleague and we presume as well with students. He seems at some distance from his wedding vows, and has managed to fool those who work closely with him in service (presumably) to God."

Clayton often wondered what might have happened had his mother stepped off the back steps and not seen the snake. Where he had been raised there were plenty of stories about copperheads and timber rattlers. As a boy he'd been told stories that seemed more tall tales than the truth. His aunt had told him of the time she had stepped on the head of a snake that had curled around her ankle, but she'd kept her heel in place and screamed for help.

He felt that he and President David Karns had uncovered a snake inside their home. They had missed that snake and had been surprised, but were now aware of the snake's presence and how it had been intent on twisting and poisoning their ideals and principles. As a result, they had contacted trusted resources, involved the chair of the trustee's board, and come away having begun a process that promised the possibility of good outcomes. Lying in bed, Clayton turned the table lamp off. He adjusted his well-used pillow and rested. He remembered his earliest sermon, the one where he had preached on the text: "I set before you good and evil; choose this day how you shall live. As for me and my house, we will serve the Lord." He had chosen, and he had no regrets. All the same, he'd had to make some hard choices.

One of the hardest had been his catching a secretary at the seminary who had embezzled money from a petty cash account. As her supervisor, he had checked the account and concluded that she had skimmed a bit each month. The amount was not large, and he was uncertain how to handle it. When confronted, the woman confessed, promised to pay back what she had taken, and pled that her husband not be informed. He had wrestled with it and decided to go with what she wanted, and it had worked out ok. In the end she'd been a valued member of his team.

Only now did he look back at those circumstances and wonder at what others could have implied by his actions. She was a beautiful woman, and with the knowledge of the arrangement he had made, anyone out to get him could have insinuated all sorts of sexual implications. He wondered if Karl really was a snake lying in wait just past the fallen tree, or if there were folk who, for some reason, were out to get him.

He remembered that he had been ordained to a ministry that believed in forgiveness and the possibility that a person who sinned could "turn round." "But," he thought, "in ministry I also saw souls who had little or no empathy, who could do things that hurt others and who then simply walked away, seemingly untouched by the pain they had caused. Was that what Karl Wolfe was capable of doing?"

The accusations he'd heard against Karl were troubling. Clayton could accept Karl's dalliance with a woman who was his age, but he could not accept a faculty member's sexual involvement with students. By definition, faculty had the power edge in such relationships. A professor might claim that this particular student was special, and that there was no power imbalance in their relationship, but Clayton doubted such equality could occur. And if there was more than one student sexually involved with him, then Karl Wolfe's behavior would have erased even that argument. Clayton was tired. It had been a long and troubling day. In the matter of sexual escapades, he thanked God he had never gone past the fallen tree. He'd made some bad mistakes, but at the end of each day he'd been able to lie down beside his wife, Kate, and not be ashamed.

He thanked God for that, closed his eyes, and quickly fell asleep.

*

Wolfe twisted out from under his gray blanket, thrusting himself upright. Seated on the edge of his bed he muttered a second time: "I am not a bad man." Shards from the sleepless night rattled round his brain. At his home yesterday a package arrived. Addressed to him and marked "Personal," the plain, brown envelope held copies of sixteen letters. His signature ("Love, Karl") was scrawled across the bottom of each letter. "My God," he thought, "how stupid could I have been?" Seven of the letters had been written on his old school's stationery; the remaining on div school paper from his office.

There were also two pictures, time stamped. Molly Hoffman with him entering a motel door and then later outside the same motel door, he and Molly deeply embracing in a kiss. Who took these pictures? Surely not Molly, but who else then? They would have needed a telephoto lens. Who had the expertise, the knowledge as to where they might be, and the time to hang around a motel to get such pictures? And why no summary letter, no demand of him, no threat other than the letters and the picture. He thought of Emily—could she have done this? Emily, once a slip of a girl, now forty pounds overweight; no. . . the letters and the picture did not come from her. But what about Max, Molly's husband. He'd forgotten him. But no, not him either; he was a wimp. Not him. But who?

He was sweating. Where had this package come from? Anyone who got a copy could stitch together a pretty devastating picture of Dean Karl Wolfe. Who would benefit? Who? And what did they want from him? And what might happen if his more recent escapades were connected to this package? "Not to put too much spin on it," said Karl, "but I've worked like hell to get to this position, and woe to whoever tries to boot me out of here." Planting both feet on their bedroom floor, Wolfe paused. He did not need to look to know that Emily was fast asleep. Her snoring— like a small motorboat with a mild flutter—was as identifiable to Karl as a fingerprint. She had once been in love with the world and with open arms for him, the rising star, the one destined for something more than the small school where her father had made a name for himself. But now she was distanced from her earlier joy, slow and cumbersome, without zest for either him or her place in the world. And was it his fault that he succumbed to those who might tempt him?

Rising from the bed, he turned to glance at the clock, now reading five fifteen a.m. "Damn," he exclaimed. He stumbled into the bathroom, peed, and then stood before the cabinet mirror; had he always looked so hard, even mean? In that moment he again sensed his physical decline, the loss of sexual competency and all the rest of it. He would die, and (perhaps) not with honor. But the face looking back at him still held a masculine appeal, a dark sharpness accented by gray flecks across a strong beard and mustache. "A face not to be taken lightly," he mused. He spoke out loud—"I am the dean of a first-rate divinity school. Those who wish me harm should look out." This was a face that was always aware of the social context and the politics involved. Looking at that face he knew he would not be willing to go down without a fight.

Six

Shaving and shower finished, Wolfe dressed and went outside. He sat on the porch, smoked a cigarette, and slowly walked down the back alley toward the university. Kicking an empty beer can, he contemplated the back yards and garages that lined the alley. "Like people," he exclaimed, "the front side has a layer of fresh paint and new windows. On that side the snow has been shoveled, and the welcome mat is out. But out back—here on the other side—the alley is remarkable only for its spilled garbage, dog shit, broken down cars, and locked fences, just like people."

"If you are out there taking pictures," he shouted, "know that I am a worthy adversary."

*

Seven

KYLIE SAID GOODBYE TO Tyler and ducked out the back door of the div school. Ten minutes later she collapsed inside *The Thoughtful Bean.* If anyone would have asked her right then what she was doing, she would have responded that she was wrestling with God, like Jacob in the Bible at Jabbock Ford, and wasn't at all certain what the outcome might be. She knew that when Jacob left his wrestling match, he had not seen God's face and was marked forever as the man with a limp. What should she do? How was she limping?

As she had first stepped on to the train that would take her to div school, her mom had whispered "don't let them take away your faith." Kylie knew her mom to have a sure faith, one that rarely questioned God's will for her life. And Kylie thought she knew what her mom had meant, because she had heard her parents talk about the "way some people tore the Bible apart." But Kylie had found Karl Wolfe's approach to the Bible exciting, probably because she could see for the first time how people had come to orally talk about and then write down their experiences of God while offering them to the discerning eye of their community. So not everything that was said or written down made it into the Bible, and a lot of what made it into the text had been edited and re-written because of communal need. This made sense to her, and as a result she had come to view the Bible as a living document.

All of this had occurred centuries ago, and Dean Wolfe's knowledge in these areas fascinated Kylie, so she took not only his required course but also his elective ones. And she also recognized that the dean had noticed her and occasionally suggested to her the reading of "a certain book" that was new and interesting that might help her in "her work here." One day in the hallway he had stopped her. "Kylie, you ought to consider the next few years as a prelude to your taking a doctoral degree in Biblical literature. I think you'd do well. There would be jobs, good positions waiting for someone like you. If you feel you might want to work with me, I could mentor you."

"Someone like her." She was pleased, even if the idea was a big one, almost too big to take in, but she thought about it. Was someone "like her" called to be a professor? A possible call into ministry was what initially had drawn her to consider the divinity school. Her church had played a pivotal role in her life. Whatever had been put in her way had been pushed aside by the trust, loyalty, and love shown her by the adults in her life, and they had all come together within her church.

Not that there weren't issues. Her dad daily encountered racism directed at his blackness. What disturbed him most was the apparent ignorance on the part of those whose words cut into his soul. She watched him struggle to not let such words beat him down. At the end of the day, sitting round their small dinner table, his presence remained one of love and not of hatred.

Kylie wanted to understand how the words of church, made real in her home, might become the centering focus for a life well-lived. That was why she had come to the div school. Here was where folk grappled with such ideas. Here was where conversations that might last a lifetime got started. And she had found the hoped for lively conversations in her classes and among her peers. "But," thought Kylie, "how can the rich, conversational practice I find in the divinity school continue after I graduate?"

Such thinking caused her to seriously consider pursuing a doctorate and a job in a setting like a seminary or a div school. But were such thoughts a betrayal of ministry? Her church was big on "calling" and "discernment," both personal and communal. And she believed that God eventually would "call" her into her own "voice." She loved the word "vocation," a word that had to do with both calling and voice. As she tried to hear her own call, her vocational direction, she recalled how back home she had worked with a woman pastor about *who* and *whose* she was and how she might be called into ministry.

As a part of that process, before she had first traveled north to the div school, she had asked several women in the church to meet on one evening with her and the pastor to help her work through these things. She knew this was a step toward the discernment of her personal future. She sought their blessing as she took this first step on her journey. Their blessing was important to her. Placing hands on her head, shoulders, arms, and back, the four women prayed for her and blessed her. She felt the weight of their presence and their words: "Know who you are, and always remember whose you are." As she got onto the train, in her mind they rode with her as she headed north and to her first meeting with Dean Karl Wolfe and the rest of the divinity school faculty.

*

Martin asked Tom Metcalf, the senior div school faculty member, to meet and discuss the deanship with him. Tom suggested breakfast at *Niko's*, a Greek cafe frequented by both faculty and students. On his way to school, Martin often would see Tom near the window at *Niko's*, working on a yellow legal pad and eating breakfast. To Martin's knowledge, this habit had yielded eight books.

An early snow was falling, each flake distinct, and as Martin stomped snow off his boots and entered the café, he was quick to brush the accumulated snow off the shoulders of his coat. He paused, aware of sounds other than what Niko called Greek "background" music. To Martin's surprise, *Three Dog Night's* "Joy to the World" was being pumped into the Café. Sliding into the booth across the table from Tom, he asked: "New music choice?" "Yeah," said Tom. "New waitress." A young woman with loose cropped, coppery hair and a nose ring approached their booth, and Martin ordered eggs, bacon, toast, and black coffee. She was polite, efficient, and very cute. "New world," said Tom. "It is that," said Martin.

"You just missed *Blue Oyster Cult's* "Don't Fear the Reaper," said Tom.

"My loss," said Martin. Then, after a moment: "You could identify that song?"

"Nah," said Tom, "but I asked her what was playing. Can't say the music helps my writing, but I appreciate the service and the server. I can only hope that when Nikos gets here, he'll orient her to the kind of customers he wants to come to his café."

"If he doesn't fire her."

"No; Nikos appreciates polite, competent waitresses. He also likes to have attractive women working the tables. Tomorrow the music will be back to normal. I guarantee it."

"Well, music aside, the reason I wanted to talk with you was to get advice from you as to what I need to know about doing the interim dean's position. I really want some input. You're the senior faculty person. You've seen deans come and go. I'm hopeful you'll tell me what might make this a doable job."

60

"Been thinking about that, Martin. Seems to me there are three things. Not to be boring, but the school year is full of deadlines. You need someone, a secretary you trust, who can put that into a calendar and mark the important things with red flags. Without that, you're dead. Second—the div school is only a small part of the university system. That means politics. It also means budget. You need to be sociable and visible and astute in those relationships. Don't get me wrong, but unless you look out for the div school, no one else will. Third. . . and finally: your door must be open to things personal as well as things academic; I mean there will be hobby horses people want to ride, and you need to have the wisdom of Solomon as to what you support. One day there will be a knock and a professor will be asking for a better parking space. Once that person leaves, a student will appear asking you why they can't keep their pet parrot in the dorm. The wisdom of Solomon, my friend. That's what you will need."

In the background *Crosby, Stills, Nash & Young* were singing about "Ohio" and the Kent State shootings. Tom nodded at the waitress, who came over to the booth, coffee pot in hand. "You a student at the university?" Martin asked. "Grad student," she replied. Tom asked: "What field?"

"Social work," she said, with what Martin thought might be a wink. Tom nodded. "Good," he said. With a smile on her face, she carried the coffee pot to the next booth. "She'll be here tomorrow," Tom said. "Let's pay and go to school." As they walked the few blocks to the university, Tom told Martin that the waitress was from a small town "down state," and that her story interested him because she had worked with the rural Native American population there. Her work with them led to a deep interest in social work. "Now she is here," Tom concluded. "Name's Shelby, by the way." "A good story," Martin said. "Yes," said Tom, "and not yet finished."

Martin asked: "Why are you so interested in narratives?" "Well," said Tom, "I mentioned Shelby because she is right here, in front of us; but every individual has their own story. You as a dean need to be aware of how these stories can come together into a common vocation. To do that, you need to know why the div school lives and breathes as an institution. It too has a narrative, a story." He went on—"Stories carry the weight of what an institution has come to mean, Martin. For example, look at the tops of the door posts in our chapel." Martin could see where Tom was headed: "And at the top of each post is a carved stone face," he said.

"Right," said Tom. "And each carved head is the image of a major donor who funded not only the chapel, but put it and the div school at the center of the university. There's a story as to what they saw as important back in the day when the ministers and businessmen got together and said 'we need some education in this God-forsaken city,' and began to build this university. They built the div school and its chapel at the center of the university."

"And today?" asked Martin.

"Today the divinity school and its faculty are outliers, a bit of an academic oddity. Remember that fact when you sit down with the other deans. They no longer see us as the center of the university. Sometimes they will support you, but not always. So maybe my second point was the important one: politics, politics, politics. You might want—early on—to find out how the university development office deals with the div school. Our grads don't earn much money, and I would wager that there are some issues based on that and how the administration and the board of trustees cut up the money raised by the development office. Check it out. I don't know what you might find, but when finances are involved maybe *The Rolling Stones* were right: 'You can't always get what you want.' Our waitress would understand."

"Right," said Martin, "But I can hope that maybe, just maybe, 'we might get what we need.'"

"Go to it young man!" Metcalf chortled, "And I'll be supportive of that hope."

*

Thinking back, early on Kylie was aware that men found her attractive. She was not sure why this was so, but it was. At age eleven men called out to her when she walked to the corner store. In high school, boys bumped her in the hallway, but she would step back, and seeing her intensity they would walk away. She knew they called her names behind her back, but she also knew they wanted her body, wanted to take her someplace and claim her as their property, their "girl." She watched a friend at fifteen birth her own baby and she knew she wanted more than the struggle and the life of a single mother. Basketball, the church, and her innate curiosity saved her. At five nine she was a good high school forward; she could dribble and shoot and she found she liked putting her body on the line. The church raised high her spiritedness; she knew in her soul that she was somebody, a young woman loved of God. Her thirst for knowledge fed her mind, and while others had no time for reading, she consumed all the books she could get from her local library.

And now she was north, far from home, trying to discern God's will for her life.

One day she had surprised Tyler and some of his friends by stepping onto the div school outdoor basketball court. Taking a quick pass, she drove the lane toward the basket, made her shot and turning, intercepted an in-bounds pass and then hit nothing but net from the top of the key. "Where did that come from?" Tyler asked. "How little you know," she replied.

Kylie liked being a bit of a mystery to those who wondered what she was and where she came from. She had not imagined that Dr. Wolfe might also have similar thoughts. Again, in the hallway after class Wolfe had stopped her. "The annual AAR/SBL meeting (American Academy of Religion/Society of Biblical Literature) will be held in this city next month. You ought to consider going."

"Would it cost much to attend?"

"Not really. They have a student fee and I have a budget line I can use to offset even that cost, so I guess it might cost you for a meal and a room for one night, but it could also open you to more deeply see some of those possibilities we discussed."

"Let me think about it."

"Here are the registration papers. Fill them out, slip them into my mailbox, and I'll submit them to the financial office."

"OK; thanks for telling me about this."

Two months later she got her conference registration packet through the mail. Studying each page, she found herself fascinated at the titles and descriptions of numerous workshop offerings. This would be fun. And then it was time to go downtown, check into her hotel room, and carry her registration information to the conference hotel.

Kylie's being downtown at a big conference made the idea of getting a doctorate more real. Wolfe's suggestion of possible mentorship carried her through some of her more awkward moments, like getting lost on the way to the conference center. She'd gone one train stop too far. Then she missed the "student registration" sign, got stopped by a guard at the main entryway and had to go back to registration for a name-badge. But then she was ok, even enjoying the book fair. The size of the event was overwhelming. Was there really this many professors interested in religion? Her conference booklet listed each hour's offerings and further confounded her. But she located two panel discussions, found her way to both, and emerged feeling triumphant. Another div school student, Karen Wexford, caught up to her in the hallway: "Kylie, isn't this amazing," said Karen. "It is," said Kylie. "And I missed breakfast, so I'm hunting for lunch. Care to join me?"

The two women stayed together until late that evening, when Karen headed back to the university. Then Kylie, tired and exhausted, bumped into Dean Wolfe. She'd always been cautious about men, but after a full day at the conference at about 9:30 PM, she somehow found herself being escorted to her room by the dean, and before she realized what was going on the two of them were inside her room and he was encircling her arms from his position behind her while cupping both of her breasts in his hands.

A growl rose deep inside as she twisted to her left even as her right hand curled into a fist and slammed into his face. The ring on her finger cut him, and he drew back so quickly that as she hit him he already was falling backward onto the floor. "You bastard," she said, watching him, her eyes angry, not shamed, not apologetic. "Get up and get out." He stumbled getting up and, pulling a handkerchief from the pocket inside his coat, tried to staunch the flow of blood oozing from a cut under his left eye. "Who do you think you are?" he shouted.

In that moment she was not certain what he might say or do next, but he yanked open the door and left, offering no more words. Inside, she sat on the edge of the bed. "What do I do now?" Then tears.

*

Eight

PRESIDENT DAVID KARNS CAUGHT Clayton early, so early Clayton had not yet walked his dog. Answering his phone, Clayton sensed concern: "Something bad?" Karns didn't need an invitation—"We're going through an audit of the last two years Karl Wolfe was with us. I mentioned to you, Clayton, that Molly Hoffman had some stationery from him imprinted with the seminary logo?"

"Yes."

"Tucked in the material she gave us were letters to her that suggested he was using seminary funds to meet her when he was supposedly on seminary business. I don't know if you remember, but Professor Max Hoffman had a sabbatical year, and he spent part of that in Germany and part in South Africa. Apparently Wolfe had several conferences he attended during those time frames, and Sally either accompanied him or met him near the end of some of them. He then billed the seminary for the use of the hotel room for one or more extra days, all with the stated intent of attending academic meetings piggy-backed onto the conference. He went so far as to detail all this in memos to his secretary."

Clayton said: "And when he got back to the seminary, he would turn in his expense report and charge them to one of his lines in the academic dean's budget."

"You got it. So we connected the expense records with the times Professor Hoffman was out of town, and we checked with a few of the people that Wolfe was supposedly meeting, and guess what?"

"None of them had any 'piggy-back' academic dean's meetings."

"Exactly. We've done this on our own with a pro bono auditor, but his firm is a good one and our trustees will be shown this and will no doubt want to do something about it." Clayton interrupted: "This is not good. Now if it was just the money, I'd say let's you and I and the board of trustee's chair and the auditor approach him, scare the tar out of him, and ask him what he thinks he ought to do. I've had experience with this kind of mess, and usually that will do it. Then you or I could go see him a second time, and dollars to doughnuts he'd have a plan through which he'd pay back all that he stole, with interest." Karns listened to Clayton. He then focused on what bothered him about Clayton's summary: "You said, and I quote: 'If it was just the money.'"

"Right. The scheme he tried to pull off wasn't so much about money as it was pulling the wool over our eyes. He and Molly Hoffman 'piggy-backed' some sexual time using the school's academic budget. Wolfe is an arrogant bastard. To put things in print that if found would lead us back to him tells me he not only wants to be found, he cares not what this might do to us and to him were it to become public."

"Neither I nor the trustees will want to walk away from this one, Clayton."

"No. I agree. But I am not certain how best to pursue it. I can't think but that the legal fees alone—how much does the auditor think he stole?"

"About ten thousand dollars," said Karns.

"The seminary lawyer could eat that up by billing you for just a few legal hours. Every fifteen minutes of conversation with the lawyer, and *bing*, more money in his firm's pocket."

"Look, Clayton. We're going to be talking about this over the next few weeks. I wanted you to know that people feel betrayed, but I don't expect them to jump up and pursue Wolfe just yet, but that might change. We're looking at a number of things involving Wolfe. I agree with you—this business with Molly Hoffman is a lot more than just a financial issue. We've gotten the denomination involved as well, and when we reach some consensus, I'll let you know."

"All right, David. Now I'm going to walk my dog and eat breakfast and try not to think about Dr. Karl Wolfe."

After hanging up the phone, Clayton whistled for Sassy, and both he and the dog got into the car. Sassy sat in the shotgun seat, and he chuckled as he remembered Kate saying: "When I see that dog in the front seat, I swear she's almost human." Kate was never far from his mind. "Sometimes I'll hear a noise in the house and I'll turn around expecting to see Kate," thought Clayton. "And more often than not, it'll be the dog." As he drove into the city, Clayton mused: "Loss isn't easy. Sometimes I'll be sitting at our table and I almost believe that if I close my eyes, she'd walk in with a plate of spaghetti for me."

Near the university he found an unmetered place to park. He headed toward the university tennis courts, certain that Sassy would find a stray tennis ball. Once she had a ball, Clayton tossed it and the dog would run full tilt after it. The ball softly cradled in her mouth, she'd hurry back, ready to start the routine once again. He liked to start at the tennis courts and work his way through the ivy-edged quadrangles into and through the sprawling university complex. Once he hit the medical side of the university he'd angle left and then left again until he eventually returned to where he'd parked the car.

Usually walking the dog distracted Clayton from the worries of his day, but tonight as he parked the car in his driveway and whistled Sassy into the house, he realized he was still thinking about just how angry he was with Karl Wolfe.

*

Sitting in class, Tyler had a hard time concentrating. Not that Professor Metcalf was boring, but thoughts about Kylie kept intruding. He'd met Kylie's mom and dad, the Ravens, and had come to believe Kylie had gotten the best of that genetic mix. From her Japanese mom she'd gotten almond eyes, a warm, relational intelligence, and a gracefulness wrapped in a slender, cocoa-hued-body, and that last part from her wiry African American dad. Her dad had also contributed tenacity, above average height, and a get-it-done attitude that seemingly had been built upon a steel inner core.

Kylie was beautiful, but she was much more than a beautiful woman; she had a directness and honesty that, on occasion, had thrown him, particularly when he seemed inarticulate about his emotions and what he really meant to say. His folks, on meeting her, had said that he had a history of dating "dismissive" women; his dad pointedly stated: "This one is a deep pool beyond your ken. Be careful, Tyler. . . she's a keeper."

Tyler could agree, but he still had issues about commitment. Up till right now he'd avoided any deeply tied relationship. Not that he steered clear of women. Far from it. But he'd never indicated to them or to himself that he wanted anything more than casual friendships. And the women he dated never seemed to call for more on either their part or his.

Until now. Now he'd found himself wondering what really drew him to this woman. Her smile? The exotic side of being "in" a relationship with a woman whose pedigree would not "fit" in rural Potter County? Come to think of it, he'd never seen an Asian (or a Black, for that matter) growing up. That only occurred when he went to the state college, and even there, he'd rarely talked with folk who seemed outside his normal Anglo crowd. Was he prejudiced?

Then too, a lot of these thoughts started with him. What about her? What was she thinking? What if she didn't want this to go further? He could imagine her saying: "OK, Tyler. Let's just be friends." Could he live with that? He'd thought a lot about what it would mean if she were absent from his life. Girls never turned him down. Sure, back in high school one had broken his adolescent heart, but for the most part, his relationship with girls (now: *women!* He remembered) was positive. . . and often more than positive. They were warm and good. He wasn't into one-night-stands, and while he often fantasized about Kylie with him in bed, he also wondered if she could be, might be the person he willingly and enthusiastically would spend the rest of his life with. "Old school," a voice kept repeating in his head. "So," he thought, "what's wrong with that?"

In class Professor Metcalf was talking about "blessing," and how we'd lost that idea as something old-fashioned and even pre-modern. "Touching someone in blessing has to do with much more than sexuality." The professor went on: "Take Jacob, that smooth man, and Esau, that one's hairy brother." Metcalf paused, waited for the laughter to subside, then continued—"You know the story. The older brother, Esau, was to receive the blessing of the two boys' blind father, but Jacob covered his arms with the skin of a young kid and, imitating Esau's voice (and probably working up a sweat in order to smell like Esau) asked the father to touch him and to bless him inasmuch as he was Esau, the oldest son. And, thinking Jacob was indeed Esau, the old man touched Jacob and gave him Esau's blessing." "Touch," said Metcalf, "can be the touch of truth, or the touch of a lie."

He went on: "You often will be asked, in ministry, to offer God's blessing. Sometimes this will be a request for the simple touch of a hug or your hand, but there will be more seductive occasions, and you will be tempted. At those moments, remember Esau and remember that in touching someone you can bless or betray, offering either God's love or the devil's curse."

There was a lot of conversation as the students left Metcalf's classroom. Tyler joined the group headed toward *The Thoughtful Bean*, but in his mind he was still wondering about Kylie Raven and what might make someone offer her a curse instead of a blessing. Why would a married man who was dean of an important institution hit on one of his students?

Tyler knew Dean Wolfe was not the best "fit" for this div school. A lot of what he had to say seemed radical, especially for Master of Divinity students who would, for the most part, wind up preaching and ministering in small or medium sized churches. This might be the big city university divinity school, but not many believers where Tyler came from would want to hear Wolf's comments on the questionable divinity of Jesus.

One day Wolfe had said in class that the divinity question about Jesus was a late decision and had been inserted into the texts because a hunted and persecuted community needed a guarantee of life after death. Wolfe said that a realistic approach might suggest that the empty tomb was a result of some of the followers spiriting Jesus' dead body away from the burial area in order to dispose of the all too human remains. The students at the university because of the PhD program were interested in Wolfe's conclusions, but those thinking about ministry within a church setting were heard to mutter: "this stuff won't preach." Wolfe's take on Jesus had Tyler wondering what the dean might say about the existence of God, but he wasn't brave enough to ask that kind of question.

Professor Metcalf, on the other hand, was a storyteller. He said that truth was often found in the narrative stories of the Bible, and that they were there as communal testimony about how a people experienced God. For them, God was a given, yet they only had story to affirm God's existence. "God," Metcalf said, "cannot be proven." Tyler thought that if Dean Wolfe was a cynical realist, then Professor Metcalf was a romantic.

But how realistic was it, he wondered, for the dean to hit on Kylie?

*

Edwin Diaz was the div school librarian. He was formally one of the university library staff, but was charged with responsibility for the div school's library. As a faculty member, he served as an advisor for a number of MDiv students, including Tyler. Being young and accessible, Edwin had more than his share of advisees, but he liked such contact, especially when a student was as serious as Tyler. In addition, Tyler had been given a work/study position in the library, so the two had frequent contact.

Tyler liked his advisor. Edwin was deeply involved in a Hispanic congregation on the far west side, and he'd invited Tyler there "to see how a good church functions." Tyler had gone on a Sunday. The church was in a large, non-descript brick building on the main street bordering a large city park. It was apparent that this was a blue-collar, working class congregation, and Tyler wondered how Edwin fit in this context. Once inside the church, he'd been warmly greeted, and then taken into the worship space. He'd not expected the family orientation of the worship service, nor was he prepared for the ready and enthusiastic involvement of the worshippers in the songs and the sermon.

Afterward, he'd talked at length with Edwin, who'd pointed out the close connections between the morning Bible study classes and the sermon, as well as the multi-aged nature of the choir. He stressed that a lot of this kind of lay-led process had been part of the deep history of the congregation, but that it had been lost and only recently been re-activated by the leadership of their woman pastor.

When asked how he'd come to be involved with this particular congregation, Edwin told Tyler that he'd actively looked for the kind of church he'd attended as a child; and that this congregation was like his home church, a strong advocate for people on the edge of the dominant culture. Edwin had gone on to share how as a young man he'd come to understand his call into ministry, and how he'd had to struggle because "book-learning" and an educated ministry were not among the highest values of his people. He had, he said, "a passion to change that."

Tyler had gone back on two more occasions, taking Kylie with him once. She liked the congregation's involvement with the world around it, and she was impressed with the woman pastor. "Reminds me of home," she said to Tyler. As she wondered about such a call for herself, Edwin had set up a dinner with him, the woman pastor (Lisa), and Tyler. Kylie was impressed with Lisa, and friendly conversation dominated the evening, much like Tyler had hoped. When Tyler and Kylie said their good-byes and were on their way home, Kylie told him that she intended to see Lisa again. "She was very helpful," Kylie said, "And I like Edwin. He is kind. And smart," she added.

Edwin's office at the div school was on a hallway between the chapel and the library. The walls of the hallway were covered with carved wooden paneling, and the first time Tyler had tried to see Edwin, he'd been confused as to where the door to Edwin's office might be located. Edwin had been in transit from the library, and caught Tyler looking lost in the middle of the darkened hallway. Laughing, Edwin had said: "This is an old building, and my office actually runs the length of the hallway, but no one can ever find my door. I guess if I was quiet, no one would ever find me!"

Between working for Edwin and meeting with him regarding class schedules and the inevitable discussions as to Tyler's academic and professional future, the two had gotten along, so it was an easy choice for Tyler to call on Edwin regarding his concern about Kylie and Dean Wolfe. Tyler was not one to beat about the bush; he was direct: "Edwin, I have a woman friend who is being hit on by Professor Wolfe. She says this is a known issue with Wolfe. I want to know if there is anything I can do to help her or any of the other women who are in similar situations with him."

"I hear your interest in helping, but has she asked you to do something?"

"No. But there must be some policy that can help, or something I can do. It just is not right."

"You're angry."

"I'm angry, yeah. And I am not pleased that one of the faculty members. . . in fact, the guy supposedly in charge. . . is doing this. I know she's not lying, so yeah. I'm angry. I'm also puzzled. I sometimes work in the library with Wolfe's wife, Emily. Does she even know about this? I have to admit that I've wondered about sending her a letter or talking with her asking if she knows, and if she does, why she hasn't acted. I think that way, but I know, a letter seems a chicken way to do anything. I'm more direct. Usually, at least. But I feel helpless right now. I'd rather talk with her, but I really don't know what to do."

"A lot of this falls to the woman who has been harassed. She has to be willing to formally charge the dean with sexual harassment. Not a lot of people really go that far. Not that they can't. There is a faculty manual that outlines the process, but unless she's really strong, it is a pretty tough road." Again, Tyler took the direct route: "So maybe I ought to read that manual, and maybe if she does want to go public, I'll need to be there for her."

"That sounds about right. But Tyler, if what you say is going on, there must be more than one woman who's been or is being harassed. If I were you, I'd ask her if she's got some other women who might act with her and together they might find the strength to raise their voices."

"Good advice. Thanks, Edwin. I mean it. I'd just like to punch him out, but that won't help."

"I don't like this either, Tyler. I can keep it confidential, but can I at least say to my faculty colleagues that a student is being harassed and does not know how to deal with it?"

"Not yet, Edwin. I don't want to out her without her permission. I was afraid to even approach you."

"OK Tyler, I'll be silent on this. But if you need someone to be an advocate, I'm willing."

As Tyler left Edwin's office, Edwin stood and looked out his window into the university quadrangle. There were a lot of students and professors hurrying back and forth. "Why would someone like Wolfe do something like this with a student," he wondered out loud. "If the woman he has targeted is Kylie Raven, I think he made a big mistake. She's no cream puff. If she's the one (and I bet that's the case), then Dean Wolfe should be afraid of unintended consequences."

*

Winter Quarter

1989/1990

Nine

ONE LATE MORNING IN December Tom Metcalf's office phone rang. Putting down the student's paper he'd been reading, Metcalf answered the phone. His mother was on the line. "Tom, your dad's on his way to the hospital; it does not look good. I need you to come."

He made some quick but necessary arrangements, kissed Megan with the added words "I'll call you tonight," and was out the door and on the train headed for the airport, the end of the train line. He was anxious, and after buying a ticket at the airport, he'd started to walk. He'd already checked his bag at the counter, and hiking throughout the terminal he hoped would ease his antsy behavior. There were people all around him, but he did not see them. He kept reminding himself that it was his dad and not his mom. His mother had cancer, and he'd expected any call from home like this one would have been to alert him to a relapse, or worse. But his dad; that had surprised him. And seriously ill; unbidden, his emotions bubbled to the surface. Tears trickled down his cheeks. Wiping his eyes, he marched deeper into the terminal. His feet hurt, and he suddenly realized that he'd have to hurry to get back in time to catch his plane. He was at the end of the line, one of the last to get on board before the doors closed, but he made it.

Flying above the clouds had always impressed Tom, and as he caught the sunset off the wing of the plane he breathed a simple prayer: "Give my mom. . . and give me. . . the strength to be there for dad." He thought about how central his dad had been to his growing into the man he'd become. All his life, he'd been able to rely on the sustaining presence of his father. Unbidden, he remembered how, one time on a date, he'd run out of gas. He'd called his dad, and a half hour later his dad had shown up, gas container in hand. While pouring the gas into the tank, he'd quizzically commented: "When I was a young man, running out of gas was a romantic tactic, and I doubt I'd have called my father for a rescue." That was his father. From an early age, Tom recognized his father as competent, trustworthy man, and that certainty had never wavered. Now his father was very ill, perhaps dying.

Connections went well, and Tom soon found himself on the ground in a rental car two hours from his boyhood home. He took the river road north toward his mother, father, and more memories. The river road was a narrow strip of asphalt tracking the river. Along the way were small cottages and hunting cabins, the occasional campground or settlement where a mountain stream had cut across the road and formed a location where a handful of homes had been built before this section of the river had been declared a national forest. When Tom had been a boy, he and his dad had built a fiberglass canoe and run it on this river. One of his dad's friends would help drive them north into the headwaters of the river, drop them off, and they would fish, camp, swim and paddle their way south to where the big bridge in town crossed the river. A pipeline underlying the river at that point made for a bouncy set of rapids. Those had been good days.

Coming off the ridge bordering the river, Tom eased the car around the downhill bend, bottoming out on the straight stretch leading into town where the old mills still stood, now housing start-ups of everything from cardboard box makers to a small, specialized, paint-brush manufacturer. While the high ridge held snow, dotted with the green of hemlock and white pine, streets near the river had been plowed free of snow, and traffic had increased. New signs posting speed limits caught his eye. He slowed as he swung the car onto the two lane bridge dropping him in the center of the town. The soft ice cream stand at the end of the bridge was closed, but two new businesses filled a fire gap that had consumed both a photography shop and an apartment building. Ahead lay the church attended by his parents. He turned right, and tourists were on the street, braving the cold and ambling into and out of the Victorian-aged shops festooned with banners and all the color required for successful Christmas sales. It was good to see the activity, he thought. When the mill had moved its poured steel division to Texas, some had wondered at the possible death of the town, but ingenuity and determination had won out. He was glad to see that *Perry's*, where he had once taken dates for hamburgers and fries, still existed.

A left at the light took him away from the river, the historical business district, and up the hill. Going up the hill, all the cross-streets were numbered— one, two, and at three, he turned right. He was two blocks from his home, a three-story brick and frame house that gave him and his younger brother and sister individual bedrooms.

When Tom had graduated college, he'd been at sixes and sevens, without a sense of what he might do. He'd been taught to think, and while most of the folk he graduated with went onto graduate schools, Tom wasn't ready for that kind of move. So with his parents blessing, he'd gone to Europe with a backpack and a few dollars in the pockets of his jeans. A year later, he was back in the states working in a camp for emotionally disturbed children located in the upper Hudson River Valley. To say that this experience changed his life would be an understatement. It was in this camp that he began to understand the power of story, and it was also where he'd met Megan, the woman he would love and marry.

The camp director was a psychologist professor from one of the big New York schools, and he was adamant that everyone come to know and understand the stories that were integral to each child. Case conferences unpacked a child's story, working on the language and behavioral responses that might be used in helping the child understand, reframe, and enlarge their own story. The camp was intentionally small and served a common purpose to assist children in the construction of narratives of hope instead of defeat. He would work there for three summers, and he would do the graduate-school route, but now with a clear sense of vocation.

Megan was a camp counselor, as was he. Her beauty, intelligence, and empathy astounded Tom. On days off, they rode the train and went exploring into the big city. If you walked and made use of cheap transportation, New York City offered wonderful things to do. They would pack a knapsack with sandwiches and fruit and set out with a goal in mind that could change as easily as a summer day. By the end of that first summer, they knew they were in love. Graduate school led to her certification as a psychologist and entry for him into the academy and the professorate.

Married for thirty-five years, with three grown, on-their-own adult children, they had paid off their own graduate school debt and had helped their kids navigate the sometimes rocky road into adulthood. Now secured in their professions, they were appreciative of having time to do those things they wanted to do.

As he took the three steps up to the gate, all these thoughts coursed through his brain. There was a light on by the door. He rang the familiar bell and the door opened. His cousin, Janie, stood there, looking sorrowful. "Oh Tom," she said, "He died; I'm so sorry."

*

Early morning and Karl Wolfe could not sleep. People were on the street outside his window getting on the train and going to work, and he was lying in bed with that thread that held him upright badly frayed. He no longer believed in a good God who watched over him and knew the number of hairs on his head.

He slowly rolled out of his bed, away from Emily, who slept soundly, quietly, without bad dreams, who still believed in God. It was winter. Three times each week he went to the hospital for re-hab. The women who directed exercises and timed heart patients like Wolfe in their routines were happy people. He spun the rotating wheel and walked on the treadmill. He tried to capture some of their laughter and make it his own, but all his efforts did not satisfy him.

There were regulars. In a way it was like church. There was the alcoholic who had a bad knee, and three more heart patients who'd had surgery like his. There was one guy who never talked and another who talked too much. But Wolfe knew what to do. Like church, he smiled, made small talk, did his exercises, thanked the staff and left. Today was one of those days when he did not go to the hospital. Still, he'd awakened early on the second floor in his home, and now he stood by the bedroom's front bay window, looking out as a December's snow continued to fall. It was cold. He should be in bed asleep under the warm blankets.

The pedestrian crosswalk caught his eye. A red "stop" digital hand changed into a digital white "cross" walking stick figure. He thought: "But why cross the street?" His doctor told him that the itch on his chest, where the scar on his sternum had not yet healed, and all the welts still healing that coursed up and down his arm and leg were good things telling him he was alive. His doctor had emphasized: "You were lucky. You had no symptoms that warned you that you were in trouble, yet you still survived a full-blown heart attack. Not everyone does."

So he was lucky.

Wolfe wondered if it was luck, or chance. He knew it wasn't the benevolent act of a gracious God. He'd once believed in a God. If God was all powerful, then maybe Emily's prayer circle made sense. Maybe he owed them for their prayers. Try as he might, he could not accept that kind of theology. Why would God pull strings to save him? If God pulled strings for every person who called on God, wouldn't the world seem crazy? He could not accept that kind of God—a God who granted favors to a lucky few—that wasn't a God he could respect.

On the street a young couple tossed snowballs at each other, at six-thirty in the morning. She. . . long, dark hair cascading around an oval face tilting in laughter toward him; he, dark jeans and fur-topped boots, twisting away, trying to dodge a direct hit from her well-aimed snowball, happily failing and closing with her, encircled her waist, tugging her away into a quick kiss and then toward the train stop; both so alive.

"Aaah, crap," he muttered to himself. Emily rolled over; he moved—slowly—away from the window and into the bathroom.

It was cold in there, too.

*

Martin Evans had been asked to preach in the church where Karl and Emily Wolfe attended. Evans assumed that this long after Wolfe's surgery there was a good chance they might be present. Norah was pregnant, and with the pregnancy had come some bad moments with morning sickness, so she had a good excuse not to accompany him. It had also turned cold, and he sensed that she wanted to rest in their warm bed.

It was the season of advent, and the lectionary readings hinted at the coming of Jesus, an expectant coming that accented how the church always and continuously waited for Jesus's arrival at Christmas. "We wait, and then he comes." So said the old, old story. It was a story of hope, of promise. "Like Norah's pregnancy," Martin thought. He had coupled one of the lectionary readings with one of Auden's poems, a poem that asked if we really wanted the "promising child" called Jesus to be born. If he was born, would we have the guts to live the way God seemed to suggest we should. This was a tougher message than a lot of the "sweet, baby Jesus" messages that seemed to fill the TV and downtown store centers. Martin intended to link the baby Jesus with the man the church affirmed as "the Christ," the one who came to save, and who winds up nailed to a cross.

He planned to end his sermon by saying, "In advent's period of waiting, believers are asked to re-examine their lives in light of the advent promise that Jesus will come and will be born anew. He not only came two thousand years ago, but comes this year and every year. His continued presence challenges us at the core of our lives. Advent is about much more than a sweet baby lying in a manger; it is also about answering a hard question: do we really want Christ to arrive, to come again this and every Christmas?"

He didn't know how he'd missed Emily and Karl Wolfe, but there they were, perhaps fifteen rows back from the chancel area sitting in a pew behind a family of several large, athletic boys. Karl caught Martin's eyes, and for a moment Martin felt the searing pain of a deep anger course through his body. Karl looked down, and Martin deliberately chose to make eye contact elsewhere, avoiding any further direct connection with Karl. After giving the benediction, Martin found himself greeting a steady stream of people who were leaving the service. Looking up from a handshake, he found himself grasping Emily Wolfe's hand. "Good sermon, Martin," she said. Behind her came Karl. He looked exhausted. Maybe it was the weight loss, but to Martin he looked hunted. They shook hands. Wolfe asked, "Is Norah here?" "No," Martin replied. "She stayed home today." "I hope she's fine," Wolfe responded, and then exited behind a final few trailing church members. Martin thought, "She is fine, no thanks to you."

In the car, headed home, his smile somewhat fixed, Martin found himself nevertheless pleased with the post-service "coffee hour" conversations he had with members of the congregation. Everyone seemed to approve of his sermon, and he felt his spirit rise as he was praised for his "graceful words." A young couple told him that they would set aside some time in the season for personal discernment regarding their lifestyles. All good stuff, he thought. But he also found himself wondering at the rage he felt at Wolfe's presence in worship. Just the man's presence stirred some deep seated anger inside him, surfacing with such force that he had almost attacked this heart patient just out of the hospital. He wondered, had he access to a gun in that moment, would he have shot Wolfe?

Martin had once served as a volunteer chaplain at a jail, and he often had found it hard to comprehend the violence that lay near the surface of some of the incarcerated men. Their stories often had to do with women and other men who, they felt, had stepped too far "over the line." "Like me," Martin found himself saying out loud.

He was suddenly aware that if a man intentionally abused, misused, or hurt Norah, he was capable of killing that person. And that very morning, in the middle of a church service, his rage had boiled up—even as he was preaching discernment and peace— and had almost spilled over. He caught himself, dismayed at how this recollection still angered him. And it was about something Norah had easily handled. She was deeply bothered by Karl Wolfe, yes, but she would be the first to say that she could take care of herself. Why, then, was he so angry?

Did he consider Norah "his," as in "his wife, his property?" He hoped that was not the case. No. It had more to do with the bonds he believed they both shared. Were he abused, mistreated, or hurt, he was certain that Norah would tap into a deep rage at whomever had done those things. He smiled. She was what his dad often called "a real pistol." And he meant that as a positive compliment. Norah had told him that he needed to beware of Wolfe; perhaps she should have added that he also needed to beware of his own feelings, his own male pride.

"Discernment," Martin said out loud. "I need to contemplate what my fantasy of Wolfe being sexually involved with Norah is doing to my insides. What am I going to do with myself and the choices I might need to make if this thing about his sexual improprieties starts to unravel?" As he said this out loud, he found himself pounding the steering wheel of his car.

He said: "I need to slow down."

*

Ten

On a Sunday afternoon during Christmas break, assistant professor Rebecca Swingle reached for the top of the book shelf in her office. There were eighteen empty cardboard boxes scattered around her office, and she finally found herself putting a final book into its place on the shelf behind her desk. "My desk," she said. "I have a desk and I (finally) have a job as an assistant professor. Hallelujah."

Unexpectedly stepping into her room, Dean Wolfe coughed. She turned; he said: "Hello, Becky." Not everyone got to call Rebecca "Becky," and certainly not the dean, but she caught herself and politely responded, "Hello, Dean Wolfe." Apparently he was back at the div school, though just for one or two days each week. Professor Martin was still the interim dean. Wolfe looked tired. Earlier pictures of him showed a more vibrant man. Today he seemed older than what she remembered. She cautioned herself to "Be careful'" of this old man even as she reminded herself how she felt when once she overheard her niece telling someone that Aunt Becky was "old."

She felt lucky to have her appointment with the divinity school. She knew that this was a critical moment in her career. First impressions were important. If, at the third year of her appointment the faculty felt she had not proved herself, she could be asked to look elsewhere. She'd be given a year to find something, yeah, but this was a polite way to say she'd been fired. But if they affirmed her work with them and their students, she could be on the way to promotion and a long career with the Div School—if she chose to stay. Dean Wolfe was a sticking point. Even with sympathy for his heart attack and the evident pain and rapid aging that attack had caused, Rebecca knew that she would keep her distance—she had just enough experience with him to realize that she neither liked nor trusted this man.

Her relationship with the university was tainted by her distaste for the man. After her initial interview at the school, he had driven her the several blocks to her hotel from, but instead of leaving, he had insisted in coming with her to the front desk. That she saw as a courtesy, but then he wanted to come with her "to check out her room." Following another couple, she had timed her approach to the elevator so that she could step inside and quickly turn round, effectively saying "good-bye." Later, alone in her room, she had chided herself: "You overreacted." Yet she found herself surprised when a month later during a "welcoming" photo session with new faculty for the university newsletter, Wolfe had slipped his arm around her waist while resting his right hand on her hip. He'd been bold in that moment, but bolder still when she had arrived late to a luncheon where her place card was next to Wolfe's chair. Feeling trepidation, she sat down, only to become aware of Wolfe's probing hand on her leg. The force of her abrupt rise knocked her chair onto the floor. She found herself brushing her hair in the ladies' room when Professor Rachel Henderson stepped inside. "Are you ok?" Rachel asked. Dissembling, Rebecca avoided eye contact. "Yes," she replied, "I suddenly felt faint." Henderson didn't buy her explanation: "Look, Rebecca. I think that something happened with the dean, and I want you to know that you don't have to put up with his monkey business."

Rebecca had passed it off—"it was of no account, really"—and had quietly slipped away from the luncheon. That evening she had called her mother, who suggested that Dean Wolfe was of another generation, and that she had to watch out for his "accidental" touch. That much was true, and several months later she found "the good dean" brushing some supposed lint off the front of her navy-blue sweater. He had ambushed her, and while she had flinched at the touch of his hand on her breast, Wolfe had passed it off, saying: "There, there; I won't hurt you." That night her mother cautioned her on "keeping clear roles" during her first year. "They don't really know you, honey," said her mom. "Keep your distance and work hard. You can more easily speak out after they get to know you." Her mom told her that as a secretary in a large firm, she too had been "accosted." Maybe it was a generational thing, Rebecca thought, but Wolfe's creepy stalking behavior was hard to put up with, and she had hoped that today—a Sunday during Christmas break— might have found him away from the school, but no such luck.

"Becky," Wolfe began. "I'm sure you want to make a good impression during your stay with us." Rebecca cringed—"How did he know what she had been thinking?" He continued: "As Dean, my concern is that you settle in, and find the resources to make your stay with us pleasant. Have you had any problems thus far?" Feeling like a schoolgirl before the principal, Rebecca responded: "The staff and the professors have been wonderful. I know my first year is important, but I think I'm ready to go. Getting my books unpacked has helped a lot toward feeling at home here."

"Well, I'm pleased that you are moving in and feeling ok, but I wanted (personally) to offer my help; that is, if you want my help." Somehow he had moved closer, and was now backing her up against her bookcase. She stepped sideways, avoiding a hand he had extended toward her. "I'm not certain I understand, sir." For several moments the room was quiet; in the peculiar warm-weather break, Rebecca could hear the "thwak-thwak" of a tennis game, but there were no other sounds. She thought: "I'm alone here." Dropping his hand, Wolfe smiled. He nodded twice, as if he had reached a decision, then spoke: "Were you to accompany me to the February conference in Atlanta, we might share a room. I'd like that. I could then be most helpful in your future rank and tenure deliberations." This was said calmly, without apparent emotional content, and Rebecca felt that some boundary was being crossed between them with his proposal and that she had not prepared for this in her wildest imaginations.

Again, she stepped sideways, positioning herself on the far side of her desk, away from the dean. With the desk between them and an open window behind her, she picked up her letter-knife. Holding the letter-knife in front of her she— with deliberation—said: "You know I'm engaged, Dean Wolfe, and while I appreciate your comments, they are inappropriate, and I intend not to advance myself that way." As if nothing of consequence had just occurred, Wolfe placed both hands on her desk. Leaning toward her, he said: "Know that I mean no harm, Becky. I'm simply suggesting that we might enjoy each other more fully were we to connect in such a fashion. Our 'connection'—he stressed the word—would reduce the stress on both sides that often gets associated with the promotion process. Think about it. Atlanta could be a lovely diversion. But if this does not appeal to you, well—no harm, no foul." It was said as if they were discussing the weather.

With that, Wolfe stepped back, and before she could say anything in response, she heard the sounds of the distant tennis match and the "click-click" of his heels disappearing down the hallway. Holding her breath, Becky slumped into her chair. "Did that really just happen?" She went to her door, closed and locked it. There was moisture on her forehead and her jaw was clenched.

"I need to talk with Rachel Henderson."

*

After his father's funeral, Tom and younger siblings, Kerri and Michael, stayed on to help their mom "dispose of your father's things." Kerri, his little sister, now grown, tried to talk her out of it, but she was adamant: "No, Kerri. I need this to happen. I want you to do this for me." Sunday afternoon the three of them had climbed the stairs, not talking, and not looking at one another. It was strange to be in his parent's bedroom, rooting around in his father's things. As a child, Tom had understood that this was their room. Somehow it violated his sense of the way it should be to be filling empty cardboard boxes with his dead father's clothing.

The big chest of drawers was neatly filled and well-organized. "Like dad," he said out loud. In the top drawer was a locked .45 pistol case. His dad had served as an MP. The .45 was probably his weapon. Tom had never seen the case or the gun, even though the town was a mecca for sports hunters. Lifting the case, he discovered an envelope. Inside were his dad's discharge papers, his parent's wedding license, and birth certificates for Keri, Michael and himself. There also was a letter addressed in his mother's familiar hand to his father. The stamp on the envelope indicated it had been sent during the war. "These go to mom," he said. There was also a second revolver, wrapped in a soft hand towel under which was a box of shells. "This one looks like the .22 target pistol he used to take when we went target practicing up by the old mill," he thought out loud. Holding it to the light he read "Smith and Wesson."

"This is hard to do," said Kerri.

"I'll take the two pistols," Tom said to Kerri.

From the right hand top dresser drawer he pulled out penknives, combs, an old pocket watch ("his father's," said Kerri), and an envelope filled with childhood pictures of them. Tom felt tears starting to trickle down his cheek as he slowly leafed through the pictures. "Mom and Dad's world," he mused. Michael took the old watch. Kerri ("our historian," Michael said.) took the pictures and a silver picture frame of them leaning against an old car. They were young, obviously in love, eyes filled with great hope and energy. Tom put the penknife in his pocket. He turned toward Michael, who was sitting in his father's old armchair. Michael held an old cardigan sweater Tom recognized as one his dad often wore. He'd also taken an old Civil Conservation Corp ring that dad had worn as a young man, and had slipped the ring onto his right ring finger. He was also crying: "This is so unfair," Michael whispered. Seeing Michael's tears, Tom put his hand on Michael's back. He said, "We're sad at dad's dying. I know that. I miss him terribly. He had a lot of life yet in front of him. It is unfair. But look at what he saved here, the things he felt were important anchors for understanding who he was. We need to mourn and yet we also need to celebrate who he was for us and for mom. He loved us, and he'd want us to help mom now." Tom paused, as if thinking about what he was about to say: "Look, you two, mom is not getting better; her cancer is in remission, but it isn't gone. I worry about her, especially with dad's sudden death. I'll say it again—dad would want us to help her."

As Tom lifted his hand from Michael's shoulder, Michael stood, nodding his head and turning back to work on emptying his father's chest of drawers. Soon three boxes were full, and there were several piles of clothing that were either folded or on hangers now lying flat on the bed. "I'll take this stuff to Goodwill tomorrow," Michael said to no one in particular. The suits, ties, shoes, and dress shirts would find quick homes, of that Tom was certain. He kept a canvas coat that had a leather collar and cuffs. He stood back from the assortment of boxes, clothing, and the few things that were important enough for his father to keep in a private drawer. Pictures, an old ring, watch, penknife, and a few documents "tell us dad's story," muttered Tom. He watched Kerri and Michael from the upstairs window wrestling boxes and loose clothes into their rental cars: "Everything else is dust in the wind."

*

Wolfe hated taking his pills. "His" pills.

After his heart attack he took them for high blood pressure, too much cholesterol, and for gout. There were eight of them, and Emily arranged them in a green, plastic pill tray with daily compartments that in total added up to a month's supply. He'd open Monday's, Tuesday's, and slowly, pill by pill, count away his days. The pills came from a mail-order pharmacy based in Texas. They weren't cheap. Today was a Sunday. He'd gone to church with Emily. Martin Evans had preached. He had to admit, Evans did a good job. He had not been surprised to discover that Evans had not been too friendly at the door. The reception line had been a long one, but Emily had insisted they stand there waiting their turn to shake Evan's hand. Was he imagining, Wolfe wondered, or had Evan's grip tightened a bit when he had asked about Norah? Maybe Evans knows.

Wolfe looked down at the green pill tray in his hand. He wondered what might happen were he to stop taking his pills, but having seen his aunt suffer and not be able to communicate following her stroke (and she had refused to take her pills), he dismissed this idea. In some moral way that he did not fully understand, he felt the pills made him weaker, at least in his own eyes. No longer could he do what he had been able to do when he was thirty or even forty years old. And the longing he had, the yearning for those lost years always came when he thought of some young girl. He knew his longing was somehow connected to his lost strength. As he'd aged, he'd been surprised at how often his body had betrayed him. He was unsure of himself, noticeably weaker, less flexible, unable to stay up late working on a class, a speech, or a journal article. He no longer could count on his body to supply the energy he needed. "Old," he said. "And weak."

He'd caught himself that morning looking out the window at the neighbor girl just home from school. She had stepped out of their house and despite the cold was sitting on the top of the steps that led down to the streets. Unusually pretty, her slender body was capped by curly blonde hair. Wolfe did not know her name, but it seemed to him she had appeared as a kind of gift, and he kept track of her comings and goings. He had little else to do, and her gracefulness and age reminded him of other women he had known, some intimately. He thought of Kylie Raven, how she had turned —like a cat—and hit him as hard as any man. But that had ended badly; looking across the street he had on occasion masturbated, but not today. Today he was waiting for Jennifer to arrive.

He had not crossed that line into senility. . . yet. He still had certain powers, real authority as a dean, influence with those who surrounded him at the div school. This power was not lightly given. And it could be taken away. But, in the moment at least, it afforded him connections with girls and women who still were in awe of who he was and what he represented.

*

At lunch, Norah asked: "How did it go?" Martin replied: "As good as could be expected."

"Problem?" asked Norah.

"Emily and Wolfe were in Church."

"Hard for you?"

"Yes. I was angry."

"Not good to be angry when preaching, I'd guess."

"I know," said Martin. "The thing is, Wolfe's sitting there, right in front of me, and suddenly it's as if I'm doing the male thing. . . wanting to get down from that pulpit and punch him out. And I'm thinking this while words are coming out my mouth about the coming of the Christ child. It was surreal."

"But you didn't go and punch him, did you? You carried it off ok."

"Maybe that's what bothers me, Norah. I did carry it off. I was in the pulpit, and I was angry enough to hit this man, and I continued to preach about the prince of peace. What does that say about me?"

"I think it says that you're human," said Norah.

*

Eleven

Wolfe was entranced by first year Div School student, Jennifer Logan. One day near one of the quadrangle intersections on the university campus he had watched her walking toward him. He had paused and caught her eyes. Seeing him stopped and waiting, she had walked up to him and said "Hello." To Wolfe it seemed like her meeting him was foreordained ("I've become a silly Presbyterian," Wolfe thought). But the way she had looked up at him—she had beautiful blue eyes—it had been obvious that she was at the university in order to be taken care of by him, and if she expected some close, even intimate contact because of his care, so be it.

She had the look of a model. A strong, almost Danish blonde glow. High cheek bones and a body that did not quit. His quick impression told him this was not the typical university student. He'd asked if she was in the divinity school, and she had said: "Yes, I am." He'd then asked if things were going well, and she'd said "OK," but with a frown, as if things were not going as well as they could have. He was cautious in this, of course; he now was cautious in most things regarding women. He'd pursued her very slowly, but soon discovered that while she had gained admittance, she had little understanding of graduate work. In a word, she was academically slow, perhaps she had certain learning issues. In any case, he was not interested in her mind.

After some weeks of flirting and occasional conversations over coffee, Wolfe had invited her to dinner at his home. He knew she would assume his wife would also be there, but Emily was not, and he said that she had unexpectedly been called away. The "unexpectedly" part was a lie. His wife was at a church meeting, and he had used her absence to get Jennifer alone in his house. Not that he could do what he really wanted to do, which was to strip her and have sex on the living room rug, but he was content to be in control, stretching the flirting to bold comments as to her body, her hair, her dress, her "good looks." Perhaps he'd gone too far, because she had left before he'd had a chance to show her his study or to share dessert.

But he wasn't surprised when she stopped by his office. She had a way of looking at him that took him back to earlier days with other young women, and he was happy to continue a quiet campaign of gentle flirting. He felt a certain thrill when he first called her "Jenny." He more easily dropped off into sleep when he thought about her—Jenny's skin across her nose was sprinkled with freckles. She had pale blue eyes, and her composure was calm, even serene. Her clothes betrayed the fact that money was an issue, not that they were dirty, but they were worn, suggesting that she was making her way with what she had, and wasn't purchasing the latest style. And she struggled with written exams. That seemed to be the real reason she did not slam the door on Wolfe's all too friendly comments. After all, he was still the divinity school's dean.

Somehow in her quiet way she had convinced Dean Wolfe of her need for an independent study in his area of expertise. This had been interrupted by his unfortunate heart attack, and the registrar had told her that all would be well as long as she concluded the study once the dean was back at the div school. But Jenny had sent him a get-well card with a note telling him she had a draft of her paper, and once he felt up to it, she'd be willing to come to his home to discuss it. She had included her phone number, and much to her surprise, he'd called, and a date was set. Dean Wolfe said he was looking forward to the time he might spend with Jenny.

Her ringing the doorbell sent a small shiver down his spine. "Jenny" he said, opening the door. "Sir," she replied, stepping into his home. "Here, let me take your coat." Wolfe moved behind Jenny, brushing her shoulders as he lifted the coat while she slid arms out of both sleeves. Hanging her coat inside the hall closet, Wolfe took her by the arm and led her into his study. Once the study door was closed, he turned and embracing her, whispered "I missed you."

Jennifer felt Wolfe's right hand sliding around her waist and under the elastic band of her panties, moving downward to cup her buttocks and pull her body tight against him. His left hand found and began to slowly knead her breast. He pressed against her, but she felt no erection. Her initial impulse was to pull away, but she fought it, intuitively sensing that the old man's impotence hopefully meant this was as far as Wolfe would or could go with her body. In the moment it was as if she had become an inanimate object, a blown-up plastic doll. She thought: "Something of no consequence."

He did not attempt to kiss her, and after tightly holding her for several minutes, he released his grip and stepped away. "We should look at your paper," Wolfe said. He turned away and without facing her grasped her hand while leading her to his study, a book-lined room near the rear of the house. Twenty minutes later he shook her hand while saying "Goodbye." She had a puzzled look on her face as she walked away from his house.

Waiting for her train to the university, she sat by herself on the deserted elevated platform. She wondered why she was finding classes at the div school so hard, and she asked herself not for the first time why she had come here. Maybe she should get out of the program. She liked young children. She knew that much. Maybe she'd do better were she to study something like child development or work toward becoming a certified teacher. Her advisor had asked her why she was in the div school, and the only answer she had was that she'd hoped to become equipped to work with children in church settings. He'd warned her that the div school might not be the best place ("or easiest," she thought) to get entry to such positions.

She knew that her initial coursework didn't fit her concerns, and all the theological ideas on the lips of most professors were just a difficult struggle for her. She'd be lucky to get past the core courses without flunking out.

In the middle of her anxiety she'd met Wolfe. From that first meeting it was clear that he was interested. "His 'A' will balance out three 'C's,'" she thought, "but I've got to get beyond this." Several other people came up the stairs and were now scattered around the platform. It was chilly, and Jennifer wondered when it would snow. Some of those who were waiting sat on a bench under an enclosed heating unit that came on and then at no particular interval turned off. One or two were reading that day's local paper, but most seemed caught up with keeping warm.

Jennifer could see the train's headlight far down the track, and people beginning to stand, positioning themselves where they hoped a door into the stopped train might open. As she stepped on board the train, a div school student she recognized came running down the platform and jumped into the same car. He took a train seat across from her: "How's life, Jennifer?" he said. Looking him in the eye, she said: "I've had better days." He wanted to talk, but her recent encounter with Wolfe had soured the evening for Jennifer Logan. Looking out her window in the train, she could see people's homes, the lights of moving cars, and pedestrians hurrying to their destinations. A sprinkling of snow crystals hit the window. As her fellow student opened a book and started to read, she thought: "I've become a whore. No, not that. I'm selling my body like a prostitute. And for a measly grade."

*

Professor Sharon Henderson looked up from the work piled high on her desk. She'd long ago given up keeping ahead of everything that came with teaching, but she was good at prioritizing, and one look at Professor Rebecca Swingle, the div school's new hire, and she knew whatever was bothering Becky was going to trump everything else. "You ok?" she asked. "Nope. Not even close." Rebecca had been hired in part because Sharon had chaired the search committee. Becky was a gifted young scholar with the possibility of an important future ahead of her. Sharon believed that she might just become the kind of bright light that would attract students, particularly women. Of the three candidates they brought to the school, Becky Swingle easily was the one who stood out. The students loved her, and the faculty were amazed that they could get someone like her to come to a school that had been written up in *The Chronicle of Higher Education* as a place "not friendly to the woman scholar." "What's wrong?" Sharon asked. There was a deep sigh from Professor Swingle. A few tears made their way down her face. Henderson reached across her desk and handed her a box of tissues. "Wolfe," said Swingle.

"Wolfe?"

"He told me that in return for 'sexual favors,' he'd help me more easily move through the university rank and tenure process." This was said through clenched teeth. "That's so stupid," Henderson exclaimed, getting up to close the door. "The man has lost his brain. I mean, he can't do that. The senior faculty makes that kind of decision. It goes to the university faculty committee, and from them to the trustees. He only carries the recommendation. That's it. Why would he say that? It makes no sense."

"I only know he did say it, and I'm at a loss as to what I should do."

"Ok. You and I are going to lunch. You don't have an afternoon class today? No? Good. Let's go."

One week later Professor Henderson closed the div school conference room door. She surveyed the small group seated round the single table— Dr. Rebecca Swingle, the university's young assistant professor, a second year master's level student, Kylie Raven, and Jennifer Logan, a quiet first year student. Henderson began to speak: "You may have wondered why I asked you to meet here with me today. I asked you because frankly, I'm angry with what is going on in my school, and you are here because you are involved in it."

"I said my school, and I meant that. I love this place. I've been here long enough to know that secrets have a way of coming loose, and that's what is happening right now." She paused, exhaled a large sigh, and continued: "Professor Swingle came to me last week because—wait a minute—what I'm going to say will need to be held in confidence until or if we decide to make it public. Before anything else, can we agree on that?"

There were three nods, though Jennifer was slow to agree. "Jennifer?" Professor Henderson asked. Jennifer's "yes" was soft, barely audible, almost not heard by Sharon, who waited. Jennifer looked up, saw that Sharon was waiting for her response, and said: "Yes; I'm in."

"Good," said Professor Henderson. "Dr. Swingle came to me last week and told me that Dean Wolfe had been inappropriate with her. She also told me, Jennifer, that she had reason to believe that the dean also behaved inappropriately with you. And Kylie, I saw the dean go into an elevator with you before ten o'clock that night after the closing session of the AAR/SBL meeting, and I saw him ten minutes later exit that same elevator. He was in such a hurry to get out the front door that he did not see me. He was holding what seemed to be a bloody handkerchief to the left side of his face. That week he told me he had been mugged *after* he'd ridden the train home from the conference. That story was a lie. I think you defended yourself from Wolfe's advances, and he was running away from you when I happened to see him and put two and two together."

She paused: "You all know me. You know my story, and you know I've written about sexual harassment and that Tom Metcalf and I have been working this year with a congregation where the pastor betrayed his relationship with several women who were church members. Neither Tom nor I support that kind of behavior. We understand how it might occur, but we don't condone it. I don't intend to sit quietly and do nothing if I suspect that this kind of thing is going on where I teach."

"Professor Swingle has indicated that she will be making a formal complaint against Wolfe. That complaint would be much stronger if you two—nodding at Kylie and Jennifer—were willing to join her. I know that even if you don't want to do this, Professor Swingle's complaint will hit the fan and there will be a huge eruption on this campus. Something will be done, of that I am certain."

"Now you. . . Jennifer and Kylie. . . you don't need to get involved in this, but I will tell you from my own experience that if you remain silent about this man, that silence will eat away at your insides, it will undermine your voice, it will deaden your talents, and it will cause you to doubt that there is a loving God. And, in addition, when you need to act, you will find it hard to be brave in the face of evil." She paused, exhaled, and looked at both students: "Do you understand me?" The two heads nodded "yes."

"This is what I hope you will do. I don't want, at this time, to hear your stories. If I do hear them, then my role in this will be suspect. Wolfe does not like me, and for good reason. So what I am asking you to do is to take one of these tablets. . .she produced three yellow legal tablets. . .and write what happened to you. Be descriptive, and give dates. Write your story. Tell how it made you feel then and how you feel now. I don't want you to leave here until you have all of it written down. And what will then happen? Professor Metcalf is waiting outside this room. He's grading some papers, and when you are done you will go to him, put your essay in one of the large envelopes he has, and both you and he will sign and date the sealed envelope flap."

"You should realize that your envelope might be unsealed in a court, or at a trustee hearing about Dean Wolfe, but if you are willing to do this, I will try to keep your names confidential (but I cannot promise that will occur). Will you do this?" Again both heads nodded "yes." Henderson continued: "Professor Swingle will be writing her story as well. She will also give her story to Professor Metcalf. There is a fourth tablet here. I will write what I saw that evening when Kylie and the dean had that elevator ride. When I am done, I will take my little essay to Tom, I'll put it into one of his envelopes, and then he and I will seal and sign our names across that seal, dating the envelope. And if it comes to it, I will welcome the opportunity to testify against this man."

*

Twelve

SNOW CONTINUED TO FALL as Martin Evans opened his second academic council meeting. His first council meeting had occurred shortly after the "hiring" interview he'd had with President Tanaka. That academic meeting had gone well. Two committees had business to transact, and some divinity school initiatives were discussed in depth. After that meeting he'd been congratulated by several of the professors, and they had trekked the several blocks to *Fritz's Bar and Grille*, the local west side hang-out for the university and the wider community.

After two beers and a lot of talk, he'd gotten home late, but was pleased, as was Norah, at his description of the relaxed feeling he'd had during the meeting: "I think my ease has to do with how uneventful it all was. I mean, we followed the agenda, everyone behaved well, there were no red flags, and we ended the meeting in less than ninety minutes. I know that almost to the second because Tom Metcalf congratulated me. He said that 'the move to adjourn' came at the eighty fourth minute!"

That was a month ago. In the weeks leading to his second council meeting, he's been aware of some undercurrents that were murky at best, but nevertheless present. He'd taken to visiting faculty members in their offices, and they in turn seemed more than willing to visit him in his office. Librarian Edwin Diaz told him during one such visit that he'd picked up some interesting scuttlebutt at a regional librarian's meeting. "It seems that Wolfe's old school has all but announced that they intend to go to court over some missing money," said Edwin, "And while that's not connected with any of our people, it suggests the mood of that school is against Wolfe."

"He's being hit hard," said Martin. "First the heart attack; now this."

"Makes me wonder," said Edwin. "Not so much about the money, but how he eyeballs the ladies. Makes me wonder."

*

President Tanaka called Martin Evans into his office on the day of Martin's second academic council meeting. "I get the regional newspaper, and that rag includes Wolfe's old institution within its area," said Tanaka. "Check this out," he said, extending the newspaper to Martin. The headline on the folded page read *Past Seminary Dean Investigated*. "The seminary's Board of Trustees must have decided to make this move," said Martin.

"I know," Tanaka responded. "I just got off the phone with that board's chair. He told me both the seminary and the denomination are in the middle of their own investigations. He said there had been a leak regarding the money issue, and that the investigations were broader in scope than that one concern. He apologized for sending Wolfe to us, but said no one back then had any hint of all this."

"Today's faculty meeting ought to be lively," said Martin.

Later, after calling the faculty council to order, he'd entertained reports from three of the standing committees, and was beginning to think that he had imagined any dark issue, when Professor Sharon Henderson, under new business, asked to be heard. She said, "By now most of us have heard the rumors floating around Dean Wolfe's supposed sexual inappropriateness with some of our students and faculty members. I'd like to have this council appoint a committee to examine these issues and to pursue whatever university policy applies in this area." Immediately a number of voices sought the floor, and Martin recognized the librarian, Edwin Diaz, who said, "We can't have a committee appointed to pursue rumors unless we have a charge. There are always rumors, and we don't have jurisdiction over rumors. If a charge has been made that falls within our responsibility, then we should form a committee to examine the merits of the charge. Has a charge been made?"

One of the newer faculty members, Rebecca Swingle, nodded her head: "I'll make the charge." She looked down the council table and said, "I charge Dean Karl Wolfe with inappropriate sexual behavior with me and with other students and faculty of this divinity school, and I ask an appointed committee to find evidence that either proves or disproves this charge." Considerable discussion ensued. Twenty minutes later, all agreed to proceed "according to The Faculty Manual." An examining committee was set up, consisting of a chair, Thomas Metcalf; interim dean Martin Evans; and Kevin Walker, the assistant professor and psychologist responsible for pastoral counseling. The council then adjourned, and the three men called President Tanaka to establish when they might meet with him the following day regarding the charge and appropriate university procedures.

*

Norah's nursing schedule included a night shift, so Martin sometimes arrived home to an empty house. Norah's absence triggered thoughts about Wolfe. Before Norah came into Martin's life, he'd had what he'd called "moments of melancholy." While they couldn't be called bouts of clinical depression, the bleakness that he'd felt on those occasions would not be something he would wish on his worst enemy. He wondered about Wolfe in that regard. Was this a crisis of the spirit? Or one of belief? Was Wolfe losing it? Maybe a mild stroke? Some form of mild dementia? He thought back to a conversation he'd had with Norah, when he'd said that he could not understand why someone would risk approaching someone like Norah, knowing that everything that person had worked for and achieved at any moment could uncontrollably explode in his face. And Norah had said: "Maybe he's bored, or depressed, or just looked at his life and decided that some of the things that once mattered and that held him together don't really matter anymore, so why not take some risks?"

And Martin had responded: "It has to be more than that, Norah. At first I asked myself how a minister and someone involved in educating folk studying for the ministry could do these things. But then I realized how stressful ministry can be. I certainly was stressed! Looking back at my little half-time ministerial position I can see signs of burn-out in me during that period. I was impulsive. I felt isolated. I think it's possible that he's spiritually burned out. Maybe his being a dean for so long set him up for such issues. On the other hand, I've also wondered about the man's mental stability. I don't think that this is a mid-life thing; I believe that he's too old for kicking over the traces, divorcing Emily, and running off to Mexico in a convertible with a beautiful woman twenty years his junior."

"Is that your dream, Martin?" He stopped, thought a moment—"No, Norah, but maybe, just maybe, it could be a dream he has but can't quite get the courage to actually pull it off. I mean, he's no young stud. Maybe all this is only a pathetic old man's dream that occasionally spills over. So let's say you're right; maybe he just wants to kick over the traces, break some taboos, go out on terms other than the ones that have carried him this far." Norah emphatically shook her head. "You're kinder than I am, Martin. It might be that what I initially suggested to you—that the man is a sociopathic predator—goes too far, but his behavior is way out of bounds. He is causing real pain out here in the real world. I am betting that you will find some nasty stuff from his past that has little to do with dreams. Please remember; I looked him in the eye and could see that he would enjoy intentionally turning my life inside out." Norah was angry, and Martin felt he had gone too far. "I believe you Norah, and I respect what you said. But why is he so open with most of what he's done? If what he is doing is so evil, why isn't he more hidden with this stuff? Most of it is right out in the open. It doesn't make sense."

"Maybe not. . . but men of a certain age, perhaps of a certain generation, particularly if they have been successful in their past sexual endeavors, often feel invisible. They assure a power relationship when considering all women. Women are there for them to use or abuse as they wish. They often have a certain sense of entitlement that goes with this perspective as well as a built in ability to lie convincingly. But even if none of what I've said applies to Wolfe, his skating close to the edge may, in fact, be exciting for him, and don't underestimate him. He just might want to get caught so that he can beat you," suggested Norah. "And if that's the case," she continued, "I think the committee you've just set up has the tools and the smarts to figure that out."

*

The next day was a Saturday, and Martin reminded himself to be on his best behavior that night while he and Norah were attending their second university dean's dinner at President Tanaka's home. Before departing for the dinner, Martin checked his familiarity with the names of the deans. "Don't forget their spouses," said Norah. "All women," said Martin.

"And all important," said Norah. Martin sighed. He hoped that at the dinner he would not stick his foot in his mouth like he'd just done. "You'll be fine," said Norah, pulling him away from a recent publicity shot that displayed and named all the deans, including him.

Once at the Tanaka's, Martin was surprised at the evening conversation. Before he'd gotten a glass of wine, he'd been asked by the dean of the law school about the harassment charge and if there was sufficient evidence to carry it to a legal conclusion favorable to the school. Several other deans joined in, and the conversation, now led by the dean of the school of education, had an edge to it that bothered Martin. After that dean left to get another glass of wine, the law school dean quietly informed Martin that their colleague had "married his student, don't you know," and that some of the conversation that had occurred then, "still smarted."

Before dinner was announced, two more deans found time to speak with Martin about the charge. Tanaka noticed these conversations, and when announcing "Dinner is served," added, with a smile: ". . . and I hereby forbid any business conversation at the dinner table." He continued: "Business can occur on Monday when we gather at 9 AM in my office. Until then, please talk about the Christmas season or our basketball team, but leave all business till Monday."

As they headed home, Norah said: "I was between the law school dean and the head of the school of social work. They were very gracious, but managed to get one or two questions about 'the charge' onto the table. They hoped it was winnable, and one dean was concerned as to how any adverse publicity caused by the charge might affect the university. I was polite, but pled ignorance on both counts, so the conversation moved to other topics."

"I knew this could be a hot topic," said Martin, "But I didn't appreciate how it might churn up old issues within the university. Late in the evening President Tanaka let me know that two of the present deans had married university students; two out of eight!"

"And," said Norah, "The dean of the school of religion let me know, in very clear words, that 'Dr. Wolfe is a fine Bible scholar.'"

"How did that conversation go?" said Martin.

"I responded as politely as I could, suggesting that he had been charged with sexual harassment by a professor, not charged with poor scholarship."

"I can imagine your soothing words might have calmed him, but this is a gentleman's club, and there were a lot of not so hidden emotions flying around that room tonight."

"I agree," said Norah. "But it would be nice if you had more ammunition to support the case against Wolfe other than just the one professor's charge. I wonder if others might come forward next week. I mean, it seems to me that Wolfe's coming on to me must mean that he's coming on to others."

"This is a minefield," said Martin. "I'm aware that our own Professor Henderson could be seen coaching Professor Swingle just before the council meeting. I know that both women—both unmarried women, by the way—have negative feelings about Wolfe, but I'm not clear as to why that is."

"Rebecca Swingle and Rachel Henderson are both attractive women, Martin," Norah stated. "Would it be easier were both women homely?" Martin let her comments hang in the air, even as he was aware of Norah's raised eyebrows. Brave enough to continue, he said: "I meant that we've got a charge that pits an aging dean (just back from a heart attack) against two attractive, photogenic beauties. I can see how a competent defense lawyer might work with those pictures on the front page of this city's newspaper. And when Professor Swingle made her charge she noted that there were students involved. No one picked up on that point, but I heard it. So there might be more fireworks to come. I don't think anyone will come out of this a winner. What should I do, Norah?"

"You will do what you must do, Martin. Do the right thing. Other than that, given tonight, I think you've just figured out that this is going to be a big one, and people have a lot invested in its outcome." With a mischievous smile, Norah continued: "Maybe you can look at it as an educational opportunity. What might people learn from all this?"

"I love you Norah, but your words seem so bloodless; I think it is going to be bloody."

*

Thirteen

THE PHONE'S RINGING BROUGHT Clayton Heron in from his back yard, where he had been putting some snow-filled flower pots he'd missed last fall into his garage. On the fourth ring he raised the phone to his ear, "Hello; Clayton Heron here."

"Clayton; I am glad you're home." Without identifying himself, the caller hurried on, "the damnedest thing; I had a call and then a visit today from a Mrs. Nicholson, and.. . ."

"Just a minute. . . is this Melvin? Melvin Jackson at the denominational office?"

"Yes it is; I'm sorry, Clayton. I guess I don't sound myself today."

"It's ok, Melvin. I bet I sound a little funny, too. I ran into the house from the garage."

"Look, Clayton; what I need is an hour of your time. I've never had to deal with something like this. . ."

"You caught me at a good time. I'll change my shirt, and if you don't mind jeans, I'll see you directly."

"I really appreciate that. Wear your jeans. See you when you get here."

An hour later, Clayton found himself on the outskirts of the city near the municipal airport. The denominational regional office was located in a suite inside one of the tall, glass wrapped office buildings. From here Melvin could drive, fly, or take a train to any number of places where he might be needed. He was the "pastor" to the ministers in a six state region, and while he and two secretaries were accountable for eighty odd congregations, two seminaries, and a retreat center, he had kept a warm contact with the school that had educated him and that school's president emeritus, Clayton Heron.

A security guard sat at the front desk, and after Clayton had signed a visitors' list and the guard had called the denominational office, he was allowed to step into the elevator. He pressed a button and rode up two floors. Getting off, he turned left toward the denominational wing of the building. Walking into Melvin Jackson's office, Clayton had the same uneasy feeling he had when first hearing about Karl Wolfe. He didn't spend much time shooting the breeze with Melvin Jackson; he got right to it: "What's going on, Mel?"

Melvin was as short as Clayton was tall. Clayton thought that the two of them made an unlikely pair. Melvin had bristly hair. That hair made Clayton think of some of the brushes he had used last summer cleaning the aluminum wheels of his car. Sometimes Melvin's nose twitched when he got excited, and what with the hair, Clayton often thought of Melvin as a badger. "And maybe that's not a bad image," Clayton thought, "given the badger's tenacity and toughness and the stuff Mel regularly has to deal with."

"The damnedest thing, Clayton. Yesterday I got a call from a Mrs. Nicholson, a woman who is a sometimes member at the church Karl Wolfe attends, you know where that is?"

"I do."

"Well, we sat down and she tells me that after her daughter's death, she was downsizing and packing things when she came across something that her daughter had written just before her death."

"What did it say?"

"Hold on; there's more. Mrs. Nicholson told me that her husband and she hadn't really attended the church with any real zeal; they were more the Christmas Eve and Easter kind of people, you know? But her daughter, Annie, got involved with the church youth group as a seventh grade student, and she decided on her own to join the church. She was a regular ninth grade confirmation class attendee. She was fifteen."

He paused for a moment, gathered his emotions, and continued: "Mrs. Nicholson opened her purse and took out a picture of Annie. She was a beautiful child. The picture showed Annie standing in a field of high grass with several young children. She has a hand on one's shoulder. The wind is blowing the grass and her long hair, and there's something about the picture that makes you sense how much she likes these kids. She cared about them. And they cared about her." Melvin had to pause for a long moment, caught his breath, then he continued: "When she was emptying Annie's room, Mrs. Nicholson told me she had come across the Bible Annie had been given in sixth grade by Pastor Jack Curtis. Mrs. Nicholson said she had been crying, and that all the promises God seemed to make in the Bible just got to her, and in a burst of anger she had thrown that Bible against the wall."

"As the Bible landed on the floor, two sheets of paper tumbled out. They were written in Annie's hand. She used lavender ink. A long story about a crush on an older man, a man assigned her by the church as a confirmation class mentor, a man who she says in the letter seduced her and had sex with her in his own bed, in the room he slept in with his wife." Again he paused: "In the letter she states that she is pregnant. Her mentor never knew." Again Melvin paused.

Clayton thought he'd never before seen Melvin so emotionally upset: "She killed herself, and not knowing why, her mother wept and then tried to begin moving on. Her mother cremated the girl, not knowing about either the letter or the pregnancy. No autopsy was called for. "

"Who is this man?"

"Karl Wolfe. She put his name inside her narrative, dated the letter, and signed it."

*

Walking home from what had been a deeply unsettling meeting, Clayton tried to sort through the information he'd been getting. By whatever measure he tried, it always seemed to negatively involve Karl Wolfe. And then there were other bits and pieces that also came into play. Like the fact that he had been a close friend of Jack Curtis, a minister who in retirement had served in the church where Karl and Emily Wolfe had attended. Clayton hadn't told Melvin that when Jack Curtis had moved into hospice care it had been Clayton who had regularly visited and watched him die. This had not been easy for either man. Both men had been raised in the Appalachians, and both shared an avoidance of outward display and flamboyance. Their taciturn approach to things personal meant they tended to play life "close to the vest." But three days before Jack Curtis died, to Clayton's surprise Curtis called and calmly asked Clayton to hear his confession. "But you're protestant," Clayton responded.

"Don't mean I can't confess, Clayton."

"Jack, God will welcome you with open arms."

"Please come, Clayton." Clayton came. His first words to Jack were "God loves you."

"I know that, but hear me out. I've got two things I need to confess. You know I served as a medic, and you know I saw action. We got overrun one night. Most terrifying moment of my life." There was a long pause, as if Jack was reliving that night and gathering what energy remained in order to continue: "And I murdered three men."

"That was war, Jack."

"Not what I did. We were overrun, and these three came at us. They shot my best friend. He was right beside me, and I knew he was dead, and I thought in that moment that I would surely die, but a grenade exploded and the three went down and I got up and shot them."

"Jack, again I'll say it: that was war."

"I don't think so, Clayton. They were badly wounded, but they were conscious, and they looked at me, and I knew that I could hold them as prisoners, but instead I deliberately shot each one in the face. I confess that all my life I've tried to tell myself that I murdered those three men because I was terrified and because my buddy was dead. But the truth is I did it because I could do it. I shot each one in the face. I shot them because I was angry, full of rage, wanting to kill someone, anyone. And it was wrong."

"Jack, I'm certain God forgives you."

Again, a pause. Then a very quiet: "We live in hope."

Clayton didn't know what to say or do, so he just sat there quietly. He wondered if Jack was being sarcastic when he'd said "We live in hope." Clayton knew that on occasion his church used those words as a kind of congregational call and response; the minister would ask: "How will we live?" And the congregation would respond: "We live in hope." Clayton wanted Jack to mean the words, but he was momentarily confused and uncertain, so he waited. Finally, Jack spoke: "Clayton, I'm sorry. I'm at the end of my string. I'm just sorry."

"Perhaps you should rest?" Clayton asked.

"No. Next week I'll have lots of time to rest." Curtis laughed, a dry chuckle of a laugh, but laughter, nevertheless.

After he regained some energy, he said: "Look, Clayton. I'm dying. I don't have much time left. They let me use as much morphine as I need, and I need a lot. I backed off some 'cause you were coming so I could tell you these things, but I need to say that I don't think I'll be here tomorrow, at least not able to coherently talk, so please listen. I need to tell you about a young girl who wanted me to say 'Even though you've chosen badly, life is good, and God still and always loves you.'"

"But I missed what she was saying. Clayton. I backed off, even though I knew, in my gut, that she wasn't just talking about her relationship with boys. I had a moment when my gut told me a man was involved, but I denied that; she was still—in my eyes—a child."

"She ended her life. She was only fifteen. She told her mother that I should do her funeral because I was kind. Clayton, I wasn't kind when I shot those men. God, I wish I had been kind. But I wasn't. And I wasn't kind when I forgot about her not really looking me in the eye and being somehow embarrassed about what she wanted—no, *needed* to tell me. I was sick; I didn't have the energy. . . no, that's not right; I'd never backed off before. No excuses. I didn't call her. I didn't follow that hunch. I let her down.

"She also told her mother that I understood her, but I didn't let myself understand her. I just did not think she would allow a man to misuse her. The last time I saw her I think that she was trying to tell me she was in some kind of sexual relationship with an older man, and I believe she killed herself because she felt abandoned." Jack's eyes filled with tears: "Abandoned by that man, me, by her parents, even by God."

Clayton went straight at him—"Jack, I'm going to say what you've said to me on many an occasion: You can't be God; you can't have complete control over others. That would make you a puppet-master, and that's not who you are. She chose to kill herself. You think she wanted you to tell her that even though she chose badly, life has been good, and God still and always loves her. And I want to tell you those same words. Believe them, Jack. God loves you for who you are." Putting his hand onto Jack's arm, Clayton waited till Jack's sobbing ceased; "Jack, can you tell me her name, so that I might pray for her?"

"Annie Nicholson."

*

Fourteen

A LARGE CARAFE, CUPS, sugar, cream, and napkins were at one end of the conference table in President Tanaka's office. In addition to the three man committee from the divinity school, Tanaka had invited the university lawyer, the university public relations officer, and the chair of the Board of Trustees. More snow had fallen, some roads had been closed, but even those who had difficulty traveling had made their way to the university.

After introductions, Tanaka spelled out the situation: "University policy in the area of sexual harassment is not very strong." Tanaka continued: "But the divinity school has made a charge and a committee for investigation of the charge has been formed. So far that's good policy. But now the person charged must be informed of the charge, and the investigating committee must do their investigation, report their findings, and then make their recommendations to the faculty and to the person so charged 'in a timely fashion.'" He continued: "The faculty must vote on the recommendations that they receive from the committee. If the person who is charged disagrees with the faculty decision, appeal to the university board of trustees is possible. There is no recourse following their decision."

The university lawyer chimed in at this point, saying: "Except, of course, in a court of law. Or, perhaps in the court of public opinion. But let me agree with the president on his review. His reading of the Faculty Manual is exactly right. I'd add one point: even if the policy in the Manual is a bit wiggly, we will follow it. Let me be clear: to invent new policy at this time, no matter how well intentioned, will not be helpful."

"What do we want to see happen, and what is the worst case scenario?" This question came from the board chair.

"Bluntly put," Tanaka said, "it's best for us if Mr. Wolfe accepts whatever recommendations are made by the faculty, and if we can assume some finding of 'moral turpitude'—the phrase used by the University Faculty Manual, he simply goes away into early retirement. I would like to think that the evidence the committee might find would be compelling enough for him to resign; but. . . on the other hand, he could disagree. He could fight."

"And", said the public relations director, "that's why I'm here. It would not be good for our brand were we to have this case blow up in public. Frankly, the public will not like the idea of professors sexually harassing students. Universities can do a lot of strange things, but we will have the dogs onto us if we can't keep our professors' hands off the student body."

"So," President Tanaka interrupted, somewhat uncomfortably, "first we alert the board. Mr. Board chair, that falls to you and me. I'll draft a letter and run it past our lawyer, then send it to you, and if it's ok we'll mail it out. Secondly, we'll need a letter detailing the charges made in the faculty meeting to go to Mr. Wolfe. The interim dean and I will work on that and get it to our lawyer today. Thirdly, the investigative committee immediately starts working. They need to identify and interview people who might help move this forward. Some of them I expect should be deposed in our lawyer's office. Overall, we need to ask: Is the charge sustainable? Did Mr. Wolfe act this way in his previous employment, or in his church, or in his denomination, and would folk who know about any negative sexual behavior on Wolfe's part be willing to give depositions and testify against him, possibly in a court of law?"

"But in all of this," said the public relations director, "we need to act quickly and not in ways that attract the media." As the three man committee exited Tanaka's office, Tom Metcalf started talking: "The media guy doesn't want much, only that this gets done quickly and silently someplace far, far away from the prying eyes of the press."

"We've got a hot potato dropped into our laps," said Kevin.

"Maybe so," said Martin. "But there it is. We agreed to do this thing, so we need to get started."

"You're right," said Tom. "I've got sealed statements from Sharon, Becky, Jennifer, and Kylie. I think we should leave them sealed. That means we need to interview each of them to see what it is that we truly have. And they need to be told that if this goes to court, we'll have to get sworn depositions. That means going to the lawyer's office and taping a lot of question and answer sessions, and it may well also involve not only our questions via our lawyer, but questions from Wolfe's lawyer. They need to know this. Agreed?"

Both men nodded agreement. Martin then said: "I want to follow up on the people from his denomination and his old position at the seminary. I think that ought to give us some broader information. If both institutions censure him, it bolsters our case." Kevin Walker added, somewhat apologetically: "I'm still overwhelmed. Who would want this kind of mess to be the capstone for what till now has been a successful career?"

"I have no answer for that, Kevin. No answer at all," said Tom.

*

By his own definition, Clayton Heron had been an activist seminary president. He had no praise for presidents who expected things to always remain calm. His activism was born of a more pragmatic nature, one that knew not doing something was in itself an action. His proclivity toward engagement sometimes got him into trouble, but he'd never backed off his conviction that a president's role was to lead. And now he felt that he had to do something about Jack Curtis's "confession."

Curtis had asked him to serve as executor, but before he'd agreed he had asked Jack about his brother, and Jack had dismissed as untenable the idea that his brother could be the executor. "He'll get a third of my estate," said Jack, "and that's enough." Questioned further by Clayton, Jack had said: "He gambled away most of his part of our inheritance, and I don't want to be his enabler."

"OK Jack," Clayton said, "whatever you want me to do, tell me and I'll do it."

"Thanks, Clayton. My brother will fight you on this, primarily because a third goes to your seminary." He laughed: "I want to be certain that you'll make that happen. Your school is a good institution, and I know how strapped for cash you've always been. Use my money well. And I've given the rest to that church I was last serving; you know the one?"

"I know it."

"I've been explicit. I'm leaving enough to permanently endow a youth and family minister. I named it 'Annie's endowment.' The choir is to get new robes. They are to sing at my memorial service. And my friend the choir director should be asked if he'd do 'Simple Song' from Bernstein's Mass. And any readings from the Bible ought to be the King James Version. Good English. All that's in the will."

"Not to be crass, Jack, but what ought I to do with your ashes?"

"This may be the tough one, Clayton. North of Pittsburgh, just under Franklin, there's a broad bend in the Allegheny River. If you're up to it, I'd like you to scatter my ashes there.

"Why there?"

"That's a big part of my story, Clayton. My grandfather had a big house in Franklin. After my parents were killed in a train accident, that house became home for me."

"I didn't know you lost both parents, Jack."

"Well, I did, and moving into my grandparent's home was hard on me. Some in town called it a Victorian mansion. Which is to say that my elementary days were marked by kids picking on the 'rich kid' who lived up on the hill and slept on piles of money. That says a lot about why I have tried to live a more simple life."

"Ouch," said Clayton.

"But that's only half of it. My grandmother was a full-blood Seneca Indian of the Iroquois federation. So I became the rich Indian kid for the mill kids to beat up." Clayton thought that this story said a lot about Jack. His eyes had a kind of extra half-covering that Clayton had been told was an important distinction for those with an Indian lineage, but he'd never really noticed Jack's eyes that carefully. He said, "I never knew any of this, Jack." Jack rolled over in his bed, obviously in pain. He asked for and got a sip of water. He looked weak, his ashen face a mask. "Not long," thought Clayton. But Jack had more to tell Clayton: "I grew up in Franklin, and a lot of my ethical underpinning I owe to my grandmother. I was thirteen, and the kids were cruel to me. She saw that I was miserable, and one day she had me sit in the living room. We had what she called 'a talk.' She was old, of course, but still beautiful and vibrant. And she told me how she as an Indian had grown up aware that she was "different." She told me that all people have times when they are twisted up inside and unfortunately often allow their pain to control who they are. When that occurs, they need healing, and sometimes, given time and a sense of what the world might need, a person sometimes is able to step away from that pain and become a healer. She said that having lived such pain, a person like me might better understand it, and be better able to deal with it. She said that she saw in me the gift of healing." He was tired, and harboring his strength, he slowed his words.

"I know that you have a canoe, Clayton. I know that you love the woods. Remember that all that I'm telling you happened when I was what… thirteen? I had a canoe then. And my grandmother knew that I could swim and that I needed direction. She trusted me enough to send me on a 'vision quest.' Yes. My grandmother told me that I had to go down the Allegheny River just south of Franklin. She said that I would find a God-rock there, jutting into the river, and that I would—she said 'would'—canoe there and camp overnight by myself. She said that even though I should stay awake, I would have dreams, and that I must listen to these dreams. I cannot fully explain it, but that's where I decided to become a minister. And part of me has always been aware of and as true as I could be to that Seneca blood that still flows inside me."

"That's a powerful story, Jack." Jack looked up from where he was lying—"It is." The two men were silent. "A deeply spiritual, religious, even mystical experience," said Clayton. Jack nodded his head: "I think that I was closer to God then," said Jack. "But I was thirteen."

That night Clayton decided he would tell someone at the university divinity school what he knew about Annie Nicholson.

*

Fifteen

WOLFE HAD TAKEN UP walking, even when there was snow on the ground. He had found a nearby mall that was easily reachable by car, and several mornings each week after the mall opened he'd join with other mall walkers. There were several walkers who were always the first to get inside the mall and walked together. Wolfe steered clear of them.

He disliked the mall. But there were two things he did like: the mall was enclosed, so all the winter weather was outside; and, there were always some mid-morning shoppers, young, attractive mothers who were serious in their hunt for the best sales offered in the mall. He liked anticipating encounters with these "yummy mommies," as he had begun to call them. At the end of one of his laps was a high-end store. At that point he'd usually catch one or possibly two older, well-heeled women exiting or entering this store. They were dressed "to the nines" as he'd heard his mother say on those rare occasions when they had gone into town for food. In Wolfe's adult experience, this was the way people often used to dress when riding in an airplane, "But no more," Wolfe said out loud.

He often wondered at the necessary mark-up to maintain a facility the size of the mall. But no matter about these minor irritations, he could hop into his car and in a relatively short time be parked for free doing what mall walkers did, a seemingly endless circling of the mall's interior. He'd been doing this long enough to identify the regulars, enough to sometimes say "hi" or raise a hand in passing. At first he found it hard to do three laps of the mall's central trunk, but today he'd gone four laps of the bottom floor and four more on the top level. He was pleased, and looked forward to what he thought of as his reward. In the center of the mall was a place to purchase coffee. He'd abandoned his one-time habit of caffeinated coffee and a roll, being told by his doctor that coffee sweetened by cream and sugar was no friend and a roll each day was a killer. Decaf coffee then; no cream. No sweetener. No roll. There was the morning newspaper, and if anyone really wanted to talk to Wolfe, on most days they'd find him at the center of the mall sipping coffee, absently scratching his scarred chest, and catching up on the news.

There was one woman who caught Wolf's eye. She was regularly behind the counter of the coffee shop, working the expresso coffee machine while Wolfe alternated watching her with reading the newspaper. He wondered why he was the way he was. When just a young man, women often made it quite clear that they were sexually interested in him. Even after marrying Emily, occasionally he'd meet someone who seemed willing to offer him pleasures outside the marriage vows. But he'd stayed faithful, at least until Molly Hoffman. It happened at a time when he and Emily were apart. She had been visiting her parents in Maine, and he was at home, leading a summer seminary intensive course.

Maybe the separation from Emily was a contributing cause of the affair, but he thought that wasn't the real reason. Maybe it was his realization that life passes quickly, and that there were things (and people) he had not taken the time or the opportunity to explore. He'd been so busy, busy with his career and his research and busy in pursuing fame and the adulation that came with being known and respected. But as he'd gotten older, he'd realized that what he'd once taken for granted, that sudden rush of pleasure when he'd understood that a woman wanted to have sex with him, that time was over. Finished. Gone.

When he'd been younger and working at the little seminary, he'd noticed (and been noticed by) Mrs. Max Hoffman, even that idea. . . having sex with Molly Hoffman, a married woman. . . was seductive, enticing, a suggestion of danger, of crossing a border heretofore verboten. And he'd embarked on that journey, a pilgrimage quite other than what he'd expected. He wondered what would happen next. He'd closed the Molly Hoffman chapter. Molly still called, but he easily avoided her. Whatever entanglement she imagined still possible did not seem realistic to him. Wolfe finished his coffee, folded the newspaper, walked out the mall to where he'd parked his car, and headed home to Emily.

Mail arrived at the Wolfe home by 10:30, and this meant Emily usually sorted "important stuff" from "throw away stuff" before Wolfe got back from the mall. He'd gotten back from the mall to discover a visibly distraught Emily waiting for his arrival, a letter clutched in her hand: "What's this about, Karl? Is what they are saying about you true?" She did not wait for him to speak, but threw words at him: "They know what you've done, Karl, and they are coming after you."

She yelled at him: "You told me that Molly Hoffman was a crazy lady trying to get you into trouble. Now the university lawyer is charging you with sexual harassment against faculty and students at the divinity school. Students, Karl. Students. How could you, Karl. How could you?" Drained by her outburst, Emily dropped the letter on the hardwood floor and still crying, turned and ran up the staircase into their room, from where Wolfe could still hear her sobbing. Reaching down, he picked up the letter. He could see the university crest embossed at the top of the first page. The letter was, indeed, a formal one. It quoted the university's Faculty Manual as well as the minutes of an Academic Council meeting that had recently occurred at the divinity school. He was accused of "moral turpitude." He was so labeled because of his "sexual harassment" of students and women who were not named.

"I need a lawyer," he thought, "and I need a good one."

*

Professor Tom Metcalf sat by the phone in the university lawyer's office waiting for a call from Clayton Heron. He'd been told that Heron could be a possible connection between Karl Wolfe's denomination and the denominational seminary where he had served as dean before coming to the university divinity school. He'd never met Clayton Heron, but he had been led to believe that Heron was a kind of curmudgeon. The person informing Tom about Heron said all this with a smile, noting in closing that he thought Tom would "instantly like the guy." His phone rang. "Metcalf here," he said. The answer came: "Heron here. I gather you folk are itching to put it to Karl Wolfe."

"Well. I don't think I'd put it that way." Metcalf said. "I chair a committee that's been charged to see if there is any truth to accusations made by both university students and faculty of his engaging in sexual harassment, and I'm told you might have some knowledge that would be helpful for us."

"Right. Anyway you put it, we got snookered by this guy; he's bad news, and more's the pity, he's an excellent scholar and is at the top of his academic game right now. We didn't know what he was doing at the time he was the dean at our seminary. But we do now. After he left here and took your position, we found out that he'd been in a sexual relationship with the wife of one of our faculty members; we're not happy campers. That said, what do you need?"

"I need people who know what he's been up to, and who are willing to give depositions as to their knowledge. This could mean giving public testimony in a courtroom. It won't be pretty."

"I'll volunteer. After all, I was president when this took place here, and I've been subjected to several lengthy conversations with both the wronged faculty wife and her husband. That was not fun." Heron continued: "I can also say that his denomination, which is fairly conservative on matters such as these, listened to allegations from several women and decided to block him from speaking engagements or positions of influence within the denomination, either paid or unpaid. If nothing else, I can testify to how that censure came to be, so count me in."

"Thank you."

"I'm not done yet; I think you ought to call our denominational pastor. His name is Melvin Jackson. He and I have talked about the suicide of a fifteen-year-old girl named Annie Nicholson. She was one of Wolfe's 'mentees' for a church confirmation program. The pastor who set that up is dead, but I think Annie's mother, Mrs. Nicholson, would be willing to testify." Heron cleared his throat before continuing: "Mrs.Nicholson has a letter in her daughter's handwriting. It names Wolfe. He seduced her. The letter is quite clear about the circumstances; the girl, believing she was pregnant because of the several times she had intercourse with Wolfe, killed herself because she erroneously felt she was at fault, and was ashamed of what had happened. In the letter she says she was too filled with guilt over all that had happened with Karl Wolfe to tell her mother. I think Mrs. Nicholson would let you photo-copy that letter."

Tom interrupted; "A fifteen-year-old girl?" Heron responded, "Yes, but that's not all of it. Her parents thought that the letter might result in either legal or civil charges against Wolfe, but the lawyers said Annie's cremation did away with any DNA evidence from the 'presumed' fetus that 'might' definitively link Annie with Wolfe. So her parents are angry that this older guy used the church relationship in seducing their daughter. They still aren't quite convinced they are without recourse, and I suspect a public thrashing of Mr. Wolfe would be greeted by their applause. So they might help."

"You also need to talk with Molly Hoffman, one of our faculty members. She's talking to anybody who'll listen, and I think she'd be pleased to tell you her story. She has love letters from Wolfe written on our school's stationery. She could tell you how long he's been at this sort of thing. I warn you, I have no idea how Max, her husband and also one of our professors, is taking this. He's pretty quiet, but that doesn't mean he'll remain so. Molly though; she's a bit of a nut, and she's a woman scorned. The Nicholsons and Molly Hoffman are people who want to take him down, if you know what I mean."

"I'm beginning to understand, Dr. Heron. What I find astonishing is how he managed to be so toxic without being discovered earlier."

"I don't know, sir; don't know. Most of the folk he worked with here in our little denomination or in the seminary, for that matter, trusted him, respected him. He was, and still is liked. I'm sure that when these charges are made public that a number of very respectable folk will be ready to defend poor Karl Wolfe."

Tom cleared his throat: "You make it sound inevitable."

"I think it is, sir. If this hits the fan, he'll come after you. What's he got to lose?"

*

Sixteen

INTERIM DEAN MARTIN EVANS was sitting in his "easy" chair, reading a crime novel. Suddenly Norah burst through their doorway: "That bastard," she exclaimed, tears streaming down her face. "What's wrong? You o.k.?" Martin was on his feet and she was in his arms. "It's Wolfe."

"What? Again? What this time?" A red heat flooded Martin's face.

"I stopped to get lettuce at the Co-Op. I saw him two aisles down, and I thought I could get lettuce without him noticing me. So I was in front of the lettuce bin looking at the lettuce when I sensed someone close, right behind me. I start—really I jump back—I turn, and he's there, right in front of me. He slipped behind me like a ghost, or something. And he's holding a peach in each hand with a big grin on his face. He said: 'I saw you, Norah, and when I saw you I thought of peaches, and I found these two. Aren't they perfect?' And he's fondling them, as if they are my breasts! I'm speechless, standing there, people all around, looking at him. I'm motionless, just staring, and he says: 'Round and soft and just perfect. . .' He holds them as if he's tweaking nipples—you know—and I turned and I ran out of the Co-Op into my car and locked the doors and came straight home as fast as I could. No lettuce tonight, Martin; no lettuce."

"The man's lost it; I'm going to his house and I. . ." Holding a wet paper towel to her face, Norah exclaimed: "No, you are not. I'm as angry—maybe more so—than you, but you will not go there and I'll tell you why."

"Why?"

"Coming home I thought about it. He wants to make this personal. He did this even though I'm obviously pregnant! He wants you angry and not thinking. He wants you to come to his house and punch him in the face and scream and yell while the police show up and he'll be on the phone to his lawyer and tomorrow's headline will read—"

"Interim Young Dean Accosts Old Dean?"

"Yeah. Something like that." Martin managed a smile: "So I can't play alpha dog?"

"Right. . . and I think you've hit on a deeper reason. He thinks you—interim dean—are occupying his territory, and he's marking it. . ." Norah paused, took a deep breath, and continued. . .

". . . Like the dog he is." Smiling, Martin carefully removed the paper towel from Norah's hands. He said: "Right again. He thinks women are his property to mess with as he chooses, so why not mess with the interim dean's woman; but how do you keep so cool? You are one smart woman."

"You don't know the half of it, sonny. You—boys and men—are always in our face, messing with us. I learned at a very young age to keep cool and walk away (or run in this case!)."

"Tell me more. I guess the guys I run with are somewhat different."

"You aren't all bad men, but a lot are. You remember when I rode the train last fall into the city and the guy sat down opposite me in one of those end seats that face each other? And he looked at me like he would rape me in a heartbeat? He said—in a full car, by the way—he said 'If you'd like to fuck (yes—'fuck'), we could exit at the next stop. I know a nice motel near. . .' He didn't finish because I was halfway down the car, moving away from him, but I could still hear his voice: 'Can't say I wasn't polite.'"

"Full car?"

"Yes; and no one said a word. It was just the way it was. No harm, no foul." Martin still had his arms around her, but then she shuddered, and he turned her, tilting her chin up so that he could gently kiss her on her lips: "I remember your anger then, like I'd never seen you before."

"Oh I wanted to kick him, hurt him, and yet I felt dirty, as if the world I've been protected from had crashed into my world. Now I'm careful about where I sit in trains. After today, if I see Wolfe, I'll walk the other way."

"You realize we talk with him tomorrow."

"Be careful, Martin. He wants you to be so angry with him that you are ineffective. You nursing anger is to his advantage."

"No lettuce, you said?"

"Right; but I have an idea."

"And?"

"That new Café. . . maybe they have lettuce."

"And maybe wine?"

"And maybe wine."

*

Another Sunday morning. Snow was still piled high on sidewalks and curbs; cars remained hidden in small cave like spaces carved out of the mounds of snow by tired commuters trying to hide their parking spaces from poachers. Even so, as snow descended on the city a month ago, Emily could have been found dressed for church and waiting by the door for Karl Wolfe, and today she is up, but not dressed to go to church. No one has said anything to her, but they know. They know about Molly Hoffman and they also know that my husband (Yes! *My* husband) has been sexually and inappropriately engaged with some professors and students here at the university.

Students! Emily found it hard to wrap her mind around this idea. She knew Karl liked to watch young women, often commenting on their appearance to her. She'd thought most men also behaved like this. When she'd confronted him once, he'd been honest in his response: "I'm just noticing the beauty of that young lady, Emily. She makes a dreary day sunny." But something had gone horribly wrong. He'd crossed a line. He'd done some unimaginable things. And what he'd done was known. Known by his colleagues, by the members of our church, and the people we know in this community. "How can he show his face in public," Emily shouted out loud as she leaned on the sink in her kitchen.

She remembered as a child when her grandmother had given her one of those little nesting Russian dolls. She had played for a long time with the doll. In her child's mind she'd thought that everything that ever mattered might be hidden inside that doll. She'd played with the dolls for several weeks until she had all the colors, sizes, and the order of the dolls memorized. She still had the set of dolls. It was on a bookshelf in their bedroom. As a child she'd wondered at how the visible doll looked so impenetrable, but back then it was magic the way there always seemed to be just one more hidden doll until you were finally holding one that was the size of a nickel in your hand.

Now she wondered if her life was like those dolls.

She had once been an attractive, energetic, optimistic person, but that doll had been peeled away, gone. A librarian, but that doll was gone, too. Now she no longer counted as a neighbor or a church member. She'd once been the dean's wife. Someone respected. But that doll was gone, too. Maybe she's that tiny doll, the one that's almost too small to really see, the last doll in her personal set of dolls, a "nobody," someone who could disappear now, and no one would know that she was gone.

She had known other women who at her age did not want to go outside; ashamed to see someone who knew her, and who might throw in her face what was happening. Once she had a vibrant sense about what mattered, what made a difference, about things cared for and loved. She'd treasured her marriage to Karl, but even then Karl seemed somehow absent. . . maybe even then elsewhere with someone seeking something he'd never found with her.

Saturday she had gone grocery shopping. She'd felt claustrophobic, pressed in, and almost started screaming while she stood among the cauliflower and the broccoli in the vegetable section. Her mind had been locked on a question: "What will I say if I see someone who knows me?" Sobbing, Emily sat down in the kitchen chair—"I was someone who loved being at the church. I was a respected librarian. I was the wife of the Dr. Karl Wolfe, university dean. My life was stable. What happened to me?"

*

Seventeen

THERE ARE FOUR CHAIRS and a table in the room. Three men will enter the room in order to interrogate a fourth man, Karl Wolfe. The room is small, with two pastel walls complemented by a nondescript carpet. A Celtic cross hangs on one wall. A brightly colored figurative drawing of Jesus meeting the woman at the well is centered on the second wall. A large window overlooking a snow covered courtyard dominates a third wall. In the center of the room is a small table with the four chairs around it.

Interim Dean Martin Evans, first to arrive, moves a single chair to one side while positioning three others directly across from it, backed by the window. He turns on two of the room's standing lights and checks the window drapes, opening them so that the gray winter light penetrates some of the room's hidden corners. He arranges three glasses on the one side of the table. A pitcher of water with some ice in it already is positioned on the table. A fourth glass sits opposite the three, in front of the single chair.

He then sits. He is not looking forward to the next hour. Over that hour or more the committee of which he is a member will introduce the sexual harassment charge and the evidence they have discovered to Dean Karl Wolfe. He will be asked to respond to the evidence. After due consideration, Wolfe will be asked to leave, and the committee will try to reach a consensus regarding what they have heard. Decisions will be made. A second man comes through the door, sits down, arranges some papers to his satisfaction, and then remarks: "Nasty thing, this."

"You're right about that, Tom," said Martin Evans, the room arranger. Tom takes a seat. Martin asks: "Have you thought about how to start this?"

"Not really, Martin," said Thomas Metcalf, senior faculty member and chair of the committee. "I think, knowing Karl, he'll be pretty forward about our role. That is to say, he won't like what we are supposed to do, and he'll let us know that. So I think it best if we agree to simply plod forward and not get distracted by whatever he chooses to do." While Metcalf was speaking, a third man enters and assumes his position on the third chair. "Easier said than done," said Kevin Walker, assistant professor and junior member of the committee. He'd arrived minutes before Karl Wolfe made his appearance.

"Gentlemen," said Wolfe. Standing in the doorway, Wolfe looked the proper academic. A blue blazer, checked shirt, and red tie accompanied gray slacks and polished leather shoes. He had lost weight, and he had bordered on thinness before his heart attack. He looked tired, as if some of his interior stuffing had escaped. Tom had the sudden image of the doctor's knife cutting a thin line down Wolfe's chest. "You want me over there," Wolfe said, nodding at the empty glass and chair sitting opposite the three men.

He sat, poured himself a glass of water, and Metcalf took charge. "You know who we are," he said. "Kevin, Martin, and I were appointed by the Academic Council to investigate the charge leveled against you of sexual harassment. We intend to move quickly, and we're glad you agreed to come today."

"No women, then?" asked Wolfe. There was just the trace of a sneer on his face as he said this.

"Right," Metcalf responded.

"And you, Kevin, a new faculty member. Interesting assignment."

"He's on in part because of his psychologist's credential," said Martin. Wolfe had been leaning back in his chair, but now he moved forward, the skin around his eyes tightening. Looking directly at Kevin he said: "You intend to give me a label? And you, Martin, you hope to become permanent dean? Would you like that?" Kevin smiled. Not a judgmental smile, but a slight, courteous smile. One signaling that he understood, but would not play the game. Martin seemed impassive. His hands were folded and rested on his lap. Ignoring Kevin, Wolfe paused, turned toward Metcalf, and said: "How do you want to do this? Take them one by one, sequentially?" For a moment it seemed as if nothing had changed from a year ago, and Dean Wolfe was in charge, conducting a faculty committee meeting. "I think so," said Metcalf. "The faculty member making the primary charge, Rebecca Swingle, says that over several interviews with her, you suggested that were she to sleep with you, you could make her rank and tenure process move smoothly and successfully." Wolfe tensed, and leaned forward: "That's just silly. You know I don't control rank and tenure." Metcalf calmly responded: "Perhaps not, but her charge seems, on its face, believable."

There had been no overt display of anger to this point, but as Wolfe leaned forward, his voice rose: "How so? Have you evidence other than her story? Or are you going to say that the accused is always a liar? She is sweet, I grant that, but I don't believe she'd be able to sell a story as naïve as this to a jury." Martin found himself thinking Wolfe had a point. Most of Professor Swingle's charge could be argued as a "he said/she said" report. There was no corroboration. Still smarting from the insights offered by Norah, he commented: "Dr. Wolfe—you seem to be the one skilled at lying. You certainly lied to your wife and your community as to your relationship with Molly Hoffman, the wife of a professor in the seminary where you served as Academic Dean."

But Wolfe seemed to have anticipated this line of questioning: "You believe her?" Martin replied: "I talked with her husband, with the seminary president, the elected leader of your denomination, and Molly herself. They all give the same story. We also have your letters and some pictures. I think that they suggest you are the one who is lying." Wolfe bristled: "You say then that I am a liar?"

"I'm saying that when four people independently say the same thing, I am more likely to believe that yes, you are lying." Wolfe pulled himself back into the chair, his face and arms rigid, a trickle of sweat visible on his upper lip. He shot back: "I would say that Molly Hoffman and I are adults and that what we choose to do is our own business and should not be connected to the charge made in this venue by Professor Swingle." There was a pause, interrupted by Kevin Walker: "Karl, can you understand that because you hid and then lied about your sexual relationship with Mrs. Hoffman, we'd be more apt to believe that you have had or are having similar sexual relationships here, in our school?" Wolfe seemed puzzled. For a moment he seemed struck that someone might make such a connection. "No," he said. "I can't see how what Molly Hoffman has to do with these absurd charges."

Committee chair, Thomas Metcalf, stated: "Let's be clear here. . . Are you saying that you did not seek sexual favors from Professor Swingle in return for the promise of successful rank and tenure promotions?"

"That's her fantasy, not mine." Lifting a sheet of paper, Metcalf noted: "Ok. We'll leave it at that. We also have a student, Jennifer Logan, who adds her charge of sexual harassment to compliment Professor Swingle's. Ms. Logan claims you promised an 'A' in your independent study with her if she allowed you to have sex with her. Can you respond?"

"Again, her fantasy, not mine."

"The registrar records three 'C's' and one 'A' for her work first quarter. You gave her the 'A.' She seems, in addition, to be intimately familiar with the furnishings of your study at your home. Care to comment?" There was an extended silence; Wolfe made no response.

"We'll move on. . . another student, Kylie Raven, states that you accosted her around 10 PM in her room at the recent AAR/SBL meeting in this city. She also says that she cut your face with her ring."

"That never happened. There is on record a police report of my mugging that evening."

To this point still calmly listening, Martin broke into the back and forth exchange: "The police log says the 'mugging' took place at about eleven that night. You were seen exiting the elevator in the main AAR/SBL hotel at ten that night, and you were reported as having a bloody handkerchief clutched to your face. The 10 PM report was signed, witnessed and dated long before you introduced the police report. The 10 PM report seems to directly contradict your testimony and frankly, I believe it." Wolfe was silent. He looked at the three men. Whatever stress he might have felt was only visible in the clenched jaw and the tiny bead of sweat that could be seen on his forehead. Martin continued: "The leader of your denomination tells us that in addition to your affair with Mrs. Hoffman, he believes you were involved with a fifteen-year-old named Annie Nicholson. Your denomination believes you had sex with her and she killed herself because she believed herself to be pregnant. Both Annie Nicholson and Mrs. Hoffman figured strongly in your denomination's finding you guilty of sexual improprieties. Would you care to comment?"

Wolfe placed both hands on the table: "My denomination's findings were to be confidential. That you have insider information shows me how this is going to go. You joined their conspiracy. I don't think anyone from there will offer testimony were this to go to court. That's not the way the denomination works. And I've already stated that my relationship with Mrs. Hoffman, as you call her, is our business, not yours. So you have no case. No case at all."

"And Annie?" asked Tom. "You seem quick to avoid reference to some of the concerns her parents are presenting to the police. Any comment?" He leaned back, as if inviting Wolfe to respond. Wolfe said: "Annie was my mentee. Rev. Jack Curtis asked me to take that role. I did so. At one point I told him that the girl was dangerously obsessing about me as a replacement for her absent father. Why and how she ended her life, no matter how tragically, has nothing to do with me." Tom Metcalf straightened, looked directly at Wolfe, and said: "I find it interesting that you call upon Rev. Jack

Curtis, who is now deceased, to be a witness for your chaste relationship with Annie Nicholsen. We have testimony that refutes your claim. I think you too easily make up whatever you believe we might accept as the truth."

Wolfe stood, and leaning over the table attacked: "I believe that all of you are engaging in a conspiracy. You, Tom, for some reason, are joining with the rest of my enemies in order to get me, and I won't have it. You, Martin have it in for me because I have, on occasion, flirted with your wife, the lovely Norah. But I can see through your anger and your complicity with others in my life who want to tear me down. But I won't have it. I won't. I know you want me gone so that you can become the permanent divinity school dean. That won't happen either. I intend to sue the lot of you."

Tom Metcalf half rose from his chair; he said: "I'd be careful, Mr. Wolfe. Let me be clear—we are not a legal court. We do, however, have lawyers well informed regarding this case. We're moving ahead with interviews, depositions, and the accumulation of some significant pictures, letters, and financial records. I know—some folk might suggest it is stupid to tell you all of this, but we want you to know that these charges, it seems to me, are backed by a lot of true testimony and hard data, so it seems at best whimsical for you to suggest that they are of no account. You do research. 'Triangulation' is the formal term used when three unconnected sources are telling you the same thing. People tend to have faith in triangulation for good reason. It has to do with 'truth-telling.' There is no conspiracy here; we in the university see the same thing your denomination and your denominational seminary sees, and that is that you are a predator."

Wolfe had grown increasingly more agitated, and by the time Tom had finished he had popped out of his chair. In a kind of boxer's stance, he shouted: "I deny that. You'll never be able to prove that kind of charge. I am not a bad man; I am not a predator." His last sentence was uttered as he stormed out of the room, emphatically slamming the door behind him. After Wolfe left, there was a sudden calm.

The three men remained. Hesitantly, Martin said "I'm too stunned to talk much; I'm angry. I'm also sad. This man has probably negatively impacted more people than we can know or ever realize. I have no doubt that everything he is charged with is true." Martin stopped talking. The three men looked at each other. Kevin sat with both of his hands resting on the tabletop; with a sigh, he spoke: "Wolfe's in denial. I think he believes he has done nothing wrong. I can imagine that those closest to him will support him, but my candid response is the same as yours, Martin. He lies, because he must. He is dangerous. He's trapped, and he will fight us."

Metcalf pushed himself away from the table and stood. He said, "I think both of you are right, and I suspect that he will carry his lies to those people and places where he can find support. We pretty well told him what we have and that he will find no support here, and he has to believe that as a committee we will confirm the charge and will unanimously recommend to the faculty that he be fired."

"But isn't that what we want to recommend?" Martin asked. Tom replied: "I'm not sure. This was a pretty emotional meeting. I'm still angry, and my anger is telling me to just do it, but maybe we're moving too fast. I don't want whatever we decide to look like some kind of rush job. Let's cool down, think a bit about what we've heard, and then meet Thursday after classes. Maybe by then we'll be calm enough to make a decision."

Walker interjected: "But whatever we decide, we'll need to think about what we say and how we say it, especially to the university faculty. I've had conversations that lead me to believe Wolfe has significant support within the university." Martin chimed in—"I'll echo that. I was neatly cornered at my first dean's university meeting. Several of the other deans did not like that the div school had leveled a charge at Wolfe. Some of those people won't like whatever we say about one of their own. I'd also think it wise to first run whatever we decide past Tanaka and the university lawyer. They will have concerns as to what gets put on paper; we always need to keep reminding ourselves that this could wind up in court." Tom agreed: "If today was a measure of what Wolfe might be thinking, I'd bet on his taking this the whole way."

*

Eighteen

KEVIN WALKER FOUND HIMSELF wondering about Wolfe's back-story. Not that he wanted to put Wolfe on the analyst's couch, but he thought Wolfe reminded him of a number of troubled ministers he'd worked with whose sexual proclivities had dropped them into hot water.

Walker was an ordained minister who had at one time found himself on a church staff directed by a senior minister not unlike Wolfe. He had become deeply concerned about that minister's increasingly erratic and bizarre behavior, so much so that he had accompanied a church member to their denominational minister's office to help in her formal charge of sexual harassment. That charge had unleashed a barrage of counter charges, including the idea that Walker was really trying to orchestrate a coup. All such counter charges had failed, however, when four more women stepped forward to join the first.

He'd quickly discovered there was a difference between someone, usually but not always a man, who while in a powerful position had slipped and found himself sexually involved with someone. Often consumed by guilt, these persons were almost always repentant, and if some helpful way could be put on the table, often their lives would shakily move forward even as they embraced their better angels and sought forgiveness.

But there was another possibility. This was the serial predator, a person who was intentional about their toxic and abusive misuse of power. This person sexually consumed people and then moved on to new conquests. Often this person felt little or no guilt about their inappropriateness, offering only glib responses when confronted. Kevin often thought about the pleasant mask worn by the minister that he had worked with those several years ago. He seemed unable to comprehend the destructive nature of his behavior. "A personality disorder," Kevin thought. What had impressed him then was how his senior minister never admitted to doing anything wrong. He was also struck by how likeable the man was, and how insightful his sermons were. However, when the smoke had cleared, Walker found himself a full-time graduate student in a counseling psychology doctoral program. His goal was to graduate, get licensed, and start a practice that would include working both with laity and professional ministers.

Now he was dually connected. On the one hand, he was a member of the divinity school staff, but on the other hand, he had a small practice as a pastoral psychologist based in a local congregation. And once again he was seeing a man self-destruct. Karl Wolfe seemed to be a ticking time-bomb, unaware at his core of the sort of pain he was causing.

Walker's own training as a therapist had a mandatory self-analysis component. He had a good therapist, and he'd spent time wrestling some of his own demons. He'd found some clues to the way he treated himself (and others) in his family of origin, sure, and he'd really had to work on his understanding role, boundaries, and his inability to say "no."

All this "inside work" had helped him better understand why in his own past he often was overworked and sought praise and gratification from those who seemed to love him, but did so in ways that, had they continued, might have put him into situations a lot like what Wolfe was experiencing.

In the church where he had served there had been several women his age who had looked at him as if he was God. These women were often fairly explicit as to what they were willing to do if he would only reciprocate their ardent feelings. He had learned the importance of open doors during certain conversational moments, and he was not willing to visit certain women in their homes during the day when spouses were at work. And not only women his own age hit on him; there had been one adolescent who had said she loved him and would do whatever he desired if he loved her in return.

Some of this had to do with his not being married and how that status made him a likely target. But once married, this behavior was still present. He didn't see himself as particularly handsome, so it was easy to think "It won't happen to me." But it did. Women, and on occasion, one man had hit on him, even though he was married. In at least one of those moments he had become aware that his being married was a kind of incentive for that particular person's actions. "Thank God," Kevin muttered, "and thank my training. I did not slip."

His own experience made him more sensitive to those persons who had "slipped." And, in the beginning of this case with Wolfe, he'd been hopeful that what was going on here wasn't a sexual harassment pattern. After the committee's exchange with Wolfe, he now felt otherwise. Kevin found it hard to judge Wolfe as someone unredeemable, even as he knew that Wolfe had to be fired. "I want to be Wolfe's therapist," he found himself saying out loud, "I want to help him even though I'm on a committee that will judge him and will find him guilty."

*

Sitting at their breakfast table, Norah and Martin read their morning paper and ate toast until Norah, putting down her paper, asked: "You got home so late last night that I didn't get to hear how your day went, and if there is anything new about Karl Wolfe." Pushing back his chair, Martin stood. "The short answer is no."

Carrying some of the breakfast dishes into the kitchen, he spoke to her as he worked: "Nothing new happened yesterday, and I'm getting really irritated by this dragging on; you're pregnant—looking good, by the way—and we are still plodding along, waiting for some shoe to drop."

He sat back down: "Meanwhile I've still got this thing called a sexual harassment charge on my plate. It's been taking too much of my time. I've had to push some other important stuff onto the back burner. I'll be really glad to see it done."

"I know it's been hard for you. I'm sure I haven't helped you, either."

"You help more than you know. Just by being you, you've helped."

"Even with this baby bump? I mean, I don't know what I'll be like when I'm twice as big and still waiting 'with child' in the heat of July."

"We'll be fine. Maybe we'll head north; see your folks in Michigan?"

"Maybe. But I don't want to be far from Dr. Jorgenson; this is my first go at all this."

"OK. Let's get a couple of window air-conditioners; maybe that can help."

"Don't dodge, Martin. I'm interested in what's happening with Karl Wolfe; tell me what you think needs still to be done." Martin put down his coffee cup, leaned both elbows on the table: "You're sure about wanting to talk about this? It really has become sort of boring in the abstract, and deadly dull in the particulars."

"No more 'smoking guns' to find?"

"Well. . . I won't go that far. There have been some rather startling discoveries. You've heard me talk about the fifteen year old that we think evidence strongly suggests was seduced by Wolfe and became pregnant, then committed suicide. Annie Nicholson. None as dramatic as that. Thank

God. And Norah, I find that girl's death keeping me awake some nights. I can't imagine how Wolfe deals with it."

"I think he has to have guilt, unless he's a sociopath."

"But you're right. He doesn't seem to be dealing with any guilt. I've been thinking a lot about that. In a class we were talking about Augustine, one of the great early western church fathers. In what is understood to be the world's first autobiography, he tells of the guilt he felt as a boy having stolen pears from an orchard. When I first read that, I was an undergraduate, and for the life of me, I thought that was such a trivial thing that I almost could not read the rest of his book. But as I read further, I began to get inside Augustine's skin. He had a strong relationship with his mother, and I started thinking how that close tie must have helped him understand a lot about guilt and responsibility. Mothers have a way of bringing that to a son's attention."

"Maybe your mother, but let's not say every mother."

"I'd agree with that. My mom had a radical sense of responsibility. She married for life, but she married well. I think a lot about how wise her choice was in marrying my dad, and I recognize that much of the weight I feel about my responsibilities comes from her. But let me talk for a minute about Augustine. We can leave my mother's influence on me to another day. Augustine's stolen pear was just the beginning. He wanted to talk about relationships and being honest with ourselves, our neighbors, and with God. Big, big topics. And he includes this simple incident about his childhood incursion into another's orchard. Not so incidentally, he gave his autobiography an interesting title: *Confessions*."

Norah asked, "I wonder if Wolfe could understand something like that?"

"I doubt it, given everything we're discovering about the man."

"What puzzles me is how he's either forgotten or walled off most of the things he's done that you've shared with me. How can someone do that?"

"Norah, I really don't know. If I go back to my mother, she'd have a lot to say about how we aren't born with insight and responsibility. She'd say we need to be nurtured into it by caring, ethical adults. Maybe that's it. Wolfe stepped over that understanding, and by his having done a bad thing once, found it easier to do a bad thing again. Makes sense to me." For several minutes, both returned to the business of breakfast: "Are you any closer to the end of this saga?" asked Norah.

"I'm waiting for a committee's recommendations. I've got a box filled with testimony, several sealed envelopes, and a list of people the committee and our lawyer are walking through formal depositions. One of the gripes I have is the amount of time and money we're spending on depositions. The lawyers want us to 'be ready,' whatever that means."

"If he decides to jump the gun and sue you and the school."

"Yeah. I guess so. And we have a very important date on the near horizon. Pretty soon I'll take transcriptions of the depositions and our accumulated evidence to the printer, and then I'll add any new stuff so that we'll have plenty of copies for the February Governing Board meeting. There will be a lot of papers distributed on that day."

"I assume that if they are distributed at that meeting, Wolfe would also get a full set," Norah suggested.

"Maybe that would push him into his own version of *Confessions*," said Martin.

"Right; but who'd have thought this was what a dean did."

"I guess I'm just learning on the job," said Martin.

"What else are you learning?" said Norah.

"I met with the provost, our lawyer, President Tanaka, and the new publicity director yesterday."

"Important meeting. What happened?"

"Tanaka's been worried about how the div school's charge against Wolfe will bubble up into the media. So far the press hasn't really pushed it, but yesterday he got calls from religion editors of two national news/ popular culture desks. Apparently a couple of Fortune 500 firms have had sexual harassment charges leveled at their CEOs, and this editor wants to run comparative stories—something like *What's Going On in Divinity Schools and the Fortune 500*."

He continued: "I don't know where this is headed, but I'm certain this kind of story is the proverbial tip of the iceberg. And we have a couple Fortune 500 types on the university Board of Trustees, so when that story breaks—if it happens— and if it hits their desk, we'll be cutting closer to the bone, and would expect some internal pressure to get this thing done."

"It's not Christmas yet. You've been dean for just this quarter.. Talk about baptism by fire!"

"It's only going to get worse," said Martin.

*

The phone rang in Tom's office. He completed a sentence he'd been trying to get right, dropped the pen on his desk and picked up the phone. "Tom Metcalf." At first, Tom thought he'd been disconnected, then: "Karl Wolfe, Tom. Thought you and I ought to chat."

There was a pause. For a moment, Tom felt adrift. What was this about? "I'm not sure you and I have anything we can talk about, Karl. As chair of the committee investigating your behavior, I don't think I should talk with you at all."

"Don't think you'd want the committee to overhear us, Tom. I'd just like to ask you a question. Remember our accreditation visit and that cute blonde you hooked up with? Would you want Megan to know about that night and her, Tom?" Another pause. Then, Tom's response, with anger: "Know what, Karl?"

"Well. . . I think she'd like to know what went on in room 509, don't you think?"

"Go to hell, Karl," Tom said, slamming down the phone. He pushed back his chair, away from the phone, away from Karl Wolfe. It rang again. He let it ring three times, picked it up. "Look, Karl," Tom said, with anger in his voice. "Tom, its Kerri," said his sister.

Taking a deep breath, he said: "Kerri. I'm sorry. I thought you were someone else."

"Yeah? Sounds as if you wanted to take his head off. What's going on?"

"Not your problem, Kerri. Are you calling about mom?"

"I think she's in trouble, Tom. I just got off the phone with her, and it was like she really didn't want to talk with me about the cancer or her health. I'm worried about her."

Kerri was in England with her husband. Tom sighed. "She's eighty-six, Kerri."

"I know that, Tom. But this is different. You were up there last week, right? Was she ok then?"

He caught her emphasis. Maybe she seemed o.k. last week when Tom had visited, but Kerri felt she was not ok when Kerri had called her this morning. Tom sighed. "I've got a few days coming up, starting with Friday. I'll see if I can make arrangements to get there. I'll call you tomorrow night and let you know how that works out. Ok?" There was some chit-chat, then goodbyes. Tom got up from the desk and walked out of the school.

"Karl's panicking," he thought. That night he'd spent with Alex was what, eighteen years ago? Karl had only seen them for those few moments in the hotel lobby. That was all he had seen. And Alex had been clear— that one night, and she was back with her husband and him with Megan and that was that. A week after the accreditation visit, he'd gotten a "Thank You" note. It said: "Tom, You were an important part of my life. Thank you, Alex."

He'd noticed the "you *were* an important part" of the note. He'd understood. She would not respond were he to pursue her. Whatever that had been was over. And he was ok with that. But Karl. . . Maybe Karl was fishing. He'd taken his best shot by floating what he'd imagined when he'd seen Tom with Alex in a hotel. Maybe Tom would bite, panicking enough to pursue Karl and try to find out exactly what he did or didn't know. Karl would hope Tom might get hooked in that kind of process. "Not today," Tom thought. "Not today. . . or any day."

He compared himself to Karl Wolfe, at least as he was beginning to understand Karl. Everyone had secret longings. Some of these were consciously recognized. For example, Megan loved chocolate, but had determined that was not a secret worth keeping. She'd made a joke about this longing, and if he found a candy wrapper stuck beside the car seat, he could ask her if she'd indulged her chocolate longing today. Others were hidden. Like the longing he'd had for Alex. Still others were so deeply hidden that their owner probably didn't know they existed. What was important was how such covert wants got translated into overt behavior. Books were written on this sort of thing, and all cultures invented ways to warn people as to the kind of consequences that might occur were such desires acted upon. Some authors were so bold as to suggest that the roots of religion are found in a culture's effort to codify the right sort of behavioral responses to such longings.

Whatever. In any case, he'd recognized his behavior as potentially destructive to his marriage, his work, and himself. Until Alex he'd been a straight actor. The words: "Always Responsible" might have been carved on his gravestone. Under pressure, he'd slipped, and had he continued down that path, he'd no doubt he'd have ended badly. So he'd told Megan. Not an easy conversation. But he felt that he had to tell her, and in the end she'd understood. He was not certain had the circumstances been switched if he would have been as gracious as she had been. And continued to be. He had not slipped a second time. So that night in that hotel, as far as he knew, had damaged no one. Karl Wolfe, however, was a different story. He'd damaged several persons. He seemed unable (or unwilling) to recognize or understand this.

No matter. Those around him had come or were coming to an understanding as to how Wolfe had broken open their behavioral expectations. They were beginning to realize that over a lengthy period of time Karl Wolfe sequentially exploited those women he encountered in his work, church, and denomination. There was little or no mutuality in these relationships, and Tom's recent phone conversation with Wolfe only highlighted the sort of tactic he might use in order to satisfy his hungers.

Tom shook his head: things were going horribly wrong for Wolfe.

*

Nineteen

Sitting at the edge of the campus, *The University Club* provided the demarcation of the border between the university's academic enterprise and the neighborhood known as *West Side Community*. A carefully manicured neighborhood, *West Side Community* was filled with middle to upper middle class professionals, many of them with university ties. Martin and Norah lived there. Homes on this side of town did not rent rooms to students. Families who appreciated stability, leafy trees, and plenty of old-fashioned cobblestone streets and a few funky entities like *The Thoughtful Bean* and *Fritz's Bar and Grille* loved *West Side Community.*

Conversation about university expansion focused on either the northern or the southern sides of the school. Not that moving west didn't have some appeal, but after the last western university expansion, any movement in that direction was met with fierce resistance. The last move west had occurred some thirty years ago. An expansionist president and board had leveled every building toward the west except the mansion that had become *The University Club.* A theater school, modern field house, football stadium and running complex rose where three story brick and stone homes once had reigned supreme. When the dust had settled, a new university president had promised, in writing, that there would be no more incursions into the west side. This pledge had been reprinted as a kind of binding promise. It was attached to every real estate contract as a good faith pledge and had resulted in a communal effort that eventually became *West Side Community.*

Everyone loved *The University Club* and its outdoor gardens. Roughly one acre had been set aside and maintained as a garden plot by the university and volunteers. *The University Club* provided a congenial spot for lunch, and administrators could be seen inside and outside hosting guests or conversing about university business. There were overnight accommodations upstairs for university visitors, while an occasional evening feast featured the chef's latest culinary ideas. As interim dean, Martin Evans held a club membership for the div school, and this came in handy for faculty search candidates and the occasional special divinity school event. Today he had a reservation for two. He was to meet Sharon Henderson for lunch.

Her hair damp from a workout at the university field house, Sharon arrived to find Martin playing pool with a friend from the university law department. "One minute, please," said Martin, even as his friend ran the last three balls, soundly beating him. "Martin," said Sharon. "You are always hopeful, even when you are losing."

"Exactly," he responded. "But win or lose, the game is meant to be played, not fought over."

"Maybe in pool or ping-pong," said Sharon as they moved upstairs into the luncheon area, "But not in a court of law."

By this time they were being shown to their seats and both made their choices from the day's offerings. Martin carefully listed their choices on a small paper slip, added his member number, and handed the order to their waiter. Turning from this transaction, Martin said, "I agree. It's not a game. This thing with Wolfe could turn sour very quickly. That's why I wanted to see you today."

"I heard that the committee met with him."

"Yes. We met. He was irritated that no women were on the committee, and he picked at both Kevin and me. He suggested that I was there to make sure he got fired. That action would make me, he suggested, permanent dean."

"And Kevin?"

"He had a jab at Kevin's psychologist credential. Wolfe basically said: 'You're too junior to be on this committee, unless they have you here to put a label on me.'"

"So the exchanges were like that, I mean pretty pointed?"

"They were. I might not have quoted him exactly, but that was the meaning of his comments." A pause; then: "He didn't shoot at Tom, though. Being the senior faculty guy, Tom got a pass. No zingers from Wolfe."

"Why so, do you think?"

"I could think of several reasons. Maybe to sow discord among us. Or maybe to curry favor from Tom. He is the best choice for chair, and he's seen a lot over the years. Maybe Wolfe thinks that Tom will side with him."

"Will Tom?"

"No. I am not the psychologist, but Wolfe is in total denial, and it was Tom suggesting that maybe Wolfe should consider what it might mean if three separate institutions find him guilty of sexual harassment. I mean, if we find him guilty, our decision will side with the judgments against him from his denomination and from his seminary. We told him we had folk willing to give depositions from all three institutions. So his back is against the wall."

"Why me, Martin? If Wolfe's back is against the wall, why am I meeting with you now?"

"Two reasons. If this does get to a court, the stuff we have—Professor Swingle, Kylie Raven, Jennifer Logan—is all 'he said/she said' stuff. And Wolfe knows that. The only thing we have that gets him angry is the idea that you saw him holding a bloody handkerchief to his face and exiting that hotel elevator at 10 PM. He knows we know that later that night he tried to fake a mugging. He will introduce the police report, and it will say that 'at or about 11 PM he *reported* being mugged.'"

"And I stand and give my testimony and the truth wins!"

"Except he knows you dislike him, and he will try to discredit you as an honest witness."

"We have a trump card—I wrote my statement, put it inside a sealed envelope, and both Tom and I signed our names across the seal. Tom has not opened that envelope. If we need to introduce it, I think it will hold up very well against his phony mugging."

"Ok. Let's say that makes sense. But you need to know that when our committee talked about his 11 PM mugging and our witness who saw him exit the elevator at 10 PM holding his bloody handkerchief, that conversation was the only time he lost it. I mean, he lost it. It's as if he has to work so hard to keep this defense in place, and along comes this single witness whose testimony could blow the whole thing up, and he lost it. He said 'I am not a sexual predator,' and he got up and walked out, slamming the door behind him."

"That gives me pause."

"It should. You have the key testimony. And what you might say in court could blow his argument out of the water."

"So the 'second point' you're telling me is. . ."

"Watch your back."

"He wouldn't dare."

"I agree. But somewhere in all this is the feeling that he really doesn't like women. And you're a woman. A woman who could potentially put him down. Be careful." Sharon seemed to want to say something more to Martin. She leaned forward, then moved back into her chair, looked up at him and said, "I want to tell you something that I have never, ever, told anyone."

She paused: "I guess I want to do this because I trust you. You didn't need to tell me what you just told me, but you did, and I thank you for that."

There was a long, quiet moment; both Rachel and Martin seemingly studied each other. Martin waited.

Rachel began to speak: "There was a time when Wolfe and I were graduate students in the same university program. He was two years ahead of me. I knew him well enough to say 'hello' to, but other than knowing that he was smart, our paths did not cross. I had one graduate level class with him, but even then we barely spoke."

"When I calculated I had about a year left before I'd complete the degree, I decided to go to the combined American Academy of Religion and the Society for Biblical Literature meeting. I participated in their job interview process. You know what that's like."

"A meat-grinder," Martin said. "Right," Sharon agreed, "but I got what I felt was a good nibble from one school, actually this divinity school."

"Really?" said Martin.

"Yes. They had an older person who had alerted them to their retirement in another year, and the interviewers said they saw me as exactly the kind of scholar and colleague who could 'fit right in.' So they asked me to come to their campus and be interviewed there with the potential of a job the following July. I was ecstatic."

"Later that same day I found myself sitting alone in the hotel bar with my head full of congratulatory thoughts, drinking a glass of Merlot when Wolfe walks in. He gets a drink and comes over to my table. He says: 'May I join you?' And I say 'Sure.' So he sits down and asks how the day went. I tell him that I'd had five interviews and was exhausted, but that one looked very, very good, and that I was excited. He says, 'Congratulations. I, too, was offered a job today.' And he lifts his glass and I lift mine and we toast each other."

Martin waited silently. He knew that there has to be more to this story.

"And then he says, very politely, 'They must have liked what they saw of you. I'd certainly like to see more of you. Maybe you and I could carry our celebration upstairs for the night?' I was dumbfounded. He had this crazy smile, as if nothing ventured, nothing gained, and I stood up and threw the wine at him. It hit him across his eyes and trickled onto his suit. I said 'Not on your life,'" and turned and walked out."

"That's quite a story."

"I'm sure I haven't gotten what he said exactly right, but I do remember the words he threw at me as I left the table. He said: 'I guess the rumor that you like girls more than you like men is true.'"

"Damn," said Martin.

"But he was right. And I'm saying this because it might surface were we to wind up in court. For twelve years I've been in a committed relationship with a woman. She works and lives about an hour by plane from here. We have a commuter understanding. And it works for both of us. But as far as Wolfe goes, I pass him in the hall and we do not speak."

"You were here when the faculty decided to call him?" said Martin.

"I was. But he has a solid record. His research is superb, and the seminary administrators sounded sad that he was considering leaving them. What could I say? That he had propositioned me some fifteen years ago? That I was a lesbian? Who would benefit from my making such a charge? I was not willing to put myself out there on that line. But now things have changed, and you need to keep this confidential unless we go to court, because if I am the key to the case, we'd need to be prepared for his digging at my reputation. If we think this might not matter, you and I could turn out to be the losers."

*

Twenty

Bursting into Martin's office, Professor Tom Metcalf angrily tossed the front section of the daily newspaper onto Interim Dean Martin's desk. "Have you seen this?" He pointed at the lower right hand corner of the front page and the headline: "University Targets Bible Scholar." Under the headline Martin saw a picture of Wolfe, holding a Bible and leaning against one of the university gateposts. The accompanying story portrayed Wolfe as the victim of a faculty conspiracy to block his important biblical research. That journalist also got a good quote from one of the school of religion profs: "He is only doing his research. What are they afraid of?"

"What he's done is accuse us as being against academic freedom. He says that we oppose his scholarship because we don't agree with it. He's totally reframed everything. He's got what amount to endorsements from three outside biblical scholars plus one from our own university department of religion. He's making it look like the divinity school is back in the dark ages and is bent on persecuting him because of his scholarship."

"Do you think President Tanaka has seen this?" Martin asked. Just then the phone rang.

Martin picked up the phone: "Evans here. Yes, President Tanaka, we've seen it."

"He wants both of us in his office now." They discussed the newspaper story while walking across the two university quadrangles toward the administration building and Tanaka's office. "Wolfe's playing us," Martin said. Tom responded: "And doing it well." Tom continued: "He knows that most university faculty members consider the div school to be an outlier, something they put up with, even as we look more for the truth to emerge in conversation with the texts of our tradition than to their scientific method. To them, we're superstitious storytellers, and they would feel better if we were all gone and the university's department of religion could get on with their more rational approach to religion."

Martin kicked a stone off of the sidewalk and, turning toward Tom said: "This isn't new. When, in 1810, the first truly modern university, the University of Berlin got started, it made room for the theologians only because in defeat the theologians were willing to accept their terms. Berlin's bargain was that it accepted ministry as a profession worth studying as long as the theologians kept 'confessional' education for ministers someplace else, like in the seminaries. But in this city the ministers got in on the ground floor. They were the ones who initially founded this university, and so we have a divinity school that gives people the option of doctoral work or ministerial formation. That's a peculiar mix, and those folk in the 'modern' university here—who ascribe to scientific belief instead of 'superstition'—find it an uneasy accommodation." Tom said, "And you're saying Wolfe fits better with the science-oriented crowd?"

"I'm saying that Karl Wolfe is not dumb, and that if he needs to fit there, he'll do that." Tom said, "That's probably why Wolfe and I never got along, but that is not, I repeat, is not the issue. The issue isn't what I or Wolfe think matters about the Bible or Berlin; it's about sexual harassment and how he has betrayed his calling." Martin could not resist: "All I'm saying is that you believe you have a calling; I'm not certain Karl Wolfe feels that way, too." By this time they had crossed both quads, and opening the door to Tanaka's office, Tom said, "You're right, but tell that to the press and I'd be willing to bet that it makes the front page."

The president welcomed them. He commented: "I can imagine that you two experienced a slow burn reading today's paper." Both men nodded their heads. He continued: "I came of age in the sixties. We quickly figured out that something didn't need to be true to make the papers. Sometimes, in fact, telling the direct opposite of what was going on often made the next day's early paper. So we tried to massage the narrative and make it favorable for what we wanted to see happen. It didn't always work, but when it did work, it would flummox those who were fighting us."

Tom said: "And that's what Wolfe is doing."

"Of that, I have no doubt. We're a bit behind on this, but Tessa Ritter, our new public relations director, has a news briefing scheduled later today. She will note that Mr. Wolfe is charged with sexual harassment by several students and faculty, and that he has been sanctioned as well by his denomination and former seminary administrators for sexual improprieties occurring in those two additional venues. Ritter won't say much more than that, but she will suggest that the formal university process needs to play itself out, and that our venue is a better location than trying Mr. Wolfe or the university in the press. She and I have also crafted a memo to all our employees. We made it very clear that everyone on the university's payroll should direct all questions from outsiders concerning this case to her (and only her). Otherwise, 'No comment.'"

Martin said, "I like it. Of course, they can spin it as much as they want to, and I'm certain that they would like more details, but I'd like to get ahead of the curve by contacting the div school faculty today, as well as sending another letter to students affirming Ritter's letter." Tanaka said: "Do it." Martin and Tom rose from their chairs. Turning to go, Tom paused and said, "I want to thank you for your steady hand in all this." The president responded, "We're not out of this yet."

*

After his father's death, Tom began to notice a quickening deterioration of his mother's health. Not that she'd admit anything, but Tom's cousin, Janie, drew attention to her loss of weight with the hint that he ought to get her to a doctor. Easier said than done, but he'd eventually gotten agreement. Then the news. . . her cancer was no longer in remission.

He'd flown home for her new surgery. Lying in the hospital bed, her frailness and diminutive stature was readily apparent. "Mom," he'd said, leaning over to kiss her. "Tom," she exclaimed. "Oh, honey, I didn't want to bother you." Then: "I'm glad you're here." There was chemotherapy and a positive report. "Remission doesn't mean that it's gone," warned her doctor. "Only time will tell." And now, only a few weeks later, here he was, on the phone with his brother, Michael.

Apparently his sister, Kerri, had called his mother from England. She had not liked what she'd heard, so called Michael who, in turn, had called him. Both sibs were worried about mom. Janie was not far behind their calls: "Tom, she's weak. It does not look good."

Tom and Megan had talked. Tom was angry. His mother was stubborn about most things, and from his point of view she was actively resisting family members who wanted to help her. Megan had noted that "perhaps she wants to be with your dad more than fight the good fight." If that was the case, Tom knew her stubbornness would beat any helping intervention from family. He remembered how that stubbornness had played out when he'd felt he had to pry the keys to the car from her. In her eighties, she still had to drive, she'd said, "Because I take some of the old women to church on Sunday."

He'd asked her to recognize how dangerous she'd become when she was at the wheel. She'd had two fender benders; what might happen were she to hit a pedestrian? She'd have none of it. In a letter to the state driving medical office, he'd complained about her poor sight and slow reflexes. That office sent her a letter requiring a driving test. After failing the eye exam, she'd walked out of that office, gotten in her car, and driven home. After some more negative conversations, he'd gotten an uncle to remove her car's distributer cap. The uncle had inserted a note inside the now useless cap. The note read: "Call me" along with his name and phone number. Her mechanic had obliged, keeping her car off the road for two weeks. The day the mechanic returned the car to her, another woman roughly her age hit and severely injured a seven-year-old. That evening Tom's mother made arrangements to sell her car to Janie's husband. Megan had said: "But Tom, look at it from her point of view." And when he'd done so, he had to laugh. That was his mother, and a large part of who he was could be accounted for in this, and countless other similar stories.

But the cancer had returned. He'd packed a suitcase and flew north, renting a car at the airport. The road home was a familiar one. Snow was still piled high off both berms, and a salt truck in front of him was working its big plow, pushing the snow further back off the road. "Expecting more snow," he thought. The front walk was free of snow (a kind neighbor), and the old house looked ok, but the woman opening the door had gotten even smaller. It was his mom, but a mother whose face showed pain and every one of her eighty odd years. "Mom," he'd said.

"Thomas," she'd hesitatingly replied.

"May I come in?"

A pause; then: "Certainly; I'm sorry. I keep forgetting things, and for a moment I thought you were the clothes washer repairman!" She chuckled, as if she'd caught herself in an unusual moment. But such moments reappeared throughout his visit.

That evening she'd told him that she was dying. "The cancer is back, Thomas, and I told them no more cutting." They were sitting at the old table in the kitchen, and he'd reached across to hold her hand. "I don't want you hanging around here," she'd said. That night he'd slept in the bed he'd used as a youth. Death. What does anyone really know? What did he believe? Some literalist friends wanted to convince him that the empty tomb was good news, but he couldn't buy that, no matter how hard they tried to sell it. As much as he was dismayed at Karl Wolfe's behavior, he thought Wolfe

was right to argue that the communal narrative was bent in order to elimi-
nate doubt as to the resurrection and Jesus' continued presence. But Wolfe
also argued that such knowledge—that Jesus was just as dead as any other
man—invalidated the Christian faith.

On this point, Tom disagreed. He believed it was the communal story
that was the proof of a lasting post-resurrection presence; the story was
stronger proof than the empty tomb. He'd felt the love that was present in
the Christian story. He trusted the universe in spite of Wolfe's dismissal of
the empty tomb. His mother did not fear death. She'd said: "I'm ready. I'll
fall back into God's open arms. That's where I came from, and that's where
I'm going." He kissed her goodbye, and headed home. Cousin Janie would
alert him when he was needed, and he knew that would soon occur. He felt
unusually stressed, and was aware that he did not know what might happen
were he to be publically accused by Wolfe of his earlier dalliance with an
ex-student.

Indeed, the morning after he had returned had not gone well for
Thomas Metcalf. He'd skipped lunch and had yelled at a secretary who'd forgotten to give him a pink call-back slip. When he made the call, he'd been
politely but firmly chewed out for not having called back sooner. Then he'd
met with a graduate student about a paper, but wasn't able to help her move
forward, not as she had hoped. By mid-afternoon he'd closed his door and
tried to read a journal article that had been resting on top of a pile of papers
he'd forgotten to read. The article either made no sense or he wasn't reading
it right. He had lost focus by the end of the second page, so he pushed back
his chair, got up, stepped into the hallway, and was about to leave when
he decided that he had to call Megan. Back in his office, he picked up the
phone, called Megan, and was amazed when she immediately answered:
"Megan Metcalf," she said. "Megan," Tom said. "I need to see you and talk
through an issue on my desk. I thought maybe it would be good if we went
to *Rosa's*. I'd suggest going home, but I really need to get away from here,
and maybe they would have that jazz combo that we like. How bout it?"

"A lovely idea, Tom. You go early. Get a good table. I can't leave till I
see one of my clients at seven, but after that conversation I'll head for *Rosa's*;
ok?"

"Excellent. I'll be the guy in the corner nursing a beer."

"I'll find you. See you there." She hung up. He had a quick image of her
in the office, talking with clients about their affairs. "Damn," he thought,

he'd not become another client. He vowed that he'd not do that to her. The thought of seeing Megan carried him through the day.

Rosa's was actually *The Blue Rose Café*, a long established jazz joint that Megan and Tom had discovered when they had first arrived in the big city. Rosa Lee Sweitzer was the proprietor, and when Tom and Megan started going there it had just a few tables and a small stage. They got to know Rosa, a woman now well into her sixties, and each time they showed up, Rosa would make sure they got a good seat and good food. She'd lost her husband to leukemia and had turned to Tom ("my pastor," she'd claimed) for help in her distress. Tom had listened, and after a period of mourning, Rosa had decided that instead of selling the place ("I'm no quitter," she'd said), she'd buy the other half of the building, a suddenly vacant space inviting expansion. One day Megan got a call; "Megan. I have decided to call my new place *The Blue Rose Café*, because after Danny died I was blue. I am no longer blue, but it's a jazz place, and blue is central to jazz. So—*The Blue Rose Café*. I've remodeled everything, please come tonight; we'll have fun."

They had gone. The new, big outside neon sign said *Blue Rose Café*, and what had been the original room was now a long bar offset against a line of six tables. A few steps down, and they stepped into a remodeled three-story tall open addition, twenty more tables and a raised stage, behind which hung several of the city-sponsored twenty foot long *Jazz Festival* banners. A "new" Rosa in a tasteful black suit, greeted them at the door. The place was almost full, but a table was located, the music was wonderful, and they had fun.

Tonight Tom's cabbie dropped him at the front door, and as he entered he could hear a group playing "So What?" a piece made famous by Miles Davis. The intensity of the refrain hit Metcalf. He slid into a chair at an empty table, and he listened to the group work its way into and through the nearly ten minute improvisation. They were good. Not Miles Davis good, but good nonetheless. He'd heard "So What" before. He'd turn on his stereo, pull the *Kind of Blue* album off the shelf, slide the thirty-three and a third record out of its sleeve, position it onto the turntable, carefully drop the needle, and then move into the kitchen to prepare dinner. He'd "heard" it, but he hadn't really sat down and quietly listened to it. "So What," he said. . .and Megan sat down. "You got here fast enough," he said. "My appointment called and cancelled. Think I left about when you did, and you've a bit more traffic to fight. Been here long?"

"No, Just sitting really listening to the group," Tom said. "I was wondering what this thing with Wolfe will mean to the school."

"Still bugging you."

"Yeah. Maybe wondering what it'll mean to me and to you, too."

"How so?"

"Wolfe threatened me a week ago."

"How?"

"That thing I let myself get involved with on the accreditation visit he chaired. He wanted me to know that he'd remembered that occasion, and that he might choose to pull that out and put it onto the table, were it to come to a court trial."

"Oh, Tom."

"I know. I know. That was what, some fourteen odd years ago, and I thought it was buried and a past issue. You forgave me for it, and I did not again have to even talk about it with you, but I can see him trotting this out and it hurting you. . .and me. I am so, so sorry."

"I'm angry. I'm angry at him, not you. You live long enough, you have regrets. No one escapes life without some mistakes, some regrets, some things you'd do differently were you able to do them again. So here's what I say; screw him and his threats."

They ordered their dinner. Some kind of cod and a salad for her; a burger and slaw for him. She wanted Merlot; he had a beer. A trio was playing, and the tenor sax reminded Tom of Stan Getz. The group played "The Nearness of You" and "But Beautiful." He watched Megan, the fine line of her jaw and the tousled hair as she listened to the warm tones of the sax. He put his hand on top of hers. She turned toward him and smiled. He thought Getz had last played "But Beautiful" in Belgium with the Bill Evans Trio, but tonight it was being played here, just for them. He was not sure what had been started at his school, but he was deep into it now, and he would play it through to its end.

*

Twenty-one

WHEN EMILY AND KARL Wolfe first came to the div school, Emily insisted they check out its numerous libraries. She'd heard of the new, big, urban, glass and steel research library, the anchor of the system and one that had been built in the modernistic style. The university had six different libraries, but the modern one was central to the system. It certainly contrasted with the undergraduate library's "romantic," two-story, stained glass windowed reading room. And scattered throughout the school were other specialized libraries, some well-hidden and never seen except by those who knew of their existence. By questioning students walking the various quads, they located the law, medical, and social work libraries. As the new Divinity School Dean, Karl and Emily had been granted entrance, but all of them were unexceptional in design and highly utilitarian in nature. Nevertheless, Karl had been impressed: "Not easy to get into, and tough to take things out. I bet if you needed something, it would be here."

Emily fell in love with the div school library. They entered through a leather-chaired lounge on whose walls hung oil portraits of presidents and others important to the history of the school. An archway on one wall opened to the main room of the library, a three-story affair with one side filled with oak study tables and tall, stained glass outside facing windows. The three other walls rose two stories, with a walkway on the second floor, behind which lay the stacks. When she had stepped into the reading room, Emily exclaimed: "Oh; it looks like I imagined it would look." Emily stood in the room, both arms wrapped around her waist in a kind of private hug. This was what she had dreamed about—a library that might be a "home" away from home.

When Karl had been hired she was the "trailing spouse," and the university had promised they would work with her to find a job. Emily was hired to work in the div school library three days each week. The end result was a split between the undergrad and div school libraries. She loved working in both places. Books had clarity and weight. She got to handle them. Mostly this involved being at the front desk. People checked books in and out and asked the kind of questions that she could answer. Occasionally she re-shelved books within the labyrinth of library stacks, some on rollers for compact use of space, but others in little nooks and out of the way places often unknown to the casual patron. For Emily, the library was another world, one of order and predictability.

Occasionally accrediting committees came to the university. Emily enjoyed being interviewed, and when the library garnered high praise in their reports, Emily felt such reviews were in part because of her, a highly competent, responsible person. The head librarian counted Emily as one of her most positive employees, and had on several occasions attempted to entice Emily into adding either additional hours or another day to her work schedule. But Emily was happy where she was and felt that adding hours might tarnish the good feeling she had each one of the days that she worked in each library.

When she had tried to explain how she felt about her work and why working in both libraries was "just right," Karl nodded his head and then went back to reading his book. He really wasn't interested. But she wasn't bothered by his indifference to her job. She knew he was troubled by his slow recovery from the heart attack. He seemed increasingly engaged in trying out a healthier approach to what they ate. Currently this involved orange juice and flax seed. Emily sighed. He'd get onto some idea and ask her to buy whatever it was only to toss it into the garbage a few weeks later. He was grumpy. And if she brought up anything related to the university letter that stated he was being investigated, he'd put on his hat and coat and open the door: "Going mall walking, Emily."

One day when she was substituting "on" the front desk of the main university library, Dr. Heron, retired president of the seminary where Karl had been academic dean, walked through the library entryway and came right up to where she was standing. "Emily," he addressed her, "I wonder if you'd let me buy you a cup of tea or coffee when you're on your break? I imagine that might be in about ten minutes, give or take?" Emily muttered something he seemed to take as an affirmation. He shook his head in a positive way and then wandered over into the newspaper corner and sat down to read The New York Times.

Clayton's first thought was that Emily Wolfe had lost weight, a lot of it. "Maybe thirty or forty pounds," he reckoned. He might have passed her on the street and not recognized her. But here she was, behind the central desk, still at her job. Clayton had to give her credit. "Surely Karl's troubles are draining her," he thought. "And now here I am, so far as she knows, someone set to nail both of them into a common coffin." Maybe it was silly, but today, here, sitting in this library, Clayton Heron felt he was witness to a tragedy, one he neither fully understood nor comprehended, a moment in time when things that should have held together were horribly askew, and that every person in some way near the disintegration would not walk away unscathed. "This thing is too hot," Clayton said out loud.

But where had Emily gone? "Not good," she had said to herself. "Seeing that man is not good at all." Stepping away from the front desk, Emily had moved into the room where employees kept their coats. "He wants to ask me what I know about Karl," Emily thought. She grabbed her purse and disappeared into the stacks into the belly of the library. Car key in hand she exited through an emergency back door, triggering an alarm, but by the time a security guard arrived, she had located her car and was on her way home. She found herself stopped at a green light, wondering why the man in the car behind her was blowing his horn.

*

Tyler picked up Kylie's suitcase. "Girl, what did you pack? This is really light."

"Not to worry. There may be snow here, but where I'm going, at midday you can easily break a sweat."

"Swimsuits and shorts?"

"Right. And skimpy little blouses; you know, the kind you like." Tyler put his arm around her shoulders. There was a promising smile on her face, and they kissed. "Christmas break, and you're heading south to see the folks; I'm going to miss you. You'll be gone what, the better part of a week and a half?"

"Yeah; traveling on this old train will peel off a couple of days, it's so slow, but I love to ride watching things change out the window."

"This is the train Bobby Dylan made famous for just that same reason."

"Come on. . .it was famous before Bobby opened his mouth, but I have to admit that his song is a good one, for sure."

"I will miss you."

"I'll miss you, too. Don't forget—I am coming back."

"That a promise?"

"That's a promise."

Tyler handed Kylie her suitcase and, stepping back from the steps that led up into her train car, ran outside the train in the same direction Kylie was moving toward her seat inside, laughing as she waved at him through the windows until she was seated, and then the big locomotive slowly pulled away from him. There was a moment when he could just barely see her face, and then her hand, and then finally she was gone.

Tyler went into the depot, purchased a coffee, and sat on a wooden bench in a corner. He was closer to making some decisions he'd been avoiding for too long. He was a latecomer to religion. When he attended div school chapel he'd stand to sing, but when everyone broke into song, he'd plod along, not really knowing the melody or the words. And the words— the archaic words adorning most of the hymns bothered him. It was as if he was not only late getting onto the train, it was as if he'd gotten on something everyone else had been forever riding without having the remotest idea as to where the train had been or where it was going.

And then there was Kylie. She had helped him unpack a lot of the language, but most of it still failed to resonate with him like it did for her. While there were students like him at the div school, most were like Kylie, life-long believers steeped in an ethos that made Christian worship what it was. It wasn't that for him. He couldn't fake it. There were a lot of things he didn't "get" about formalized religion. But if someone like Kylie helped him "get" it, he'd often believed "getting it" was o.k., particularly if he was riding alongside her, but what if he was supposed to lead worship in a congregation. Could he fake it? And was that fair to those who knew and who were looking to him to help them not only with their relationship with God, but their relationship with each other and the world outside their congregation. Was it worth the struggle he had in re-formulating the ancient words into something a little closer to the current century? So much just did not connect for him; he hated being so lost.

But the core ideas saved him! He was able to visualize how a theological idea moved over the centuries into present day understanding, and he got excited. He had begun to work at the idea of becoming a theological historian. Not that anyone was saying there were a lot of jobs in the field, but that had not stopped him before, especially when he'd decided to pursue something. He thought about Kylie as he walked down the city street, away from the train depot. The ache he felt filled his chest.

*

Twenty-two

MARTIN GAVE HIMSELF AN extra half hour in bed, but found he could not get back to sleep, so rolled out of bed, stretched on the cold floor, did forty sit-ups and slipped away before Norah woke up. She was putting up with his long phone conversations and crazy office hours. Today was another departure with the way things used to be. It was Christmas break, and the two of them usually spent a few leisurely days getting final gifts, and then making their way to the Michigan town where luckily her parents still lived. But not today. Today Martin trudged up to the div school's administrative floor where the dean's office was located. No one else was in the building, and he was all too aware of the old story about an earlier dean who had come in on a Saturday, gotten onto the elevator, only to emerge around suppertime when a janitor, frantically called into service by a worried wife, had discovered the irritated dean stuck between floors sitting inside a broken elevator.

His office was roughly eighteen by twenty-four feet, certainly a major step up from his old one, a space no bigger than eight by fifteen feet. That room had been in "faculty row," and his first spring in that office found Martin in awe at the appearance of numerous scantily-clad and sometime nude young women seen worshipping the sun god's rays that fell on their dormitory's flat roof next door. Tom Metcalf noted, tongue in cheek, that "Such views have been known to keep the younger faculty more regularly in their offices during spring." Tom, now the senior faculty member, occupied a corner office that dwarfed those of "faculty row." Eight similarly tiny faculty offices had been on Martin's side of the hallway outside his door. On the opposite side there were seven offices and a common bathroom. On the bathroom door hung a home-made reversible sign that on one side read MEN, and on the other: WOMEN. This room engendered considerable conversation.

Sitting in the more spacious dean's office, Martin considered his current position and sighed; things seemed simpler when he was an assistant professor. His new office might convey a certain status, but the complexity of the school's current situation wasn't like anything he'd encountered in the academic world. At one end of the room was a working table and several chairs. An old but exquisite leather couch and matching armchairs lined the wall behind his desk. Across from where he sat were windows that opened onto a small balcony. "Like the pope's," offered Norah when she'd looked at his "new digs," as she put it. But with the office came administrative work, the like of which he had been unaware until accepting Tanaka's offer. Martin looked at the divinity school's mail and the internal university correspondence piled high on his desk. He wondered whether being interim dean was worth it. This thing with Wolfe certainly was intrusive. Martin's job was now consumed by it. He'd met with concerned students, had conversations with university deans, was involved weekly with President Tanaka and the university lawyers, but still found dozens of letters from graduates asking him to explain how "their school" could mistreat the good scholar Karl Wolfe.

Today, however, he'd decided to compose recommendation letters for six master's level students who were applying to doctoral programs at some excellent graduate schools. He knew that the admissions committee carefully read such letters when students applied to their doctoral program. He accordingly viewed each letter as potentially life changing. Mid-morning he made himself a cup of coffee and began reading the stack of papers from the students in the class he had just finished teaching. In earlier years, he'd be reading these at home, probably while Norah puttered in the kitchen. Later they would sit at their round kitchen table and make final Christmas lists. "Some things," Martin muttered to himself, "I miss more than others."

The phone that was his direct line rang. It was Clayton Heron. "Clayton," Martin said. "You caught me at a good time. I was grading papers, and needed a break. Why are you calling me?"

"I mentioned to you that there might be more than just sexual shenanigans with Wolfe. At the time I wasn't able to say more, and while I doubt that you'll be able to directly use what I will tell you, the attendant press hoo-haw may be publically beneficial for your case "

"What did he do, plunder your endowment?"

"Close. The man left a tiny trail that a pro bono audit tracked. It led to misuse of the regular academic budget."

"The budget controlled by the Academic Dean?"

"Exactly right. Our audit turned up evidence that the academic budget financed some prolonged stays overnight at conference hotels well past the closing of each conference. And. . .you'll find this interesting. . . we have proof that Molly Hoffman was his companion during these post-conference sojourns."

"Not exactly kosher."

"Again, exactly correct. But here's the place where this might help your situation, and frankly, the folk over here released me to tell you this because they feel, we feel, that we shipped him to you and that we would not have done that had we known the havoc he had caused here."

Clayton continued: "The trustees have recognized that the amount of money he misspent isn't the issue. They feel pretty strongly, however, that his misuse of funds strikes at the integrity of the seminary, so they are willing to spend a good deal more to sue him."

"And you think that your suit will go public."

"No way to hide it. It will make the court's docket, and some enterprising journalist will put pen to paper, as they say, and. . ."

"What you are suggesting is that his portrayal of himself as a mistreated biblical scholar might well be questioned when this hits the media."

"At the very least, it complicates his version."

*

Wolfe was late getting home. He'd met with his lawyer, who'd promised good results. Wolfe had told him his version of what had happened, but even to his ears it sounded grim. He had not shown anyone how unsettled he'd been by the investigative committee's interrogation. Their questions depressed him. Apparently he could not trust either his old seminary or his denominational officials to keep their mouths shut.

He had his fingers crossed that both groups were fixated on his affair with Molly Hoffman. He'd be willing to bet that their conservative issues about adultery were the sticking point for the denomination. Well ok, he might be able to argue his way through those concerns. He could say that the affair with Molly Hoffman had been a thing of convenience. She had been present and available. She approached him. He'd slipped. Who among them had never slipped? Who would cast the first stone? Given how long it had continued with no one guessing (well, maybe Max, her husband. But he was a shy, diffident man, and accepted the lies Molly fed him) it might be hard to argue that it had been a one-time slip. But no matter. He'd dodge and weave on that one. He could win that one. That affair hurt no one. No one.

But the issue presented by the young girl—Annie Nicholson—was different. She was fifteen. Surely he knew that, given that she was in his church and he had seen her with all the rest of those kids who had mentors. He had been her mentor. The church saw it as a covenantal thing. So the covenantal aspect of the mentor program would be used by a lawyer to say that he had not simply "slipped"—his being sexually involved with Annie was something else. It had been a formal connection, and while she was dead he could be nailed on that one connection, that one girl, that one underage relationship. But—maybe he was lucky. The denomination looked at that situation too late to do any real digging. Both Annie and Jack Curtis were dead. And no autopsy. No fetus. No DNA.

Her journal meant nothing. Her words could be spun. She was, after all, just a kid. Sheer luck. He'd remembered Jack's calling him late one night to ask for some help with Annie involving a mentoring program. When he'd seen Annie's picture in the church photo-book, he'd been quick to agree. Later Jack called again. He said that he had "a soft spot for this kid." He told Karl that he was dying, and that he was worried that she had gotten into "some kind of mess." Jack had said: "I know you two are pretty close. Take what I'm telling you as a heads-up. I would not want to see her get hurt." At that time he could still get an erection when he was with Annie. "Heads up," he remembered.

He was sorry she had killed herself, but that must have been caused by something that had happened earlier in her life. God knew, when he was in bed with her, she behaved like a woman. There had been some rough patches back at the seminary, but he'd found it incredibly helpful to spend time with Annie. A lot of what bothered him got released when he was in bed with her. There was much she had to learn, and he was a good teacher. When he'd learned of her death, Wolfe had cried. Such a loss. Such a beautiful loss. He had attended the funeral service in the chapel at her church. Jack Curtis, still alive at the time, had been there. He looked destroyed. As the service ended, he'd approached Wolfe: "I know how you feel," he'd said. "She'll be missed." He'd not seen Jack Curtis again.

He had not pursued any students or other professors than Molly while working at the seminary job. Aside from his dalliance with Molly Hoffman, he felt he was clean on that side of the ledger. So let the seminary and the denomination come after him. He could beat them. But—the idea of a "ledger" jarred him. No one seemed interested in pressing him about the loss of money due to his tinkering with the books, and he guessed he'd been lucky there, too.

That left the university divinity school and the young professor, Becky Swingle, and the two students, Jennifer and Kylie. What had he really done? He smiled. He would like to have a night with all of them. But he was past any confidence in his being with nubile women. In that regard, the heart attack and his poor veins had taken its toll. His having intercourse with any or all of them was just that, a fantasy. So what had he done? Why were they after him? It couldn't be helpful to have that kind of publicity, yet they had welcomed it. Of course they had their stories, but they had no real corroboration. Maybe he'd made a mistake with Kylie. She'd fought him. He'd read her wrong, and she was someone to worry about. He'd only wanted to touch her, or perhaps hold her. He'd thought Jennifer was close to allowing that, but Kylie must have talked her into coming out in public. Good thing he had thought to get the police engaged that night. But thinking about Kylie Raven, he found himself pacing back and forth on the ground floor of the house he shared with Emily. Someone—perhaps Rachel Henderson—had seen him, bloodied and leaving the conference a long time before he'd connected with the cops. Maybe she was the weak link. He'd think about it.

It was still snowing, though weakly. The forecasters were saying spring would be late this year. Still, if he'd been in a better mood, owned a dog, or had grandchildren near, maybe he'd have thought of talking a walk outside. Perhaps Emily would want to do that, he thought, but where was she? Standing at the kitchen sink, Wolfe looked out the window that overlooked the back yard. This was where Emily had her flower garden in the summer. And there she was, sitting on her bench, snow silently falling on her uncovered head. Wolfe wondered how long she had been sitting there, and if she was cold. He also wondered what he might say to her.

*

Twenty-three

KYLIE'S MOM AND DAD picked her up at the train station. She found it easy to fall back into being at home, even if home seemed a bit smaller than she remembered. Every day she ran. There was a route she had started running when she was in high school, and it apparently had etched itself inside her brain. She unconsciously knew where she was going. "Would that life was this simple," she told herself.

Her second day home she found her feet carrying her toward the church, intuitively putting her onto a remembered route. Entering at the back door (always open), she stood for a moment in the large semi-circle of rooms. The two levels of rooms surrounded a small stage which backed into the chancel area of the sanctuary. Built in the old "Akron-style," the church was designed so that everybody could gather for a common assembly and then disperse into the dozen rooms for small group Bible study. She chuckled as she noticed the two doors on either side of the stage. These doors would open, and just as the choir was starting to sing the introit, the church's two ministers would sweep into the sanctuary.

Lost in her memory, she'd almost forgotten why she'd come to the church, when a voice called her name: "Kylie; look at you, girl. You are looking fine. It is good to see you." The Rev. Kendra Blackstone had been the first woman pastor Kylie had ever known. She had been there for her when Kylie had bumped up against some fairly sticky occasions. After big hugs and questions about the div school and her trip home, Kylie said, "Kendra, I got myself into a situation with a professor I thought was my mentor, but who wanted me to have sex with him."

"Not good, Kylie; how did that turn out?"

"Two div school students, and I'm one of them, plus a faculty member have accused him of sexual harassment, and I've been really bothered by the whole affair."

"'Bothered' means what?"

"'Bothered' means—on one level—being the target of students who think this guy is being unfairly targeted; and, on another level, wondering who I am, and why I'm there, and do I even want to go back and finish my degree?"

"Not good. Before this happened, everything was ok; no hassles; no problems?"

"Basically, yes. Well—let me qualify that too quick answer. There's this man. . . and I think we love each other. . . and that complicates things. . . but it's a good complication, if you get what I mean."

"Kylie, what's going on in that relationship? Are you ok with it?"

"I don't want to mess it up because of this other thing, you know?"

"You don't want the sexual harassment thing to get so big that it intrudes upon your relationship with this man?"

"That's right. I tend to talk with him about important stuff, so we talk about this. . . and we talk a lot. But the bigger issue is do I really have a calling? I mean, this guy who said he'd be my mentor told me I could easily get a doctorate and become a professor, but I kinda think he was using that to pump up my ego and to get me tied into his world. Ugh. Before he hit on me, in my mind I was all set to become a professor, but now. . ."

"Now you are suspicious as to the real reason for your thinking about becoming a professor. You are thinking that because this guy hit on you, you might just chicken out on becoming a professor, and you might back into the 'safety' of the ministry. Am I right?"

"Just saying it out loud makes it less powerful, somehow. I think I may have been obsessing about this. I didn't expect a divinity school professor to hit on me; I mean, come on. . ."

"We need to talk some more on this, but I think I see you're beginning to understand how something like this undermines self-confidence."

The two women continued their conversation until the Pastor noticed the time; she said, "Kylie, I've got an appointment and I've got to go; can we talk later?" Kylie was quick to respond: "I want to think some more on this, and I think best when I run. Can I catch you in the morning Wednesday after I run?"

"As long as you won't make me run."

"You've helped, Kendra. . . you really have; some of the weight just got lifted off my back."

"Don't think I did much except listen. I do want to say that if you become a minister, I'd be proud to be in ministry with you. And, I also say that if you were to become a professor, I'd very much want an autographed copy of your first book. Now get out of here; go run."

*

156

Christmas break was now in the distant past, and while no one was willing to break faith with the university policy ("No Comment"), every day was filled with media reporters and articles accusing the university divinity school of strange things, chief among them the fact, one opinionated editorial suggested, that there was a conspiracy against Wolfe. How else could such a well-thought-of scholar such as Karl Wolfe get raked over the coals for his "scientific" biblical research methodology? One such story clearly was based on a reporter's conversation with several students in a Kevin Walker class. Walker had set up role plays focusing on mediation. Toward the end of one role play, a ministry student had suggested that maybe mediation might work with "the Dr. Wolfe situation." Another student rejected the idea, suggesting: "mediation would not work because mediation needed two somewhat equal entities, both able to give a little." The first student replied: "That's correct, and Professor Wolfe is on one side and the div school is on the other." Two other students said "Wait a minute. Students and professors have charged Wolfe with sexual harassment. And the div school has to follow university procedures when something like that occurs. So you don't have equal sides here; instead, you have two unequal parties coming before a kind of judicial review being performed by the div school. The div school has nothing to mediate. The div school has to sort out who's lying." And the guy who brought up mediation as a possibility in the first place said: "That's not the way I heard it." The reporter interviewed some of the students and published his story with the title "Divinity School Rejects Mediation Offer."

There were counter narratives, but most of them had to rely on less than the truth, simply because those who knew the inside story had ethical and legal reasons not to turn the media spotlight on the three women who brought harassment charges against Wolfe. Not known for hyperbole, Kevin Walker suggested: "It's like being in a knife fight with your knife hand tied behind your back." It was unfortunate, but the div school was a "got to have it" story. This did not sit well with those who worked at the university. In particular, it did not sit well with the university's donors and trustees.

President Tanaka met with the Provost and the various deans, including the div school's interim dean, Martin Evans. Reading out loud excerpts taken from several articles, Tanaka took one particular story in the home town newspaper apart, skewering it with facts. The deans, however, were worried. "Unfortunately," one offered, "Perception is reality."

"I know," responded Tanaka, "And I've invited a journalist to come talk with me. He's someone whose column often impacts what's believed in this town. Let's see how he deals with some of these facts."

"Be very, very careful," said the law school dean, "Factual statements are one thing, but if the journalist attributes opinions or falsehoods to you, we're in trouble. And once it hits print, there's no way to get it changed. So be careful."

"I realize that," said Tanaka. "I will be careful."

After the meeting, the provost walked out of the office with Martin. "Don't take this the wrong way, Martin," he said, "But I'm beginning to get some of your students arriving on my doorstep to complain about the 'Wolfe case.' This tells me that he is busy convincing his followers that he is the victim here, and they are mobilizing and supporting his cause." Thanking the provost for his warning, Martin slowly walked back to the divinity school.

Whatever Wolfe was planning, life went on, and that meant teaching classes, assigning and reading papers, and the advising of students readying for graduation and potential employment. Interim Dean Martin Evans reminded himself that this was the work that always attends good graduate students. But as faculty did their work and personally interacted with students, the veil of secrecy about "the Wolfe case" was pulled down, at least a tiny bit. This resulted in some students becoming even angrier with Wolfe. They coalesced and went into the interim dean's office. After they were seated and had been served coffee, Martin told them that their cause was clear; if persons called into ministry were faced with injustice, they needed to respond, and the power imbalance suggested by a professor hitting on students and junior faculty was a clear example. "But," he said, "The University Faculty Manual has a set process in place and we will follow that process." After some further conversation, he escorted the group of still angry students out of his office.

That some of the doctoral students, who had attached themselves and their future to Professor Wolfe's coattails, still felt that Wolfe was being unfairly treated could be understood. These students saw the process differently. That this occurred ought not to have surprised anyone, but it did. Consequently some of the arguments that were observed by faculty members were loud and just a few words shy of fisticuffs. In anticipation of a media coup, local TV reporters set up shop outside *The Thoughtful Bean*, and interviews with students regularly adorned their evening news reports.

At the same time, some reporters who were in fact no older than the university students they sought to interview regularly dined in the university student cafeteria, a place where conversation could easily be converted into articles and opinion pieces. While no one ever said that graduate school was fun, the friendly spirit that was once pervasive in the div school seemed to have disappeared.

*

The end of winter quarter found a break in the weather. Snow melted in fifty degree heat, and cooped up students emerged from Friday's morning classes to blue skies and mild winds. "All's right with the world," Tyler said to Kylie. "And it's the perfect day for a picnic."

"A picnic?" Kylie exclaimed, questioning this northerner's behavior. "It can't be more than fifty degrees out here."

"I'll keep you warm."

"I'm game for it. The picnic, I mean." They joined others who were walking toward the lake. Along the way, they stopped to buy what Tyler called a "picnic" lunch; two sandwiches, a sack of chips, a container of water, and one apple. "Looks like what my mother packed for me in elementary school," said Kylie.

"Two sandwiches?" responded Tyler. "You ate a lot in those days. No wonder you're so tall." Ten minutes later they were resting on a worn picnic bench that the park district had forgotten to pick up before winter hit. The bench sat on a rocky point reinforced by huge cut stone blocks. "This is really nice," said Kylie. "See," said Tyler, "I'm not so crazy, am I?"

"Never said you were, Tyler, but I never would have believed I'd be eating lunch out here in the middle of winter."

"I keep forgetting; you southern gals enjoy the heat."

"You got that right," said Kylie. "When I first got off the train up here, it was already cold. And that was the end of August! And it's only gotten colder." She shivered.

Sandwiches eaten, Tyler sat across from Kylie at the picnic table. "Kylie, I'm sorry Wolfe came on to you. I'm sorry you've had to put up with all the nastiness in the div school. I've been so proud of your willingness to stand up to him, but I know it's been hard." Quietly: "I'd like to punch him in the nose," said Tyler.

"But," Kylie said, "I already did that!" They laughed so hard both stood, and standing, found themselves kissing, holding each other tightly, hopefully. Breaking apart, Kylie said: "I'm glad we're doing this."

"This?" Tyler laughed; then kissed her again, and again. "I'm so happy," he said. Pulling her onto his lap, Tyler said: "Kylie, I know one thing for certain: I want whatever we decide to be our decision, but I want wherever we wind up to always have me standing beside you. I love you. I don't know exactly what that means, but I want to grow old, have children, and always be with you. And I'm scared and excited at the same time. Kylie, will you marry me?" Kylie wiggled deeper into Tyler's embrace. "I love you, Tyler. And I don't know what our future might hold, but I do know I want to spend my life with you. Yes; I will marry you." For a long moment they held each other. Then Tyler stood, and with Kylie in his arms spun round and round shouting: "She's going to marry me; she's going to marry me!" Several people standing near them clapped; one older man shouted: "All right!" Kylie poked Tyler in the stomach. "Tyler, there are other people here."

"I don't care; they ought to know: (loudly) she loves me; she loves me!" Later, walking back toward the university campus, Tyler said: "Hey girl; last time I asked, you still weren't certain. Minister or professor?"

"I'm still not clear, Tyler. I think I'd make a good minister. But I'm not at all ready to say 'that's me.' Could I deal with all the politics of ministry? I mean there is a tradition in some black denominations of women pastors, but even there what I've observed is that authoritarian male pastors rule the roost. Am I called to deal with that? I don't know. I admit, though, that if I had in front of me the particulars of a real church, I might feel differently. I could fall in love with a particular congregation and its mission."

"So still mixed: maybe, maybe not?"

"Yeah. And I was raised to be bi-culturally savvy, so I know I could function in a predominately Black, Anglo, or Asian congregation, but in any case, the gender and racial issues I'd face could be disconcerting. Some of the women ministers I know tell me that's the hardest part."

"So that other vocation—becoming a professor—that's still a possibility?"

"Yes. I've gotten past the Wolfe as bad mentor thing, and I've come to realize that the problems I might face in church could be seen as strengths for acquiring a position in the academy."

"How so?"

"Well, I'm a believer, a Bible scholar, and a bi-racial, bi-cultural woman. If I'm a competent Bible scholar, given who and what I am, I believe the doctorate could open a host of possibilities. Maybe the academy is a bit ahead of the curve here, but I think I can see more openings there for people of mixed heritage like me, bi-racial folk who offer methodologies of research that are more grounded." Tyler looked thoughtful. He asked: "Can we do this together? You know I'm thinking about going for an advanced degree in history. If we're both in school, it won't be easy."

"No. It will be hard. But it will also be wonderful. You love me and I love you and with God's help we'll find a way." As they neared the campus their sunny afternoon darkened, turned colder, and both noticed the return of a wintery sky. "Hey. Here's an idea," said Kylie. "Karen's gone for the weekend. Come to the apartment. I'll make dinner."

"I'd like that," said Tyler. "Maybe you could stay the night," said Kylie.

"I'd like that even better," said Tyler.

*

The phone rang as Tom and Megan entered their home after a mid-morning break at *The Thoughtful Bean*. Tom answered: "Hello?"

"Tom. It's Janie."

"Hi Janie. This about mom?"

"She died at 8 AM, Tom. She went into a deep sleep last night. The hospice nurse and the morphine helped. I was there, and decided to stay the night. She just slept away, Tom. I'm so, so sorry." There was a moment of silence, and then Tom responded, "No, Janie. We shouldn't be sad. Last time I talked with her was three days ago. She said she was ready to go, and I've got to think her pain had increased to the point that she welcomed death."

"You're right Tom. I guess my first response is for myself—I'll miss her cheerful voice. And I know that a large part of me does feel sorry for all of us. But you're right; she was ready. Your dad's death has been so much with her—it was as if she just wanted to be with him. I know that doesn't make much sense, but for her it did. You know she had no fear of death. Not that she courted death, but his absence weighed heavily on her. We've moved her body to *Higley's Funeral Home*. You'll need to call him. There are a number of details he'll want you to provide."

They continued to talk, eventually setting a date for the funeral, deciding that his mom would like the service to be at the church, and worrying about Kerri coming in from England. When the day had ended, Tom found himself thinking about cancer. It seemed omnipresent. His mother had known of the cancer two years before his dad's death. Whatever caused it—genetic predisposition, diet, chemicals, or modernity's stressors—cancer took more and more victims.

"Even canine life," Tom thought. Rarely did a week go by without troubled dog owners talking about the tumors that their pets had acquired. He fell asleep that night wondering about cancer, his father and now his mother's deaths, and he began to think—once again—about how he and Megan would eventually end their lives. Nevertheless, he slept well, and the plane ride the next morning was uneventful. Driving north, Megan encouraged his telling stories about his mother. "She was socially intelligent. She knew everybody in the church, and not as a busybody, but as someone who cared for the people that she knew. And she had grit. She was tough. When they first moved into the house on Third Street, she discovered a sewer rat in the basement. She didn't call dad, but dispatched the rat with a baseball bat. Dad came home from teaching. He measured the rat. He said: 'Counting the tail, sixteen inches long.' Then he added: 'Maybe her pounding the rat added a few inches!'" Megan and he laughed. They took the river road, and he re-called rides made on his old Schwinn bike.

They crested one long hill, and he remembered a spring near the bottom where people used to take water jugs for filling. As they drove by they realized that the spring was still there; a man was unloading several jugs for filling. Entering the small town flooded Tom with memories. The ice cream parlor, still there, where he'd had a first "date." The local theater, now converted into a mini-mall. The park near the town's center, now covered with winter snow. The water fountain where, as kids, he, Michael, and Kerri would load water balloons and chase each other. This was his boyhood home.

They unpacked at their hotel, and he went to *Higley's* to finalize arrangements. When the details were finished, he picked up Megan. They drove to the cemetery where his dad was buried. "Loving Husband and Father" the gravestone read. He'd called the cemetery office before they left home, and he was pleased to see their preparations had been taken care of. A windbreak of white pine trees whispered and crows called as they got back into the car. They passed the new high school and the snow-covered hillside where the school he had attended once stood. "Some things change," he said to Megan. "And yet, some things never change," she replied.

The church's big lot had two cars parked in it. "Probably Pastor Harper and Joe Dunne, the janitor," he said. Megan nodded. They got out of the car, slipped into overcoats, and walked to the rear entrance of the church. The sanctuary was on the far side of the building. On this side were classrooms, library, lounge, and administrative offices, including the pastor's study. Tom knocked on the door of the study; "Come in," a voice said. Pastor Harper was a slender, gray-haired man "around sixty," Tom thought. A firm hand-shake, some words of concern expressed at his mother's death, and the three were seated. "I expect a lot of people," Pastor Harper said. "She was well and truly loved," said Tom. He continued: "Are the arrangements I spoke to you on the phone ok?"

"Yes. The women's society will host your friends and family for a simple luncheon once we return from the cemetery. Our organist is set. Time-wise, the funeral here at 10 AM, then to the cemetery."

"We've been there," said Tom, "And it looks as if they are ready."

"I've spoken with *Higley's*, and they assure me that they have those details well in hand," said Pastor Harper. "A simple grave side service, then return here around 11:30 for lunch."

"Can we expect good weather tomorrow?"

"Yes. No late blizzards or heavy rain. There is no snow to slow us down." He paused: "You know, Dr. Metcalf, your mother was a remarkable woman. She served two terms on our board of elders, and she probably knew every-one in the congregation, especially the children. She was remarkable," he repeated. He went on: "I wanted to ask if you thought it a good idea to open the service to testimony from those gathered. I'd like to announce that, and I'd suggest at that time I say you would conclude the service. You'd say whatever you wanted to say, and I'd return to invoke prayer, and then move the service to its conclusion. Is that ok?" Tom agreed, and he and Megan got back into the car and drove the five blocks to his old home, where Janie, Michael, and some of Tom's relatives had been invited for supper. Kerri arrived at 10 PM, husband in tow. There were many stories told, and both Megan and Tom were tired as they fell into their beds that night.

The next morning found Tom in Pastor Harper's study when a man in a dark blue suit tapped on the doorframe: "Funeral hearse is here," he said. He and Pastor Harper went outside. Six male relatives stood near the rear door of the hearse. Another man in a dark blue suit opened the door and slid the casket out. It sat on a wheeled gurney, and the six men moved the gurney into the church and to the front of the sanctuary. Tom watched as bright red roses were placed on the top of the casket. Other floral arrangements were positioned behind and on either side. The line into the church was long, and Tom knew many of them. There was the man whose car's paint had been washed away as a result of the "Church Youth Carwash." Apparently it had never been washed before. There was Violet, a woman he could not remember until she embarrassed him by relating that when they were twelve, he'd kissed her in the tree house he and his dad had built behind their home. He'd forgotten that kiss, but she had remembered. Everyone in line had kind words for his mother.

When the moment for testimony arrived, Tom listened as person after person told stories about his mother. When he stood to talk, he'd had to pause, but he was emotionally able to finally say the right words, and he felt good about what he'd said. Both his mother and his dad would have understood. He was not ready for what Pastor Harper had to say. "Tom," Pastor Harper said, "Your mother did not really understand what you do in your job, but she was taken by a conversation she had with you about describing how some members of the Jewish tradition were writing living wills. These were documents that made an effort to name and pass on to relatives the virtues that the person dying felt had given their life meaning. That made sense to her, and she worked on one for you, Kerri, and Michael. You'll get to read it in full later, but I want to share some of what she said in that document."

He paused, then continued, "She said her children were fine, grown adults. You, Tom, and you, Kerri—and remember, these are her words—you have both married solid, moral persons. There will be times when you, being human, will fail, will argue, and will be angry with those you love, but I (she said) will to you the tenacity of real love. That is, I hope that you love so strongly that no one and nothing will ever defeat that love." Harper paused. "And Michael, your mother said that you were stronger and far better than you realized, and that her living will for you would be that you might discover your passion for a vocation worth your life. Would that you might find your north star—she said—and finding it, embrace and love it truly and deeply."

"She wrote much more than these few words, but I believe she wanted them spoken in this sanctuary. She wanted you to hear them among your relatives, friends, and family gathered here. She worked on what to say, even as she was dying. It would be easy for me to say that death does not matter, but it does. Death changes our lives. Your father died, and you mourned him. Now we who live are living without the presence of your mother. And we'll naturally miss and mourn her. Her death is our loss. But she did not fear death. She believed death was a part of living. She knew some of us live in fear of dying, but not her. She lived life fully, and when she was dying she trusted God and let go, knowing that letting go was ok." Tom put his hand on Megan's. There was a prayer, they rose to sing a hymn, and the six men slowly rolled the casket down the center aisle of the church, out the door, into the waiting hearse.

*

Spring Quarter

1990

Twenty-five

Tom Metcalf called each committee member, and they met at the div school. After exchanging pleasantries, he asked where Kevin and Martin stood. "But before you talk, let me tell you what I think," he said. "I suspect, like me, not a day has gone by over the break and into this quarter without your thinking about this mess. We've been asked to consider the charges against Karl Wolfe and to follow the evidence as best we can. We're then to make a recommendation to the Academic Council, and that will be voted up or down. If it passes, our recommendation might well go to the university trustees." He paused for a moment: "And possibly beyond that to a court of law," said Martin.

"Yes," said Tom. "So we've two quite specific things to do. The first has to do with the charge and the evidence. What can we say here? And I'll go first. I think the charge is justified. The more evidence we uncover, the more likely it is that what was alleged in fact occurred. A second thing has to do with whatever we recommend to the trustees regarding Wolfe's continued employment. Up to me, I'd terminate his contract." As he ended his comment, Tom happened to be looking at Kevin. Kevin spoke: "I've really struggled with both points. I agree with you Tom, but I need to say that this has put my two professions in stark relief, at least as I look at them. As a psychologist I see his brokenness, and I want to help him; but, as a faculty member, I see his toxic behavior and the evidence we've gathered as destructive to what we hold in trust, so like you, I vote to not only censure but fire him."

"I think the two points Kevin just made are the pivotal reasons we must do this," Martin said. He continued: "In some ways, Wolfe's toxic behavior might have been considered as normal behavior a few generations back. Back then women often were treated unfairly. So sexual harassment kind of went with the terrain. We've come pretty far. Back then men could get away with some very bad behavior. Not today. A div school cannot condone such behavior. It is destructive. It undermines the core of what we as theological educators hold in trust. On the first question, I believe our evidence sustains the charge of sexual harassment. On the second question—I also vote to fire Wolfe."

"Three votes saying the evidence we have found sustains the charge, and we are also unanimous in recommending to the faculty that Karl Wolfe be fired. Is this correct?" With the nodding of the other two men, Metcalf continued: "Our next task is to present this recommendation to the academic council. I suggest we determine how it ought to be composed, and that we work at it until we are all agreeable with a final version." Each man agreed to an overall framework for producing draft paragraphs.

A week later, final product in hand the morning of the academic council, the three men anxiously awaited their turn on the docket. Before the council was called to order, librarian Edwin Diaz dropped into the empty chair beside Tom Metcalf. "How's it going?" He asked Metcalf. "Can't complain," said Metcalf, "but I'll breathe easier when this report is out of my hands."

"You needn't worry. I think everyone here will vote to both censure and to fire Karl Wolfe," said Edwin, "And if your report needs a second, I'd be honored to volunteer." When that time came, discussion was short, it went as Edwin had predicted, and the three men were relieved that their faculty colleagues unanimously agreed with their recommendations.

Karl Wolfe had been censured by his colleagues; in addition, they unanimously recommended that the university trustees remove him from the div school faculty.

*

Emily was devastated. She did not know what she could do about Karl's transgressions. What made all this absolutely terrible was the young girl's death. At first Emily had accepted Karl's complaint that the denomination and his old school were both involved in trumped up charges against him, but as weeks passed, many of the newspaper's stories were too explicit in their stories to have been fabricated. Then one day in the mail there was a picture of Karl and Molly Hoffman kissing outside a hotel Emily recognized as being located near the seminary where Karl used to be dean.

What was strange was that on the back of the photocopy was a message from Molly: "Emily, Get out now. Don't support this man." It was signed, "Your friend, Molly." Molly was not Emily's friend. Emily had early on been all too aware that Molly flirted with Karl and was over the top in her praise of him, but still—this picture, and this note. She confronted Karl and he confessed: "It was once, and only once." She almost believed him.

But then the university letter also had to be considered. It not only alleged sexual harassment with professors, but what really bothered Emily was the statement that "students were involved." She had blown up at Karl, worried over the technical language involving hearings and judgments to be made, and time tables to be met and what all this might mean for her. That was when she started to lose sleep, not eat, and sit on the couch and stare straight ahead at nothing in particular. She had been on that couch one day when a rather timid knock caused her to look out the side window at the couple standing at her door. There had been any number of reporters who had wanted to talk with her, the "wife of the now infamous dean." She had stopped opening her door to that ilk, but here was an older couple, definitely not reporters. "Hello," said the woman. "We hoped we could talk with you. We're Annie Nicholson's parents. Karl was her church mentor." These words were delivered quietly, but Emily saw that their sorrow would soon become hers, the only question was in what way.

Emily opened her door: "Please come in," she said, "Would you like a cup of coffee?" There are moments in every life that change the way we see ourselves and our place in this universe. Emily had made a kind of un-easy peace with the mounting evidence regarding Karl's sexual escapades. She'd tried to wall it all off. She had her work; Karl had his. Their unspoken contract had worked, but recently she'd been wondering if Karl really had gotten "trapped" (as he claimed) by these women. She still had some sup-portive women from the church. They saw her as the wronged wife and wanted to help her. Karl rarely went to church. She felt that she might actu-ally survive, if he'd tell her the truth. With this hope, she'd begun to sleep again. Her appetite had even returned.

But what this weeping mother and angry father told Emily was too horrible, too dark, and very wrong. Annie had been fifteen. She became pregnant. Karl was the father. This most likely in their bed. And this act had occurred under the eyes of God and everyone else in the church com-munity. Karl Wolfe, Emily suddenly realized, had lied about Sally Hoffman, lied about those divinity school students, and had hidden what had hap-pened with this child from her and from himself.

Emily was enraged.

*

171

The phone rang two times before Clayton Heron picked it up. "Hello," he said.

"Clayton?" Martin Evans asked. "That's me;" said Clayton. "Is this Dean Evans?"

"It is. I'd like to meet and share some news with you. If you're willing?"

"Fine with me. When you thinking? Today could work."

"This afternoon today, if that's ok?"

"Why don't you meet me at the little coffee place at the corner of Washington Street and Liberty Avenue. They call it the 79B Café since the route seventy-nine B bus stops there. The coffee is good. About three?"

"Works for me; see you then."

Martin found a place on the street where he parked his car. He got out, locked the car, put money in the meter and made his way toward the 79B. It was only a short distance, but he found himself avoiding several chest-high piles of snow that had been plowed off the street and now blocked the sidewalk. "I'll be glad when this winter finally ends," he muttered to himself. What had a few weeks ago seemed like the harbinger of an early spring had not been real. Snow had returned with a vengeance. Steamed over coffee shop windows overlooked the deck. Probably well-used in summertime, today the deck held a few snow-covered plastic chairs and tables. Martin stepped inside, got a mug of coffee, found a chair in a quiet nook, and was just finishing a look at a newspaper when a tall, angular man clothed in what appeared to be a red-checked shirt, beat-up hunting jacket, khaki slacks, and worn L.L. Bean boots entered. Martin caught the man's eye and lifted his mug. The man gestured at the counter, letting Martin know that he'd join him once he had gotten his coffee. They shook hands. "I'm glad to finally meet you. I've been hearing good things about you," said Clayton.

"And I you," said Martin. "I thought I ought to talk with you before this weekend, before you heard any rumors. Our investigative committee met. They recommended the censuring and firing of Wolfe to the faculty, and they agreed. I now expect Wolfe to make his appeal to the Trustees."

"He could skip that and just go to court."

"He might, at that," Martin said, "but whatever happens, I wanted you to know that you helped in this process and that we might —I say, might— need to legally move from our stack of sworn depositions to courtroom testimony. I needed to see you and find out if you're still willing to stand up and testify in public. And I also wanted to thank you for your help thus far, and to ask what your community has done and is doing, given the public nature of this thing."

Clayton seemed agreeable; Martin waited for his response, "I'll certainly testify if I am needed, Clayton said. "As to our community, we've had some moments. Here are some of the highlights. The money thing is in the court system. We think we'll see progress there in roughly two months. Molly and Max Hoffman are getting divorced. No one other than Molly came forward at the seminary to make any charges along the lines you're dealing with. Nevertheless, some of our more pious constituents are giving President Karns a hard time. I think he'll survive. But in the aftermath of all this, he's told the faculty that they will need to craft a sexual harassment policy that includes procedures for both faculty and administrators."

"Mrs. Nicholson?" Martin asked. Clayton responded: "She is in the process of moving. You remember that her 'downsizing' led to the discovery of Annie's letter?"

"I remember," said Martin.

"Well two weeks ago she sold her house, put everything she wanted to keep in one of those storage sheds, and is now looking at places to purchase in the Carolinas. Her husband was here for maybe a month, then disappeared again. This time she intends to leave no forwarding address. She is heading south. She told me she's 'available' if needed in court or whatever until mid-July. She hopes to be long gone and on her way immediately after then."

"People move and life goes on," said Martin." Clayton continued: "The one person I truly feel for in all this is Emily Wolfe. I was shopping in the local market last week, and she came through the door, saw me, and literally turned and ran back outside. She did the same thing earlier when I stopped at the university library. Her escape from me took her out one of the main library's emergency doors, and I have to tell you, that's probably the first time Emily has ever done anything illegal. I mean the library doors are wired, and all the bells and whistles went off. It was a racket!" He paused for a moment, and then said, "I don't know what she was thinking, but if I put myself in her position, I'd either be in total denial—telling myself that all this stuff about Karl is not true—or I'd feel shame, and shame can be a powerful emotion."

There was a pause. Both men seemed caught by their own deeply felt emotions. Martin broke the silence: "I think a lot about Emily. I also think a lot about Annie and the three women in my div school. They were hurt, through no fault of their own. I can't fathom why someone like Wolfe could do the things that he did."

"It isn't that difficult to understand," Clayton responded. "All of us have fantasies about things we'd never allow ourselves to do. But sometimes powerful people say: 'Why not go ahead and do this?' They often believe power makes them invisible, that no one can see them. Or, if they are seen, they believe they are powerful enough that no one will say anything about them." There was a lengthy pause; then Clayton continued: "Maybe that works for a while. But someone once said that though the wheels of justice grind exceedingly slow, they will catch up. I believe that no one is invisible."

"You are an optimistic person, Clayton. Sometimes justice is hard to locate. And when it is located, it sometimes grinds the wrong people." Martin put down his coffee cup. It was still warm. Clayton looked hard at Martin—"You would like Wolfe to be found guilty in a court of law, but what is bothering you, Martin? Are you afraid that your actions are the ones that will grind Wolfe into dust?" Clayton sipped his coffee and watched Martin's eyes. He thought Martin's voice seemed somehow older, as if he was no longer a young man. Martin caught Clayton's eyes watching him; he said: "It seems too simplistic, somehow. Is it that Wolfe is just an evil man? That's too easy for me, too black or white, and yet I know that he has done these things and that he ought to be held accountable for them. I guess I want to believe that there is some gray in this thing." He broke eye contact, looking down at the two coffee cups sitting on the table, a folded paper napkin resting between them. Feeling for the young man, Clayton said: "Look, Martin. I take it you're a Presbyterian?"

"Yes, but. . .?" queried Martin.

"You know John Calvin, that French lawyer who became a theologian? He knew the law and he knew theology. No one has written as much stuff that bears on this issue as he did. And when all of it was written, he could be said to have anchored a lot of his work on a pragmatic acceptance of man's sinfulness. He really founded your denomination. I mean," continued Clayton, "I mean folk don't like that old word 'sin', but here we are, and it seems to fit, so why not say it and use it?"

"Maybe you're right, Clayton. I may find it hard to condemn him, but I can agree that Karl Wolfe sinned, and in particular, that the death of Annie Nicholson was a sad result of his sinful behavior. But Calvin also speaks of the grace of God, and maybe being human means we are a crazy-quilt mixture of both sinfulness and blessedness. And maybe someone such as Wolfe. . ."

"Someone like Wolfe needs to understand that living with other humans means. . ."

"Means that relationships matter, and that a caring community will call you to task if you become a toxic member and don't care who you are hurting." The two men continued talking until Clayton rose: "Time for my dog's afternoon run. Got to go."

"I'm glad we met today," said Martin. "I'd like to think the next time we see each other, it'll be around better circumstances."

"A friend of mine sometimes said a kind of blessing whenever he was up to his neck in worry," said Clayton, "It's a call and response affirmation. Maybe you know it. It goes like this: How shall we live?" And Martin replied: "We live in hope."

"And I say Amen to that," Clayton shouted as he went out the door, waving goodbye.

*

Twenty-six

NORAH WOKE AND, REACHING for Martin, felt his absence. Carefully balancing her pregnant body, she rose from their bed and went to find him. He was sitting with all the lights out in their living room. "Martin. Are you all right?"

"Sorry to scare you, Norah. I'm just puzzling about some of the things I teach students here, things like grace, forgiveness, sin, and love."

"This thing about Wolfe is getting to you, isn't it?"

"It is. Early on I wondered just how forgiveness and Jesus' admonition to turn the other cheek fit here, but now I think he'd approve of directly confronting someone who refuses to admit that he has done anything wrong. Even as I say this, I'm not so sure that I'm ok with all this."

"I know it's churning inside you; it's three am, and you're sitting in a darkened room by yourself."

"I was thinking about some of the comments I heard today. You know how some of us are having brown bag lunches so we can sit and privately talk through a lot of questions. We teach both ministerial and doctoral students, and it's no accident that we have misgivings as to how all of this is unfolding. I had mentioned at lunch yesterday that the word Jesus used that we often translate as '*conversion*' actually meant 'to turn around; to go in the other direction.' I wondered out loud if someone like Karl Wolfe was still open to that kind of transformation."

"What happened?"

"One faculty member said that she hoped what I said was the case for Karl, but that a too easy forgiveness can be a cheap response when people do horrific things. She said that was her response to faculty members who are too easily willing to forgive Wolfe's misuse of students. She felt he needs to be confronted. That, after all, speaks about power and the relational integrity that lies at the heart of what we do."

"This is hard on you; you care—deeply—for your students and these professors."

"I do; but not a day goes by without someone suggesting that those of us confronting Wolfe are engaging in a vendetta against him."

"Are students and faculty split as to what they believe?"

"Not split, but I think Wolfe has been able to move the goalposts somewhat so that he's seen as positioning himself on the side of truth. That makes those of us who are against him the bad people who are only interested in putting him down."

"Are you making predictions as to what is going to happen?"

"No; but I am clear about one thing: come next fall, Wolfe will not be a member of this faculty."

*

Martin felt that the negotiations leading up to the board meeting were overblown, but he'd come to appreciate the agreed upon format. Tom would present the divinity school's case first. Then Wolfe's lawyer would respond. Then the divinity school would have the opportunity to rebut the lawyer's presentation, and finally, as the defending party, Wolfe's team would give their concluding statement. All presentations were to honor and abide by a carefully negotiated time frame, with no exceptions to be asked for or given.

After a dinner the night before, university board members the next morning slowly trickled into a large conference room where the hearing would take place. At each trustee's seat was a heavy folio of carefully selected material provided by the university divinity school investigative committee. In that folio was a listing of eighteen persons germane to the committee report as well as a set of photographs and a brief abstract describing each person's possible testimony. Along one side of the room were tables on which rolls, coffee, and several stacks of University Faculty Manuals had been assembled.

Members of the board quickly moved to claim their spaces, positioning name card holders onto the linen covered pristine table rectangle. Several trustees could be seen sorting through the various papers they had removed from their folios. The board chair opened the meeting by saying that this was a hearing regarding the charge of sexual harassment against Professor Karl Wolfe. He stated that this was not a trial, but that both sides had determined the order and the time allotments for presentations, following which the board would meet in executive session.

Tom Metcalf started the proceedings by stating that a formal charge of sexual harassment had been made by one divinity school faculty member.

He continued: "Two students joined the faculty member in that charge. Their sealed, dated, and witnessed testimonies are on the desk in front of me, but in summary, a new, junior faculty member, Rebecca Swingle, was asked to trade sexual favors for the support of Mr. Wolfe toward future rank and tenure decisions; in addition, a new divinity school student, Jennifer Logan, was promised the grade of 'A' in Professor Wolfe's courses if she submitted to his advances; and, finally, a second year master's student, Kylie Raven, was sexually accosted in her room by Mr. Wolfe at an annual AAR/SBL meeting."

After pausing for a moment, Tom continued: "A three member investigative Divinity School committee, chaired by me, believes this testimony to be a true account of what took place, and in tracking alleged similar behavior in the Dean's previous seminary and denomination, discovered that Dr. Wolfe was being investigated by both of those institutions for sexual improprieties. In addition, Dr. Wolfe's old seminary continues to pursue Karl Wolfe for the misuse of seminary funds used to facilitate some of his sexual behavior."

"Of special interest to this committee in its decision making process was the record of his denomination regarding charges of adultery involving a seminary faculty member, Molly Hoffman, as well as the death of a fifteen-year-old girl, Annie Nicholson, who had allegedly become pregnant because of a mentor/mentee confirmation class relationship with Dr. Wolfe, then a member of her church." Tom continued, finally concluding his remarks by stating: "It seems that Dr. Wolfe has pursued his predatory behavior in a variety of locations without being caught for a long, long time. On hearing the evidence connected to each charge, the faculty members of the divinity school unanimously voted that termination of Professor Wolfe's contract be recommended to the university board of trustees. As chair of the investigative committee, I so move in the hope that you would accept and act upon the advice of this committee." He sat down.

Wolfe's lawyer wasted no time. He attacked the charges made by the young faculty woman and the two students as "he said, she said" testimony. He summarized: "Dean Wolfe clearly denies that these things happened." He continued, "Dean Wolfe will admit the adultery charge, but what happens between two consenting adults, no matter how unsavory, should have no bearing on university policy."

Wolfe's lawyer also debunked the testimony regarding the AAR/SBL incident. He stated that they had a police report that would explain the cut on Wolfe's face as the result of a mugging that night and not the result of a woman defending herself. And as for the girl who committed suicide, "Dean Wolfe was shocked at the mother's allegations as to his behavior. He knew that this troubled girl had an adolescent crush on him, but he rebuffed her advances, and since her body unfortunately was cremated, any suggestion that she was pregnant or that he is somehow responsible for what happened in that regard cannot be proven."

Then it was the university's turn. The university's lawyer stood and introduced Professor Sharon Henderson, who related her observation of the date and time she saw Dean Wolfe rapidly exiting the conference hotel with a bloody handkerchief held to his face. The university lawyer added: "We also have testimony from Dean Wolfe's secretary, that when he appeared the day following the AAR/SBL incident, he told her that he had been mugged. But you have also heard Dr. Henderson relate that she saw Mr. Wolfe exit the hotel with a bloody handkerchief held to his face, and I want to stress that this was earlier than the time the police reported the so-called mugging incident to have occurred. Her testimony directly contradicts the time sequence as reported by Mr. Wolfe, and certainly contradicts the veracity of his comments to his secretary on the day following the incident."

He concluded: "Mr. Wolfe would have you believe that he was the victim of a late night mugging, but in fact Mr. Wolf staged the mugging in order to misdirect any accusations that might have followed his assault on our student and her subsequent testimony that his facial cut occurred when she hit him with her ring hand." He then noted that Wolfe's denomination had censured him, blocking him from denominational office and forbidding him from ministerial service in any denominational church, seminary, or institution of higher education. He related that ". . . a denominational representative would confirm these actions."

After looking directly at every member of the board, the university lawyer continued: "Dr. Karl Wolfe is recognized by this faculty, the seminary where he was dean, and also by his denomination (all three institutions) as a sexual predator. This man has not shown one iota of sympathy for any of the women he has harmed. I would repeat the charge brought before you by this school's faculty—censure him and separate him from this institution." The lawyer sat down.

There was a lengthy pause, during which time Wolfe seemed to be arguing with his own lawyer. Finally Wolfe stood up. He apparently had convinced his lawyer that he should make the final statement. He stepped away from his chair and said, "I am not a sexual predator."

Looking directly at the assembled trustees, Wolfe continued: "I apologize for my poor behavior with the wife of my ex-seminary colleague, but we are two adults, and the actions of two adults should not be of concern here." Clasping both hands behind his back, Wolfe leaned forward and said: "I know Professor Henderson dislikes me, and she is the cause of some of the strongest testimony against me, but I did not know that she would lie about something—a mugging—that happened when I got off the train at my stop the night of the AAR/SBL meeting. I submit to you that the lie is hers, not mine. And as for the girl who committed suicide and the testimony ascribed to my two ex-students. . . who can tell what fantasies led them to the tales they invented. I'm not proud of some of the things that I've done, but I did not do the things that they say I did."

Again he paused. He stepped toward the assembled board members and with a smile on his face completed his argument: "It is unfortunate that the divinity school faculty dislikes my research approach to the complex stories contained within our Bible. I am, frankly, being maligned by a few disgruntled faculty members who'd like to see me leave, and to leave under a cloud. Nevertheless, as it has been made clear in recent news reports, others are willing to honor me as the first-rate scholar that I am." With those remarks hanging in the air, Wolfe sat down.

*

Everyone not a board trustee was then asked to leave the conference room. It was time for the "executive session," a closed meeting during which board members would privately discuss things. Their conversation continued throughout the afternoon and ended at five thirty. When President Tanaka stopped by his office at six, he found the three members of the faculty's investigative committee camped outside his door. "Come in," he said.

"This will need to be quick," Tanaka began, "Because I am to be at dinner at seven. Let me give it to you as simply as I can. You might not have recognized him, but the one person not a trustee who stayed inside for the executive session was the representative of our insurance company. After a long discussion, he said that while we had a good case, and could probably win, if Wolfe sued, no one could guarantee exactly how a court case might turn out, so the insurance company, in order to avoid the possibility of excessive costs, would be willing to pay Mr. Wolfe to go away."

There was a stunned silence. Tom exploded: "You mean he gets to leave and take with him a fat check? How just is that?"

"I get your meaning and I share your anger, but with lawyer's fees and a possible loss worth much, much more, the board agreed with our insurer's proposal and called Wolfe's lawyer. There was some back-and-forth, but the lawyer reported that Mr. Wolfe would 'graciously accept what to him seemed a reasonable conclusion to this sorry affair.' At least, I believe my words here get the spirit of his comments." Tom interrupted Tanaka: "So Wolfe accepted the offer. Does that mean that he is separated from university students and teaching, in a word fired, and barred from the premises?"

Tanaka replied: "Yes, but both he and we cannot disclose any of the particulars of the case. That's it." The three men were shocked. Unable to find words adequate for the situation, they stood in silence, staring first at the floor and then at one another. President Tanaka stepped to his office door, and bowing to the inevitable, they exited. Still speechless, they took the stairs to the ground floor at a run and stepped out, onto the quadrangle. As the three walked across the university quadrangle, Tom waved his arms, stopped, and said: "Now I know what it takes to retire well; I need to do something so horrific that the school will buy me out. That's the way it works, right?"

There were nods and shrugs; Martin broke their disappointment. He said: "Come on guys, we need to go to *Fritz's*, and I, for one, am going to have a beer. Will you join me?" At *Fritz's*, Martin commandeered the payphone and called Norah with the news. She said: "Glad it's done, but sad it ended this way." He told her he was at *Fritz's* with the committee, and would be home late. She "would be waiting to hear more." Martin then joined Kevin and Tom at one of the round tables; "While I'm ticked at the way this ended," said Tom, "I'd like to drink a toast to the committee and its work." He lifted a glass while saying: "We did ok!"

"I think I learned something in all this mess," Martin said. "Tanaka warned me that the institution would protect itself. Not that it isn't for justice and all that, but he told me that bad publicity needs to be cut off at the knees, and woe to those who see it otherwise." Kevin looked at Martin and said: "You think you should have seen this coming?" "I think so," said Martin. "Right up to the end I thought the trustees were with us, but they weren't; they were with the university. They followed their rules, and we followed ours. Both rules are honest ones, even correct ones. But we (and here I mean we faculty) saw it differently than they did. And the big buck decision stops with them, so no sense being angry about it. That's the way it went down. It's done." He raised his mug of beer as if to salute a vanquished foe. "It is done," he said again.

"Well, I'm still ticked at the decision," said Kevin, "But I'll toast the fact that Karl Wolfe will not be here with us on the faculty next year or for that matter, the year after that." There was laughter, and they drank. "I'll join you two with that toast, but I don't feel good about what happened," said Tom. "I'm betting he got enough money from us to be comfortably retired and laughing all the way to the bank. Let's add it up: a small ministry pension, his TIAA/CREF stock, Emily and his Social Security, plus this settlement and whatever he has in his home. . . Hey, the man never even had to say he's sorry!" Sometime later, after more commiseration, Martin got up and used *Fritz's* phone to call Clayton. "Clayton Heron here."

"Clayton. It's Martin. It's over. The insurance representative said we had a good case, but that they feared we might lose in court, so they paid Wolfe to go away. So he's gone, but both sides have some sort of confidentially agreement and we're not supposed to talk about it. You didn't hear it from me, but the good news is that he's out of here, can't come onto campus, and can't use our name in any public statements as to his future employment, his writing or any public promotions he might make. I don't like it, but that's the end of it."

"Well, he's gone. Gone, but not forgotten. Quite a year for you. What now?"

"I think I'll let this go for maybe twenty years, and if I'm still alive at that point maybe I'll write a novel that could lift the lid just a bit so that others might catch a hint as to what this was all about."

"Sounds like you might sometimes be a dean, but you'll always be an educator," said Clayton.

"Thanks," Martin said. "I'll take that as a compliment. But let me say one more time—thanks for your open and honest support. I have appreciated your advice and willingness to go the extra mile here. Again—thank you. I'm tired, and I'm going home to see Norah."

"A good idea. And the next time I see you, I'd expect you'll be the permanent dean. Least that's what I hear," said Clayton. Martin hung up the phone and went back to the table. Looking at Tom and Kevin, he said: "I'm glad we did what we did, and now I'm heading home. I'll see you tomorrow."

*

Twenty-seven

WALKING HOME, WOLFE RECALLED his lawyer and the university's negotiations. He hadn't liked any part of it, but now, walking away from all the stress, what had resulted seemed like the best thing that could have come out of the situation. He laughed. A cousin had once marveled at his ability to get out of escapades, unscathed. One day after a pretty bad episode that cousin had said—"Karl, you'd fall in the crapper and come out holding a rose."

Wolfe remembered pacing back and forth in the lawyer's waiting room. A one-man, two-room operation, his lawyer had left his office door open, so Wolfe could hear each time the phone rang. The phone rang a lot, but each time the lawyer raised his hand as if to stop Wolfe from entering his inner office. At maybe the sixth or seventh call, the lawyer raised his hand once more toward Wolfe, but this time with a gesture to come inside: "Say that again," he said to whomever was on the phone. "No penalty, a year's salary, barred from the university, a confidential settlement." He paused. Nodding his head about whatever had been communicated to him, he looked at Wolfe and said: "Ok; I'll get back to you." Gently lowering the phone into its cradle, he turned toward Wolfe, and reported—"You heard the primary points; the insurer does not want to go to court. This is a good offer. We might get a few more dollars. They probably low-balled us, but I don't think you can dicker too much with them. Think it over for a few minutes. Then we should call back." He turned back to the pile of papers on his desk. Wolfe stepped back into the waiting room, this time sitting in one of the four nut-brown chairs.

"So," Wolfe had thought, "it's over. And all that stress for nothing, really. Not that he wouldn't miss some of the power connected with being a dean, but my god, he had escaped the worst of it and here he was, getting paid off. He could pay what he owed this lawyer and stash the rest with a nice brokerage firm he knew. It would be o.k.; even better than o.k." He stood in the lawyer's doorway. The lawyer looked up. Wolfe said: "You think they'll go higher?"

"Not much. You've got opposing forces. The school wants this—and you—to go away. But I was there today. I heard what they have against you, and they have a case." Watching Wolfe, he emphasized—"Look. I know that the story you told me is the one you told them, but they have a lot of stuff that counters your points. So. . . maybe go back at them one time to see if they will budge. Maybe add in two year's salary? Maybe. Maybe not. But we need to be careful. We don't want to push too hard. I know their insurer doesn't like the idea of a jury trial, but neither should you. Whatever they offer next, my advice is that you take it and run." And that's what Wolfe did. He exited the lawyer's office into a late afternoon rain. Whatever snow had remained was being washed away. And it was warmer. "Spring," Wolfe breathed in the damp promise of spring and a summer without obligation. "No responsibilities," he thought. "I'm free."

That evening Karl Wolfe tried to convince Emily that he'd been found innocent of all charges. She was having none of it: "I don't believe you, Karl. I read the papers. I saw your letters and the pictures of you and Sally. I know how people on campus look at me."

"But Emily, they dropped the charges. How many times do I need to say it—they dropped the charges, found me innocent, awarded me a handsome sum for their libel. I'll retire. I'll write a book. We can travel. You'll see. We'll be fine."

"You think so, Karl? You think we can erase all this and go back say, ten years? I'm not dumb, Karl. They want you gone, so they fired you. Immoral behavior. And you, a church-going religious man. I don't even know you anymore."

"Emily. . ."

"They cut their losses, Karl." Quietly: "They paid you off. To Leave. To leave. I don't know what to do." Wolfe reached toward Emily: "Don't, Karl. Do not touch me. Did they say that I could keep my job, Karl? I got that position because of you. I was at the front desk when the newspapers came. I read the headline—about you, Karl. Can you begin to understand me? Can I walk into that library? With my head held high? Can I, Karl?"

They argued into the night. At two in the morning he had shuffled off to bed. At 7 AM Karl awakened. As he passed the room where they kept the television set, he saw that she had slept the night on the couch, her shoulders and hips covered with an old-fashioned multi-colored blanket. He left a note on the kitchen table: "I'm walking till nine; perhaps we could meet then at *The Thoughtful Bean*. Love, Karl." He went outside to sit on the front steps and smoke a cigarette. He no longer dreamed about the hag, or for that matter about Kylie, Jenny, or Becky either. He had not dreamed. Maybe all that was over, too. Maybe they could sell the house, move to a place that was warmer—no snow. He liked that idea. Maybe that was what they could talk about at the coffeehouse.

Tossing his cigarette, Wolfe started walking. He'd pretty much fully recovered from the heart attack. There was some damage, but when there was snow on the ground he still walked in the big mall. Three times each week. Those walks had added up. He felt newly healthy. On a spring day like this one, he was ready for a long hike. He'd aim to reach *The Thoughtful Bean* by nine. He passed dog-walkers and early risers heading toward the commuter train. Two men wearing suits and carrying briefcases passed him.

"No more of that," he said. As he neared the park's tennis courts, Wolfe noticed an unusually scarred tree. Cracked and carbuncled bark segments girded the tree's circumference. Wolfe wondered at what kind of disease had clawed its way from inside the tree's heartwood onto the surface. There was nothing about the tree to indicate it was alive. Someone on the sidewalk called out: "That tree is dead." Ignoring the caller, Wolfe touched the bark; it was burnished and thick like some of the armor he had seen in the nearby city museum. But if the tree had been well armored, its defenses (nevertheless) had been breached. It was dead. He wondered if a tree could get something like leprosy. Saying nothing to the stranger on the sidewalk, Wolfe marched onward.

The Thoughtful Bean had summer chairs and tables set up outside, though no one had yet been brave enough to sit there. Wolfe sat, facing the street. Several persons entered and exited carrying coffee in various containers, "heading for the university," Wolfe thought. A surge of sadness took Wolfe unawares. Tipping his head downward onto his chest, he began to weep. Out of the corner of his eye he caught a glimpse of red. Wiping his eyes, he saw the bright turquoise t-shirt, red shorts, and long legs of a young pony-tailed runner, a woman, probably a university student. But she was slowing, "perhaps cooling down," thought Wolfe. "Maybe her work-out is complete, and she'll stop here for coffee."

As the woman drew near, it appeared to Wolfe that she would pass Wolfe's chair: "Come, sit," Wolfe said loudly. "Come sit, young lovely. Talk with me. I'll buy you a drink." Startled, the woman registered Wolfe's presence and words. She turned away and re-commenced running, not looking back. "Too bad," Wolfe called after her. "You'll never know what might have happened."

*

Early that same morning Tyler was to get two cups of coffee at 8:30 and then meet Kylie outside the library. She'd pled tardiness on account of a late night final paper, but had promised on the phone that if he got coffee she'd meet him at the library. Then the two of them could sip coffee while sitting on the stone wall out front while enjoying this first day of warm spring weather.

Stepping into *The Thoughtful Bean*, Tyler noticed Emily and Karl Wolfe sitting at a table near the rear of the shop. Emily was unloading a stack of papers from a large library handbag sitting beside her chair on the floor. As Tyler watched, Emily stacked papers on the table and leaning forward, seemed to ask Wolfe something. Tyler decided not to stare, and turning back toward the counter, ordered two coffees.

Someone entering the store triggered the hanging chimes, and the resulting noise caused Tyler to look back toward the open door. Out of the corner of his eye he saw Emily Wolfe jerk back as if someone had struck her and then reach down into the library handbag and slowly pull out a gun. Thinking "that's a revolver," Tyler watched, paralyzed, as with a shaking hand, Emily Wolfe shot Karl once, and then twice more.

Wolfe slumped onto the table and Emily stood, firmly yanking most of the bloody papers from under the dead man's body. Stuffing the papers and her blood stained spring jacket into her oversized handbag, Emily grasped the bag in her left hand, the gun in her right, and as if nothing had happened, walked to the front door. At the door she turned, paused, and loudly said: "Pardon my interruption; I hope I have not disturbed you on this beautiful day. If I have, I ask your forgiveness." And then she was gone. When the police arrived, Tyler was asked if he saw where "the woman" went after leaving the coffee-shop. Tyler said, "I saw her walking that way, toward the train stop."

Exiting the train at her stop, Emily Wolfe purposely strode down the street toward her house and the garden she cultivated each year. It was spring, and there would be daffodils coming up. Perhaps a few would still feel smothered by some left over, decaying leaves. She could fix that. She was good with a rake. There it was, on the corner. Her garden.

Twenty-seven

Emily Wolfe sat on the old wooden bench in her garden. In a corner of the garden, snow was still melting from the remains of a once large but now stained and dirty snowdrift. Spring was here. Brave yellow and white daffodils proudly stood where winter had once ruled. Emily fed the small fire she had started on some freshly turned earth. The pages she had torn from the family photo album easily caught fire.

In the background, Emily heard sirens. A pistol lay beside her on the bench.

*

Epilogue

Early Summer

1993

"In the end, it's all gone. In the end it's what we
cared about and how we lived."

KIRK RUSSELL, *REDBACK*

Twenty-eight

FLYING INTO DULUTH TOOK some time, and Clayton Heron found himself wondering how Martin and Norah's baby girl was doing. "Baby girl," he snorted. "Going on three years old now." Martin was now the permanent dean (no more "Interim" thought Clayton), and Tom Metcalf could still be found each morning at Niko's eating breakfast and scribbling another book onto a yellow legal pad. Kylie and Tyler, and in fact all of the people Clayton had come to know from the div school ". . . were just fine, thank you."

"Then there's Karl and Emily," Clayton thought. Karl Wolfe was buried without fanfare in a small cemetery near his birthplace. In addition to the cemetery helpers, Clayton and two others were in attendance. Emily Wolfe had been found guilty of first degree murder—"she planned it," Clayton thought. But the judge had sentenced her to a minimum security facility where she had been assigned work in the prison's library. In an ironic twist, with funds realized from the sale of the Wolfe's home plus Karl's invested money and a small Social Security payment, Emily was slowly adding books and carefully building a very good small library. Clayton thought it was amazing that life found a way to continue even though all this had taken place years ago. "That's all done," he said out loud. A cabin attendant came to where he was sitting and said: "Can I help you, sir?" "No miss," Clayton responded. "What you heard was just an old man reminiscing." She smiled, and moved down the aisle.

In Duluth, Clayton rented a car, stowed his gear, and drove north along Lake Huron toward Tofte, one of the gateways into the lakes and rivers of Canada's Quietico Provincial Forest. In Tofte he had a decent lunch and once finished drove westward on a gravel road to an outfitter who would rent him a canoe, provide a permit, and put him onto Cherokee Lake. He pitched his tent at a site and with nightfall had drifted into an untroubled sleep.

Early the next morning, Clayton thrust his head through the space made by the unzipped tent flap. During the night it had snowed. Maybe an inch, no more. He remembered the outfitter's warning that spring up north came late, and that man's worry that he was going into the wilderness by himself. "Never a good idea," the outfitter had said. "You could get hypo-thermia, have a heart attack, and die in there."

"I know."

"Then there's the fact you're no spring chicken. You're old."

"I know that, too. And I'm letting that comment slide because you and I go back a long time. Stop worrying. I know where I'm going. I've got good gear and I'm healthy." The outfitter was a friend, the son of the man who helped him take his first canoe trip. That trip had led to most summers spent working in the Boundary Waters. He'd taken Kate and their kids on canoe trips onto those same waters into southern Canada, despite protesta-tions from both mothers. He'd sent a postcard with a picture of a black bear home to his mother. He'd written: "Dear Mrs. Heron. I want to thank you for your son; you raised him well. He tasted good." This was where he and Kate had spent their honeymoon.

But Kate had stepped off the wrong curb at the wrong time and been dealt a grievous blow by a kid driving a stolen car. Two weeks in a coma, then Kate had died. She was cremated, as she had forcefully made her wish-es clear long before. Kate's ashes rested in a small cedar box tucked deep inside Clayton's pack. Those ashes would be scattered onto the lake where they had camped and talked long into the night of dreams, life together, and old age.

There had been more conversation, but the outfitter had finally agreed, even as he had made certain of Clayton's planned route and exit date. The two men shook hands, and Clayton had carried his canoe to the dock and slowly paddled down Cherokee Lake to his first campsite. Early the next day he pushed his body outside the tent and stood upright. An angular, tall, and older man, his leanness and the lines on his face seemed to accent his determination to do this thing. Once dressed, he cupped a match under a handful of dry tinder, slowly adding small dead spruce branches until he had a fire worthy of breakfast.

Two days later, Clayton sat in the canoe on a river. The river had sharply turned north and he could see almost a hundred yards in front of him. He was riding a swollen membrane of water, secured on left and right by tipped-in-alders. On either side beyond the overgrown alders and marsh rose gray and brown stone walls punctuated by occasional cliff-like over-hangs. Taking a mental picture, he treasured his solitary presence within the wilderness. He felt secure in his knowledge, experience, and ability for paddling the compact canoe. It was snowing, some large late spring flakes drifting down, each visibly twisting and dissolving in the water the canoe rode upon. Two lakes and four portages later, Clayton entered a large lake with an island site he hoped had not yet been taken by anyone. It was open, and he paddled into a small eddy behind the island. After securing his camp, he built a small fire and ate supper. Standing on the rocky point that lay toward the west, he watched the last light of the day recede and night emerge. Seeing no other campfires, he felt it likely that that he was the only person on the lake.

Later that evening, looking back over the day's route—certainly for the last time—he remembered how it had been when Kate had exclaimed, and not for the first time—"It's so beautiful." "Katie," he sighed. This had been their honeymoon campsite. They had been so young. Before he went to bed he sat beside his fire for a long time. He offered a quiet prayer of thanks, and then carried the small wooden box containing Kate's ashes to the water's edge, where he gently sprinkled Kate's remains. A wind came up and caressed his face, even as tears trickled down his cheeks onto the still water.

That night there was no snow, but the next morning had a sharp overlay to the wind that greeted his canoe. The weather would change, and he could not overstay his welcome. He angled his floating canoe toward the first portage of the new day. Once on dry land, he ate a nutrition bar. Stomach satisfied, he carried the canoe and his Duluth Pack over the short portage, only seven rods (seven canoe lengths). Checking his map, Clayton saw how the next river now bent south and with luck led him into two lakes that headed west and the outfitter's location. He knew that this meant the westerlies would likely be kicking up resistance in his face as he crossed those bodies of water. Unbidden, he remembered a bad day with twenty-four mile winds and whitecaps in his face. He had kissed the dry ground as he rolled out of the canoe at the end of that day. "No matter," he told himself, "pay attention to what's on your plate just now." On the far side of the portage, he loaded, slid the canoe away from the shore line, and was not surprised to sense Kate's presence still with him. She seemed to be in his mind: "Watch the rapids, Clayton," she said. "Rapids change each year—just like life." He cautiously drifted into the river's swelling flow.

Initially the river twisted, full of rolling water and frisky over hidden rocks, testing the banks that held it in place. He positioned the canoe between two large boulders while riding something like a three foot drop. One or two eddies, a short run in the rapids. Then it settled, stretched out, and in the distance, perhaps eight feet above the river, Clayton was surprised as a white spot appeared. It was larger than any snow flake, and with squinting he made out the stubby, powerful wings and black tipped coloration of a winter-white owl flying toward him down the river's center through what was now no longer snow but instead gently falling spring rain. Clayton's jaw dropped.

The owl seemed to recognize that the puny human in his canoe meant no harm. "He's flying this river as if it's his own personal runway north," mused Clayton. "He's headed back for colder weather." The owl kept coming. A hundred feet from Clayton and the canoe the owl's presence seemed to sharpen, black beak and speckled feathers clearly visible against the determined white wings steadily beating regular strokes north.

Resting his paddle on the canoe's gunwales, Clayton stood upright, waiting. On came the owl, increasing in size and without deviation. The owl was no more than five feet in front of the canoe when, with wide-spread feet anchoring his exuberance, Clayton reached skyward as if to touch the bird with outstretched arms. He shouted, "Yes!" Then the owl was gone, receding behind the canoe, a large white dot still moving north in the falling rain.

That night he sat by a warm campfire, listening to the haunting call of a loon. He mused: having returned Kate's ashes to the universe, as he sat in a canoe on a river in southern Canada an owl had flown over his head, and at that time he had felt judged in some powerful, mystical way. . . as if his and Kate's life together had been affirmed and valued as a testimony to a life well lived, one that had been good. He knew, even as that big owl passed over his canoe, that his life was complete, and that he could die in peace.

That next morning he woke and stood near the end of the river opposite a rocky point that fell away below the palisades. He could see the bare bones of the cliffs that rose well above the spruce and occasional white pines. The cliff was a sharp face, unforgiving, yet near its base was a flat space where someone centuries before had stood in a canoe, and as if to say "I was here," placed an ochre-stained hand on the rock's face. Early one morning he and Kate had found that handprint, and Katie—standing in the bow of the canoe— had placed her hand on top of that earlier traveler's notation to the future.

Unbidden, an image of Karl and Emily Wolfe intruded. Clayton felt no satisfaction at the dean's demise; he instead found himself saying a prayer for Emily, that she might find peace and that right soon. He struck his tent and using sand scoured his breakfast utensils, packed his gear, stowing it for better balance toward the front of the canoe. By 8 AM he was back on the water. "If the weather holds," he thought, "I'll be home in four days."

The river bottomed out into a marsh, and a red-winged blackbird accompanied him as he worked his way over two beaver dams. The blue, open expanse of a lake lay just ahead and was welcomed. Sitting and resting a hundred yards off shore, map in hand with compass balanced on the Duluth pack, he was surprised when a loon, perhaps the one he had listened to last night, scudded onto the surface of the water immediately in front of his canoe. It commenced diving for its breakfast. Watching the loon working the lake this close to the canoe, Clayton quietly said to himself: "Life is good." Then leaning back in the canoe, he shouted: "And how shall we live?" The loon squawked, and—after an impressive flurry of wings—with a stumbling run over the water—achieved flight. Air-born, it suddenly banked to the left of Clayton's canoe and settling in, once more returned to breakfast. Watching the loon, Clayton quietly said: "We live in hope."

He would miss this place and the memories it held. But he had no complaints. How lucky he and Katie had been. They had lived a full life—together. And she had died. Muttering a brief prayer: "God be with me," he pushed off, the canoe and him, slipping away, then silently gone, enveloped in the lake's morning fog.

*

www.ingramcontent.com/pod-product-compliance
Lightning Source LLC
Chambersburg PA
CBHW072355030726
47505CB00014B/1839